HOW I
BECAME THE
MR BIG
OF PEOPLE
SMUGGLING

Martin Chambers was born in Perth, the son of two journalists. He is married and has two adult daughters.

He has worked as a biologist, a tour guide, a whitewater rafting guide, a lab assistant, a publican, a kayak designer, a ferry skipper and in mineral exploration. He once had a job at the Swan Brewery with the rather good title of 'Quality Control'. Contrary to expectation he never got to sample product. Quality control was about checking labels were on straight and testing the twist force required to unscrew the bottle tops.

Between episodes of cycling, kayaking, sailing or travel, he writes. He is the author of four novels and two non-fiction books, and his poetry and short stories have been published in various anthologies. *How I Became the Mr Big of People Smuggling* was shortlisted in the T.A.G. Hungerford Award in 2012.

Visit the author at
www.facebook.com/MartinChambersAuthor
www.martinchambers.id.au

HOW I BECAME THE MR BIG OF PEOPLE SMUGGLING

A NOVEL BY **MARTIN CHAMBERS**

 FREMANTLE PRESS

1

I picked up the gun. It was cold, heavy. I picked it up only as a way to break eye contact. To avoid looking at him I casually sighted across the yard, aiming at the first thing that stood out, the sign above the canteen door. *Hotel California.* I squeezed the trigger.

BANG!

'Jesus!'

'Shit. I didn't think it would be loaded.'

'Fucking hell, Son. What the hell you doin', Son?'

'It's a goodun.' The shot was still deafening my ears, ringing in the silence. The wave of birds that I hadn't seen fly off settled back in the tamarisk and on the windmill. I gestured. 'Bullseye.'

In truth I didn't know if I had even hit the building, let alone the sign. I doubted his eyes were any better than mine, but he turned to see. He grunted.

In the nanoseconds after that first shot there was time to notice that the hole left by that shock of noise had not been filled, to realise that Cookie would be in the canteen unaware, doped up with Wagner at full volume as he conducted his dishes of ingredients around the stainless bench. Spanner was under one of his vans working to fix some part, and Margaret and the girls were sunbathing down at the waterhole. I could see myself and all of us from above: the camp, Cookie in the kitchen, Spanner's legs protruding; further out, the girls sprawled on the rocks and Margaret supervising from her canvas chair under a sun umbrella. While the world stood still I was flying away, up, and from higher I could see the lacework of roads, red-brown against the drab green scrub, then the pit, the pit, where the ground was redder, where time and the sound stopped forever.

He was turned away from me, pretending to look at the canteen door. His bull neck had small beads of sweat and rolls of fat and wispy hairs and I could see the pulse of blood in some veins that stood out. I remember seeing all this in great detail and slow motion and 'Hotel California' playing in my head.

You only get one chance and I took it. I shot him. I put the gun up close to the back of his turned head and in the white heat silence of an outback day there was a spray of blood and brains across the chair and onto the floor as his body flew backwards into the mess and fell with the chair – and the strange thing was I didn't even hear the shot and suddenly the world was going at double speed to make up for all the slow motion leading to the bullet in his brain.

2

The first person I met at Palmenter Station was Spanner. If it weren't for him I wouldn't have survived those first weeks. I remember how desolate the place looked as I drove along a few kilometres of hard dirt track to the station settlement. I saw two vans similar to mine parked outside a low prefabricated building and I was glad of that. These other vans might mean there were others like me here, school leavers or backpackers up for the season to earn a few dollars.

A sign on the door said 'Canteen', and handpainted above the door someone had written *Hotel California*. I parked next to the other vans and, like a sigh of relief, the engine rattled to a halt. Four thousand kilometres faultlessly and now, as if home, it shuddered.

Music was coming from inside the canteen. Muffled, it sounded out of place. As if the canteen were a spaceship that had landed in some alien world and inside the adventurers huddled in fear, playing loud music to keep their spirits up. It was midafternoon and the heat had gone from the day. The thought of a look around the deserted grounds was less intimidating than the idea of entering a crowded canteen full of strangers.

The canteen formed one side of a courtyard guarded in the centre by a solitary tree with a wire fence around it. Opposite was an older more conventional building with wide dark verandahs and a high-pitched tin roof. To the left was a row of seven prefabricated units. Each had five doors. That was a lot of rooms – if they were for accommodation perhaps this place was busier than it looked.

On the fourth side was a water tower – a skeletal pipe metal structure with an enormous fibreglass tank on top – and next to it and even higher was the largest windmill I had ever seen. On the other side of the water tank was a vegetable garden and beyond that was a large open-sided shed full of agricultural machinery. Some trees behind the shed looked enticingly shady but the overall impression was of desolation. I felt suddenly temporary, as if not only were this homestead a fleeting thing on a timeless landscape, but so too were I a momentary stranger in a world where I did not belong. How could anybody live here?

I could see a man working in the shed so I decided to go that way to allow my head to clear the echo of road noise. The man stood from where he was hunched over the bench, arching his back to straighten it, and walked to meet me.

'Saw you come in. How's the girl going?'

I didn't understand. He pointed.

'Betsy. The van.'

'Oh. Fine. They gave it to me to drive up here.'

'Obviously.'

'Yeah. It made a funny rattle just then when I turned it off. I'm Nick. Nick Smart.'

'Wayne. Everyone calls me Spanner. Anything 'round here broken, I fix it.' He looked me up and down. 'Mechanical, that is. I don't do hearts or paperwork or computers.'

'Oh.'

'My advice: if you want those, you head right on back out of here.'

Had he assessed me with that single look, written me off? Was he serious I should leave? Dad had warned me the outback men were hard and rough and so I had been trying to look tougher than I felt.

The bloke led me back into the shed and continued tinkering with the engine part that lay dismantled on the bench. He had a beer open and took a swig but thankfully he didn't offer me one.

'I'm a jackaroo. They told me to drive the van up and I could start as soon as I got here.'

'Jackaroo. He does that.'

I wondered what he meant by that and who 'he' was. But the man stood up from bending over whatever part he was toying with.

'Fucked if I know what's wrong with it. C'mon. I'll introduce you to Cookie. No one else here. You can chill until Palmenter gets here. I don't know what he's got in store for you. Pick yourself one of the dongas over there. They're all empty. I live back of the shed. Cookie's donga is over there. The girls are put in the bedrooms in the homestead when they are here. Place fills up coming up to muster but most time it's pretty quiet. Good if it suits ya.'

He led me towards the canteen and as he walked past my van he patted it affectionately on the bullbar. 'Heya Betsy.'

There was no one in the canteen except the cook who was sitting smoking by the back door. The music was loud, classical, some sort of military march. *Empire Strikes Back* or something. I felt absurdly inspired.

'Cookie: new bloke.'

'Nick. Nick Smart.'

Cookie shook my hand. His grip was soft, his hand felt like pastry. He was smoking dope and I could see a substantial plantation thriving between the back of the canteen and another prefab building that must be Cookie's room. He saw me examining the plantation.

'Anytime, mate. Help yourself. It's a community garden.' And he gave a little laugh, as if that in itself was a helpless joke. It was not the meaningless giggle of a pot smoker. It was more forlorn. It was the antidote to the uplift of music.

They pointed me towards the prefabricated rooms that were called dongas and told me to pick one and settle in, dinner at six, ask if I needed anything. I was left to myself for the rest of the afternoon. I lay on the bed and turned on my phone but there was no reception.

The next morning a guy about my age arrived. Jason. He arrived in another campervan as I happened to be walking across towards the canteen. We confused each other for a while until we worked out that neither of us knew what was going on. He was a newbie too.

'Apparently the boss arrives tomorrow,' I said.

I showed him the rooms and the showers and introduced him to Spanner who I found again in his shed with a beer and an engine part. While I was showing Jason around I learned that he, like me, was taking a year off. Next year he would go back to study medicine. In the canteen when Cookie discovered that, he offered Jason some 'medicine' but Jason declined.

Palmenter arrived the next day with a bloke called Simms who turned out to be a third newbie. Simms didn't seem so bright, in a harmless sort of way, and Palmenter bossed him around no end. Fetch this, do that. Simms took a room opposite mine but that was it. In our spare time – and there was a lot of it early on – the three of us would sit around and talk. Simms did not say much and he rarely volunteered anything extra. When he answered a direct question he would look around anywhere but at you as he answered.

'You worked up here before?' Jason asked him.

'No, not really.'

'Did you work down south with Palmenter? He's got some business interests in Melbourne, hasn't he?' Jason probed. He didn't seem to pick up the vibe of the place.

'No. I don't think so. Don't know.'

Simms was older than us, and rake thin, and everything he did took too long. In the showers he would wander in and take forever to set out his kit on the bench, then shave, slowly like each scrape of the razor was a deliberate thing, then he'd pack that bit away and sort out things for a shower, get undressed and lay his clothes neatly on the bench. It was frustrating, because I was in and out, and to hang around and talk was as if I was hanging around in the changerooms and he was naked in the shower and you just don't know on these stations what people get up to. But it was frustration in a kindly way because I wanted to help him, partly because everything seemed such a difficulty for him and partly because Palmenter bullied him so.

At the station you kept to yourself and everything was fine. But somewhere under that layer of civility was something not said, as if, perhaps, everyone was on the run from the police. Or like Jason escaping from failed exams. Or me, running away from something I could not really explain. I wanted someone to talk to and Simms was the best I could do because Jason would have asked me too many questions.

Palmenter interviewed me the afternoon he arrived and it felt as if I didn't have a job at all, I felt I was reapplying and might be refused and sent home if I said the wrong thing. At that time I was keen to stay, prove myself, like when you are pushed you push back, so even if I didn't want to stay at that stage I would have tried like anything to be asked to stay, then say, 'No, I don't want to'. People are funny like that. You can get them to do all sorts of shit they don't want to by hinting that they are not allowed to.

Anyway, Palmenter took me into the office and grilled me about many things, asked me why I wanted the job. I knew I would be pretty hopeless around the place until I learned the job, and I said so, but he was more interested in my school results and that I was interested in studying business.

'Nick Smart. Smart eh?'

I smiled.

'We need someone smart 'round here, Son. Someone who can think for themselves. You could do accounts and take over some of the management for me. I have to spend a lot of time away, sorting out other parts of the business. If you're interested in commerce, you'll learn more here than in your classroom in the city. You stick with me, Son, and I'll turn you into a businessman.'

I nodded. I was wondering what limited business skills I might learn all the way out here in the middle of nowhere, but then I remembered Jason asking Simms about Palmenter's business interests in the city and I thought if I could do six months or a year here, maybe Palmenter might have a part-time position for me back in Melbourne while I studied.

'How old are you, Son?'

'Eighteen.'

'You look older.'

'I get that a lot. Anyway, it won't affect how well I can do the job. I learn quick.'

He made a noise to acknowledge that I had spoken. I was about to add that I'd be keen to learn some of the accounting but realised it didn't matter what I said. Palmenter was someone who made up his own mind and he already had about me.

'Son, I don't want no fly-in fly-out. You work here, I look after you, pay you well, lots of bonuses and benefits. It's a great life out here, you just gotta want it, appreciate what we've got. But if you don't want this life, you leave now. Don't waste my time.'

'I've signed up for the year and I'll do the year.' I said. His gaze was challenging me. 'I believe in keeping commitments,' I added.

He kept looking at me and it made me uncomfortable. It was not that he was reading me or assessing me or considering me, it was that he had already done all that and I was irrelevant, I was nothing. I was signed up for the year and that was that. But he made no move to produce any paperwork or to end the interview.

'I was hoping to call my parents, tell them I've arrived safe and all that.'

'You're in the outback now, Son. No landline out here and the satellite phone is expensive, only for emergency. Write them a letter. I'll see it gets posted next time we do a run into town.'

Who these days does not have a landline? Why didn't I offer to pay for a satellite call? Why oh why didn't I walk out then and there? But like I said, it was early days and there was no way I was heading home with my tail between my legs. I did not, however, mention anything about paperwork or actually signing a contract.

I had done quite well at school, well enough to be offered a place at Melbourne University to study commerce. It was my brother who suggested it would be a good idea to defer for a year and work on the mines. Simon was working at a mining camp and loved it. He and a group of his friends had rented a house in Fitzroy and rotated through the house. Because they all worked some variation of weeks on and weeks off there was always a party happening there.

'Easy work, good money,' he said. 'Get some money together so you can pay your way through university. Fly-in fly-out is great because you don't miss out on anything, plus there is a real shortage of workers at the moment so it's easy to get.'

I found a recruitment agent that specialised in mining and outback jobs. After quite a long friendly talk the recruitment man told me that the problem with fly-in fly-out was although you earned big money you also spent big amounts during the time off and he suggested I was better off doing something like station work as a jackaroo. Well-paid, all food and board and no expenses and if I worked out a full year, great bonuses. I had never been to the Northern Territory and there would be days off with the freedom to explore so it sounded pretty good. He told me of a job on Wingate Station. That was what they called it. It was only when I arrived that I found out the current name.

I discussed it with my parents and they were not happy. Dad said it was a waste to take a year off and thought if I did, then I'd never go back to study. Mum didn't want me to leave home.

'What's your hurry? Plenty of kids nowadays stay at home while they study. You won't have to pay rent so you don't need a job.'

Graduating from school is such a confusing time. I can't really say what was the real reason I had set my mind on this year away but the more we argued, the more determined I became. I can say that I was not happy at school and that once the idea of a gap year had taken hold I could not forget it, and the more I thought of escaping to the north, the less I could explain why I had chosen to study commerce. I didn't even really know what commerce was.

Our argument simmered over the summer. Mum insisted that I stay home and enrol at university. I think Dad would have been okay with my moving out and renting a place closer to uni but he knew he had to side with Mum. One time when Mum was out shopping he told me, quietly, that if it made the difference he would increase my allowance but that I was not to tell Mum.

'But you must go to university, Nick. It is a great opportunity. Thousands of kids don't get in. Don't turn it down just because you want to have some time off. By the end of summer you'll be itching to get back to study.'

'Lots of kids take a year off, Dad. I'll defer for a year, that's all.'

But after Christmas I felt even less like going to university and that was when I arranged a second interview with the agent. When I told Dad I had taken the job he warned me about the hard-drinking hard men of the outback.

'The Territory is the worst of it. Hard men up there, harder than most places. They don't take easily to strangers, outsiders, people who ...' and here he was for a moment lost for words, '... people not like themselves.'

I don't think Dad was worried I would turn into a hard man of the outback. He knew me too well. Although I'm quite physical, he knew I didn't have the tough streak it takes to be one of them. After all, he had watched me through all my school years.

Every school has its bullies and ours was Dan Taylor. He and his buddies picked on everyone, not just me in particular, although it often felt like it. Many times I would be hiding in the library reading rather than face him in the courtyard. The funny thing, though, is that Dan would be shocked to know I learned so much from him. Dan, the thick-as-two-short-planks bully! I survived at Palmenter Station because Dan taught me how to become invisible, how to pick up when was the right or wrong time to speak or to ask for things, and how to think quickly and talk my way out of situations. He taught me to notice who was where and doing what, because when Dan was on the oval extorting lunch money I could safely walk from the library to get my own lunch. And later I knew, because of Dan, how to use thugs to get my own way when I wanted to and even how to pretend to be a thug myself.

I told my Dad I was going to take the job. What he had implied was that while I might look the part of the hard-drinking territory men, I wouldn't fit in and I'd be pushed around just as Dan had pushed me around. Funny that, for the very same reason that I did not want to go directly to uni, I now felt challenged, to prove that I could cope to live away among the real men, as if there was some test I had to pass and the only way to pass it was to head directly to it.

'Think about it for a few days. Maybe we can see if Simon's work comes up with any better vacancies.'

'Dad, no one is leaving at Simon's work. They just don't get any vacancies. Plus, this is better. Full board, full-time, I save everything instead of coming back to the city fly-in fly-out and spending everything I earn.'

He tried to persuade me to take a few days to consider, but my mind was made up. If I rang them and said I was unsure I would probably lose the offer and I had agreed I could start immediately. I was supposed to collect a company car the next day as I had agreed to drive it to the homestead of a place called Wingate. In return for that I had free use of the car for the next two weeks. This sounded like the sort of place I would want to work. There was no way I was turning it down.

Next day I got up early and left. I turned off my mobile. I wrote a note to my parents telling them that I'd call them with all the contact details of the station as soon as I got there, because all I knew at that time was it was called Wingate and it was in the far north of the Northern Territory. I wrote for them not to worry, that I would be home in six months when I was due a return air ticket as part of the contract, but I underlined that I'd be working the full year because the bonus for completing the year was an extra three months pay.

The agent had given me an address in Geelong and told me we could sign the paperwork later. That didn't seem at all unusual to me and when at the address – an old warehouse out the back of Geelong – another man gave me the van and a map and instructions how to get to the station and told me all the paperwork would be done when I got to Wingate.

'No worries mate. Jackaroo, eh? Do it when you get up there, chum. They do all the office shit up there. I just look after the transport for 'em. Take your time, don't push it on those outback roads.'

I didn't know exactly what a jackaroo did but it sounded good. Jackaroo. Like I was going to do a particular job and learn some specific skill. The bloke at the warehouse gave me a choice of the vans and said again I should take my time getting there. He gave me cash to pay for fuel on the trip up and when I asked about receipts he laughed.

'S'pose so.'

The van was a bit of a comedown from the company car I had expected but as it was set up with camping gear and a small stove I could see it had some advantages. There was no reason not to leave immediately.

I drove out of Victoria via Ballarat and Mildura and could not believe how flat and barren the land was. I had never been this far from the city before, this far from the hills and forests of southern Victoria and Tasmania where we spent our family holidays. I called home that night and told them that I was okay, that I'd phone when I could. I drove through Port Augusta and on to Alice Springs. I stopped along the way, at Uluru and Kings Canyon and all sorts of other places. In the late afternoons I stopped by the highway and camped, watching the sunset and darkening sky and listening to the racket of corellas and parrots and then the remarkable silence as the stars came out.

A few days after my interview with Palmenter, a truck arrived with several more campervans that we unloaded and drove into Spanner's shed. Spanner's shed was becoming my regular haunt after work. My work was easy general stuff, helping out in the kitchen, some gardening, fixing reticulation to the vegetable and the 'herb' garden. It was pretty slack and in the afternoons I would go down to visit Spanner. He always had an open beer on his bench and by the end of the day he was quite chatty, asking about my family or about Melbourne or something else in a way that didn't seem intrusive. Often I'd find myself telling him something from school or about Simon and his mining job, but I can't remember Spanner ever telling me anything about himself.

Spanner didn't have dinner in the canteen, and neither did Palmenter, who I rarely saw, so it was only Simms and me, and Jason until he left after the first muster. And then Charles who had arrived with the truck. I liked him but found him difficult to understand. He was not English at all like you'd expect a bloke called Charles to be, he was Indian or something and he spoke exactly in that singsong way we used to send up at school, and he wanted to be called Charles not Charlie. He even had little swings of his head from side to side and he spoke so quickly you couldn't understand a thing he said, or you'd have to think about it after he said it like your brain was catching up with the words that had gone in.

A woman named Margaret had arrived at the same time as Charles but I didn't know this until a few days later when the girls arrived. I was surprised because one morning something felt different around the place, and Spanner said it was the girls. He said that they always arrived shortly before muster. Later that day I saw them from where I was working in the garden, they were cleaning the empty dongas and later sitting on the verandah of the homestead with the woman called Margaret who reminded me of a protective mother duck. Her glare was every bit as fierce as Palmenter's.

I never talked to Margaret. She was older and lived in the homestead with the girls. She would arrive with Charles or Palmenter a few days before each muster and depart as soon as it was over.

3

Spanner helped me drag Palmenter's body across to the 4WD and bundle it in the back. He was a heavy bastard. I remember thinking that television cop shows never show how difficult it is to move a body, particularly a big fat one. We finally got him into the back seat by folding him in. He sat there as if alive but snoozing in that head forward uncomfortable way people do in cars.

'You drive him out to the pit,' Spanner said.

'I'll need you too.' I didn't want to be out there alone, to do it by myself.

'I'll bring a van. We'll torch the car.' He looked at the car. It was all white, unnaturally clean, gleaming, with almost black windows. The interior smelled of leather and pine and was cool even though it had been parked in the heat for an hour or so.

'Shame. Lexus hybrid.' He gave a little laugh. 'He musta cared for the fuckin' environment.' He said it in a voice that confirmed he didn't care at all for Palmenter.

Spanner walked off without saying any more. He got into one of the vans. I drove off. The whole way, I kept looking back at Palmenter whose body was bouncing around the back seat. His knees were bent up and his arms had fallen behind and his head rested forward so I could not see the gaping hole in his face where the bullet came out. He looked very uncomfortable but alive and I kept expecting him to wake up, to fly up at me and beat me, yelling abuse and smashing his fists into me, or worse, to start talking again. A rise of panic would flood through me and I'd turn back to check. Yes, he was still there, still dead. I couldn't believe he was dead. But I had shot him. Me. And a different panic would hit me. What would I do now? What would happen if someone found out? Could I trust Spanner not to tell?

I'd force myself to relax. No one would ever know. Spanner hated him as much as I did. I could trust Spanner. He had been here all this time, had been party to all the goings on. He knew about the pit. If ever this came to light he would be in just as much trouble as I was.

Who was I kidding? Spanner hadn't shot anyone and I could hardly claim self-defence. Gunshot wound in the back of the head? There was a big difference between shooting someone in the back of the head at point-blank range, and pushing a load of sand over the bodies of illegals who had perished in the desert. I was in big trouble.

Spanner's van caught up to me and was following closely. I drove on automatic, fluctuating between near panic and total calm. I remember that the car smelled of that pine fragrance. I remember pine, and calm, and panic.

Funny how the mind works, what things it finds to notice when it's trying not to notice something else, like the lurching body of Palmenter that at every bump shifted and wobbled like a monster awakening. That pine fragrance was calming in a familiar way and I tried to remember it, identify it. Perhaps it was something my mother used. I liked it. It would be nice in my room. The drive seemed to take a long time.

At the pit Spanner looked over the car as if considering what parts best to strip off it and keep. We had no plan; we were making it up as we went along, but whatever we were going to do we had to be quick. It was the middle of nowhere but we both knew there were people everywhere, the nearest several kilometres away. That was too close. Mustering crew would be back after lunch. Chopper would arrive tomorrow. It would bring the first of the imports an hour after dawn. That was too soon. Nearest road was twenty kilometres, nearest town three hundred and fifty. That was too close. Too close. We had to hurry.

'Probably best if we don't take anything.' Spanner pointed to the other side of the dozer where he had recently extended the pit. The new bit was deeper and had steep edges. 'Park it there. Leave the brake off, outta gear, windows down. We'll push it in, bury it.'

'I thought you said burn it?'

'Musterin' crew'll see the smoke. Chopper too. Due anytime. That pilot is a nosey bugger. Not sure about Newman either.'

Newman. What Palmenter had said. Should I tell Spanner? Maybe, but right now we had to get rid of Palmenter and his car.

'They're not due till tomorrow.'

'Today. Tomorrow. Who knows? They'll be nearby someplace. They might come out this way anytime. Any one of them could see the smoke, come lookin', see the burnt-out shell. Won't be able to bury it till after it's burned and tomorrow the place will be crawling. We'll bury the whole thing right now. Come on.'

I drove the car to the edge as he directed. I had barely got out and closed the door and he was pushing it, rolling it to the edge. In the movies it is so much easier: they push the car over the edge and it tips easily, plummets off the cliff, and bursts into flames before it hits the bottom. We pushed hard but as the front wheels went over the edge, the sand collapsed and the bottom of the car hit the ground. It was stuck half over with the front wheels midair and its belly resting on the dirt.

Spanner swore. He went to the dozer and started it, rammed into the perched car so that it slid over the edge, bounced a couple of times and rolled onto its side. I tried not to look to see Palmenter. Spanner pushed sand in after it until it was buried, then parked the dozer. It was done quickly, efficiently.

'Grab some of those bags, some of that shit and stuff, throw it all over, cover the fresh sand so as it doesn't look like something's just been buried here.' He pointed into the main pit that was full of garbage. It was foul smelling and revolting. Most of the bags had split when dumped, or been torn open by wild dogs and dingoes. 'C'mon, do it.'

While I was tossing bags of garbage over the newly scraped sand he broke off the branch of a shrub and dragged it around where the dozer and 4WD tracks were, obliterating them, or at least confusing them so they looked like long-ago tracks. A few months, after the wet, and there'd be no trace of a body in a near-new Lexus 4WD under sand in the middle of scrub that stretched unchanged from here to the Gulf.

Nothing had changed at the homestead. Spanner broke off a couple more branches and showed me how to sweep the sand to hide our drag marks, the footprints and blood. Not that the blood showed, you'd have to know what you were looking for. Unless you knew, the area looked like dirt. But I kept seeing stuff. Patches that might have been blood. Or flesh. Bits of skull and brain. Already the ants had invaded. There were lines of them on the sand and up the two steps onto the landing, across the boards. I wheeled out the firehose and washed the boards down.

We had just finished when the muster crew came in. Two old utes roared up in a cloud of dust and stopped right at the canteen door. Bodies tumbled out of the tray and cab and into the canteen. I was thinking you'd have to do more than fire a gun and spray blood and brains over the ground for them to notice, and as the dust settled on the wet boards I was thinking that that was the end of Palmenter, that was the end of it all. Good riddance.

'Better go about as if nothin's happened,' said Spanner. He was reading my mind. We would come to rely on each other more and more, and this understanding we had of what the other was thinking was later to save my life. But that was in the future and I was wondering what I should do next. Could I leave? I wanted to get as far away as quickly as I could. Maybe we shouldn't have buried the car, I could have taken it, abandoned it in Katherine. Or even gone as far as Alice or Darwin before it was missed. I could have dumped it somewhere in the city. Cities are much better places than the wide open spaces to hide things. Perhaps I could take one of the vans.

'For Christ's sake don't do a runner,' Spanner said. 'Play it cool for a week or so. If anyone comes lookin' for him, notices him missing, be suss if you've scarpered.'

Spanner wasn't the mind-lazy slob that most people thought. You know, a lot of the people you meet outback are smart. They just look and talk rough and drink like they're thirsty but underneath they are real decent and thoughtful and have a pretty good idea what is going on. I looked over to the canteen and wondered about the muster crew inside. I'd wait a week.

Early on in my first year, every week had been my final week, but now it really was. That was it. Palmenter had always had a good reason for me to stay a week longer. 'Just see out this week and then you can go,' he'd say. He could be friendly, like it would be a favour to him, and as I was owed all my backpay it felt impossible to say no. Or he'd promise a bonus, a swag extra if I saw out whatever it was that was urgent in the coming week. Always something. Later he was less friendly. Plus, he controlled the vans and the comings and goings. It had been impossible to leave without his blessing but now I had no reason not to go. I'd lie low and wait the week out.

'You hungry?' asked Spanner.

Food was the last thing on my mind. I shook my head.

'Good. We gotta bring all the vans up. I got six ready. Park 'em up here, ready, like it was meant to be. Got to fuel 'em up, have 'em ready.'

'Before the mustering crew's gone?'

'Have to. Be suss, not having Palmenter strutting around during the import, but if we look and act like it was planned all along we might get away with it.' He signalled towards the canteen. 'They'll never notice anyhow. They've finished muster now, canteen'll be wet, they'll be pissed in no time. If we don't get the vans up now, first chopper'll be in the morning while we're still doing it. Tonight we'll have to be doing the licences and transfers, draw up maps for them. In the morning, driving lessons and then we send 'em different ways so's they don't end up in a convoy.'

He seemed pleased with that for some reason.

'Like in the old days,' he said. 'We used to bring in a few, sell the van to 'em. Tell 'em to drive to Sydney, or Melbourne. Not so many then. Five or six at a time, just one chopper load, maybe two. Once or twice a year. Not this many, not like now. Gave 'em a chance. At least they had a chance.'

I looked at him. I wanted to thank him for his help, for standing by me, because, after all, I was the one in trouble and if he hadn't helped there was no way I would have got away with it. But I didn't. I could say I thought carefully about it and that there was a reason I didn't say thank you. But really, you just don't say thank you to a bloke.

Like I say, it takes a while to get to know these outback blokes and Spanner was one of the best. Maybe he was on the run from the grey side of the law, but that didn't make him a ratbag. Plenty of law-abiding ratbags around the place. As we fuelled up and loaded the kit and then shifted the vans from the shed to the car park I had time to think about Spanner and how not only was he a great mechanic but he was also a thinker. Once, I had suggested he write down his thoughts. He had laughed.

'I told you, I don't do paperwork.'

It was one of those long slow afternoons when the sunshine seems golden and the whole world is so at peace that the hours go on for longer. The air was sweet with the smell of spinifex in flower. We were at the gene pool, the collection of things piled behind Spanner's shed. It was mostly cars and vans and parts of them, but there was also furniture, bits of wood, old kitchen equipment, anything that Spanner deemed too useful to throw out but that he had no current use for. Everything else went to the pit.

Anyway, on this afternoon we were trying to unbolt some bench seats to put in the back of the 4WD work unit, Bitsy. While most of the vans outwardly looked to be what they were, a Toyota HiAce or a Mazda or a Ford, Bitsy was a bolted-together amalgam of all sorts. She had no bonnet and a roof from something too long so that it projected out behind and shaded the boot area. The boot lid was welded open with two metal bars that helped brace the roof, and wooden planks formed a platform extending back from the boot so it could carry a load. It looked a lot better than it sounds as I describe it to you, and it ran well. When we drove to the waterhole we would all pile on the back with beanbags and beers and today Spanner had decided it needed proper seats.

Spanner would often get me to help him salvage stuff from the gene pool. I discovered that all of the roadworthy vans were called Betsy and in Spanner's mind this was because by now, after years of transplant surgery, they were all of the same genetic makeup. The original Betsy was a Toyota Commuter bus at the centre of the heap; virtually nothing on it was transferable to the smaller campervans. When I pointed this out to him he laughed.

'It spreads out through all of them while they are waiting.' He waved his arms at the pile, mimicking the DNA flowing from the centre to the edge like he was smoothing out sand in the creekbed. Or mixing colour into paint.

'She's the grand old dame. Plus, don't bet on it. I can make any bit fit onto anything. Lots of her making trips to and from Melbourne each month. Ain't that so, honey?' He looked up at the central wreck as if addressing a matriarch.

'But why call all of them Betsy? Children have different names to their parents.'

'It's just easier that way. Plus, they are not children. They are ...?'

'Clones?'

'No, not that. Donors. It's transplants. She lives on in them all.'

'Like Frankenstein?'

'Hey, don't be rude. They can hear you, might go into a sulk, refuse to go for no other reason than they don't like you. They have feelings you know.'

He was underneath and I was on the top, holding the bolthead as he tried to turn it. We had to speak between efforts and between his cajoling.

'Come on ya bastard.'

'So you call them all Betsy.'

'Sometimes this is how I feel. That we're all on some rubbish heap. Parked out here, someplace, waiting for the chance to be useful.'

I thought about that. I had only come out here for the year then intended to go back to Melbourne. Would that make me more useful? Certainly, stuck out on a marginal station helping to unbolt a seat from a van on top of a rubbish pile was not too useful. But what was useful?

'What does it mean to be useful?' I asked. He didn't answer for a while.

'Do your bit. Contribute to the good of humanity. Fucked if I know. If you knew, you could set off to do it.' He made some banging noises and swore some more.

'Sounds like that bolt doesn't know how to be useful.'

'Oh, he's bein' useful all right. Sometimes, resistance is put there to test you. Check ya resolve.' Some gentler tapping sounds. 'Might need to get the grinder onto this one.' He made a long hard grunting noise. 'Arrrgh, got you! See. They always give up as soon as they know you're serious.'

'You should write your thoughts down. Collected wisdom from the gene pool.'

'Very funny.'

'No, I'm serious. Write it down before you forget stuff.'

But he had laughed at the idea that anything he thought about would be part of his way of being useful to anyone.

'Nah. I'm a mechanic.'

It took us three hours to get the six vans ready. By then it was late afternoon and I was hungry. In the canteen Cookie was angry, and he took it out on us. The stockhands sat at one of the tables talking and joking loudly and already there was a crowd of empty beer cans littered about. There was nothing Cookie could do about the stockhands so he ignored them. It was Spanner and I who copped it.

'Lunch! Nearly dinnertime. You come back then. I'm not here now. Afternoons is my time.'

'Why are you here then?' I asked. We knew he wasn't going to leave the canteen unattended.

'C'mon. Let us go make a sandwich,' Spanner said. 'You can stay out here keep an eye on them.' He pointed to the drunken muster crew who were racking up for pool and a long session.

Very clever, Spanner, I thought.

'You tidy up,' Cookie said. 'Then I might. You're not setting foot in my kitchen without me.'

Cookie didn't like muster time. When it was only the few of us on-site he could smoke until he was off his face and still cook wonderful food but when the crews were all crowding around and drinking he had to remain sober. It was the only way to deal with the influx of hungry workers, who insulted him by insulting his food. They made a mess and raided his 'herb' garden and argued about the girls. But to Cookie, who daily made fresh bread and rolls, the highlight of civilisation was the sandwich. To him, anyone who knew how to load fresh ingredients in the correct manner onto a crusty roll was okay, and the chance to have us there with him while the crew drank themselves stupid in the dining hall was too good to pass.

'Where's Palmenter? I thought he was here. S'pose he wants one too?'

'He's gone.'

'Took off.'

We spoke at the same time.

Unlikely. Palmenter would never have left without eating. Cookie raised his eyes.

'Oh?'

'New plan,' I said before Spanner could speak. 'Whole new way of doing business. We're going back to the old way, the vans, small groups driving to the city. He had some urgent things to organise. He's left me in charge. He's on his way back to Sydney to run that end, needs to get some things set up before the imports start arriving.'

Cookie was looking at me. I could see he was trying to figure out whether to believe the rubbish I had just garbled. I kept talking.

'Six vans, so you'll need to make up six food packs. Like before, we'll send them off a day apart, four or five in each van. Sorry about missing lunch, but as you know, when Palmenter is here, well, what can you do?'

Cookie continued to look but not speak. Spanner backed me up.

'Go on, make us a sandwich, Cookie, I've got a hunger now. We've still got to write up all the paperwork, too. Be well into the night, just be thankful all you have to deal with is a few empty cans on the floor.'

'Well, okay,' he grumbled. If he didn't agree he would have just said no, or asked for more details, but he said, 'You want herbs on your sandwiches?'

'No way!'

'Gives you energy.'

'Gives you wings,' I said. Wouldn't I have liked to fly away.

Spanner and I sat in the kitchen with Cookie while he made sandwiches. He heated us one of his beef pies too. I liked Cookie, although he and I had rarely had a chance to talk alone. Partly I guess that is the nature of running a station kitchen. Up early, sleep afternoons. As I watched him work I thought he seemed happy with what we had told him, and that perhaps, if he ever learned the truth, he would not be too quick to condemn me.

4

Spanner, Cookie and I had been here the longest. We were the old hands and knew a few things we preferred not to but it was Cookie who seemed best able to ignore it all.

A couple of years before the shooting, it was morning, just after breakfast. A muster and import had finished a few days ago and we were all relaxing. Arif and I were in the canteen, him talking at me and me pretending to listen. Charles and Simms were there too. Spanner was down in his shed and Palmenter was in the office. We heard the rumble of a car approaching on the gravel. That in itself was unusual and I stood to look out the window.

A police car drove up to the canteen building and stopped. No one got out and in each of the buildings curious eyes must have been watching for what would happen next. The police never came out here. For them to do so now, something must be serious.

'Better hide the harvest,' called Arif to Cookie who was chopping leaf in the kitchen. Arif was serious, but the joke was that an entire plantation thrived immediately out the back door.

'Someone must have been caught,' Cookie said as he came from the kitchen casually wiping his hands on his apron. He peered out the window.

Perhaps he was right: one of the previous imports had been picked up and then said something, given up the station and Palmenter and all of us. Unlikely, but I was wondering what this would mean for me, if I'd be charged, if we'd all be charged, with people smuggling.

Palmenter admitting anything? Ha! We'd all be for it. He'd find some way of pinning it on us and getting off scot-free. I wondered what the penalty for people smuggling was. A few years jail? And here was Cookie calmly packaging up serious quantities of dope, a crime I suspected carried a far more severe penalty, again, a crime for which Palmenter would deny all knowledge and for which I could not claim innocence.

Hopefully the police had come about something else entirely but I realised suddenly how things were. The truth was I was working on a station that routinely broke the law and each day, by my silence or inaction, I became more complicit. And there was no way out, I was trapped. I should go and get in the police car, lock myself in it and tell them to take me away.

But life is not that simple. Palmenter was a bully, an arrogant bastard, he was a ruthless money-hungry opportunist preying on the weak and dispossessed. Yet these people had no choice and at least they now had a chance at a new life, a better life, and I wasn't going to be the one to end that hope. I wanted to get away, but I had to do it on my own terms.

Palmenter strolled over to the car and two policemen got out and I could hear friendly deep voices, laughter, howdyados, as Palmenter led them towards us. We drifted like ghosts back into the kitchen as they came in the canteen door. Palmenter opened beers for them at the bar while we listened from behind the swing doors.

'We hardly ever see you out this way. Don't be strangers, always a meal or a beer here for you. Anytime.'

I couldn't make out the reply because just then the freezer motor started up. Cookie scurried out to turn it off. Last thing Palmenter wanted was cops dropping by unannounced, so him telling them not to be strangers, to drop by for a feed and a drink anytime, that was plain bullshit. I wondered if there was more going on here. It was a bit much to believe that boats could land and helicopters fly between the coast and here and not be seen. At some time someone must have reported something and Palmenter was most likely paying off the cops to keep them quiet. Probably only as a precaution. It wouldn't be too hard to turn a blind eye when your patch is one hundred thousand square kilometres.

We had crowded closer to hear better when Cookie came in from killing the freezer motor, slamming the door. We all jumped and he laughed and instead of joining us he continued to chop and wrap the crop. He neatened it into piles that he wrapped in alfoil the size of a half brick and then put all but two of them into the freezer.

'Youse lot, garn, get outta here. See my illegal activity.' But he didn't mean it. He laughed then stood at the swing doors with the rest of us, weighing the packets in his hands in a way that made it obvious that this was for the coppers.

'I'll sort it, Trent. Be gone by morning. It's all over, no problems.' Palmenter stood, dragging his chair noisily. 'You want some steaks. We just finished the muster, killed a couple.' I didn't hear an answer. 'Plenty there, I'll get you both a package,' and before any of us could move he was in the kitchen, glaring at us.

'Get some fucking steaks for these boys. Where's Spanner. Shit, he's going to pay for this. This will cost us, boys.' No one had moved. 'Fucking steaks, NOW.' Not loud. Meaningful. Cookie handed him the package and sprinted into the freezer. Palmenter pointed to me and Simms.

'You two, soon as they've gone, at the machine shed. And get fucking Spanner. Sober. The rest of you, get outta here. Go find something useful to do.'

I found Spanner in the generator shed where he was changing the oil in the second generator. He had earmuffs on and so I signalled him to come outside. He shook his head and pointed at the machine, but I insisted. He followed me out.

'What?'

I told him about the police car and what we had seen, and that Palmenter wanted us all right away. We walked around to the shed where Palmenter was already waiting with Simms. Spanner was muttering under his breath, 'This is not gunna be good.'

The van was lying on its side by the edge of the track. It was one of the seven-seaters. They are more difficult to control on the softer tracks, but what had caused them to leave the highway and venture out here we would never know. What made them crash? Could have been a roo, suddenly jumping out. They had no experience of Australian wildlife. It wasn't a blowout.

Spanner swore nothing was wrong with the van. Steering, brakes were perfect. He serviced each of the vans thoroughly before each trip. He might not have been one hundred per cent behind the operation but he knew as well as all of us that if the van broke down on its way to the city, if the people got into trouble, most likely someone would start asking questions. Spanner had built a nice little retreat for himself here at the station. Why, I didn't know. An ex-wife? On the run? In any case Spanner seemed happy to spend his days alone in the shed and drinking a steady supply of free beer, sleeping it off from early evening and then doing it all again the next day.

They must have survived for some time. They had propped the rear door open and set up the mattresses inside. One body lay in there, shiny plastic-looking and bloated. A tarpaulin was tied between the wheels and angled with string to some shrubs. The cooker, boxes and suitcases were arranged in the lean-to and two people were leaning against the van, looking as if they were resting, except for the flies around their faces. Empty water containers were scattered around and we could imagine the slow-rising dread and the increasing thirst. The desert heat. Flies buzzed around the bodies and the open tins of food. We followed a network of footprints to another body that lay under a shrub a short distance away. Maggots crawled in open wounds. A few metres further a shallow grave had been dug up by dingoes. Half-eaten bits of body and clothing protruded. Must have been the first to die. A frypan and a pot lay nearby and I could see them weakly trying to dig a hole with the utensils, to bury their friend with the dignity he deserved. The first one to succumb to the heat and thirst. Was he their friend? I knew that many of them ended up travelling together with nothing in common but the desire to move to a new country. Thrown together by circumstance, by a small boat and even smaller van, now burying someone they might not even know the name of, but knowing that all too soon it might be them.

'How many in this van?' asked Palmenter.

'Dunno,' said Simms.

Palmenter hit him. He swung his arm full-length and caught Simms on the jaw. Not hard, but deliberate.

'What the fuck, don't know,' he yelled. 'It's your job to know.'

'You said not to write anything down.'

Palmenter hit him again, this time hard enough to knock Simms to the ground. 'You remember. Don't write it down. How hard is it to remember?' He looked around at the scrub. 'We got to know if this is all of them.'

'Five, boss,' I said. I had no idea, but then neither did he. He looked at me. Spanner had moved away when Palmenter hit Simms but I stood my ground. 'Five. This was the last van to leave, I remember it had five.'

No such thing, I made it up but it must have sounded believable. I had counted five bodies and I did not want to spend any longer here scouting around for more. Palmenter grunted.

'Well done, at least someone's got a brain. All right then. Spanner, get a rope on it to pull it back up. You two,' Simms and me, 'put the bodies in the back. Quick smart. Lucky for us no one is ever going to miss these blokes.'

We dragged the bodies into the van. We had to climb inside, then back over them to get out, but it would have seemed disrespectful to just shove them in. We wanted to lay them out carefully but it was difficult as the bodies were putrid and flyblown. Simms began retching when we dragged the maggoty body from under the shrub. It had been eaten, an arm came off and although I tried to avoid looking it was impossible not to look at the face that was half-chewed and crawling. Simms was vomiting but something in me allowed me to hold my breath and keep going. I was thinking how unpredictable Palmenter might be, what he might do if we both stopped working and knelt in the sand with spit dribble, dry-retching. Spanner rigged the 4WD and pulled the van upright, then hitched up a towline.

Simms was quick to volunteer when we needed someone in the van to steer it. It might have been an attempt to redeem himself or perhaps it was to avoid being in the car with Palmenter. I couldn't tell. He kept touching his jaw and it looked more like the pathetic subservient gesture of a minion than for the soreness he might have felt. Anyway, I breathed a sigh of relief. I didn't want to be in with those five stinking bodies that, despite our reverently laying them out, had all tumbled to a mess on the floor as we righted the van.

At the pit Palmenter instructed us to unhitch the van and push it over the edge and torch it. It rolled to the bottom and parked itself remarkably, as if someone had driven it there. Palmenter stood at the top of the pit watching while we gathered a few clumps of dried spinifex and climbed down to stick them under the wheels. Spanner took off the fuel cap and drained some fuel into a tin. He splashed this around inside the van and onto the bodies, then he flipped the seat and pulled the fuel line from the motor and let it fall to the ground. Petrol began to leak out and soak into the ground.

'Stand back!' he called.

He dribbled a line of fuel and lit it. The flame marched slowly across the sand towards the van and almost went out. Simms was halfway up the slope but Spanner and I stood together watching, only metres from the flame that seemed in no hurry to arrive. I thought Spanner was going to say something about the bomb about to go off but he didn't.

'Farewell, you unlucky buggers,' he said.

By the time we got to the top of the pit we could feel the intense heat on our backs and smell blistering paint. Neither of us looked back.

On the drive back to the station Palmenter regained control.

'Good job, boys. Could have been a monumental fuck-up.'

The tension in the car was thick. Spanner was fuming because Palmenter had accused him of not fixing the van properly. I was worried what would happen if he spoke up.

'What were they doing on that road anyway?' I asked nobody. 'You need experience to drive on these sand tracks. In future we need to make sure they only go on the highway, give them a good map, maybe escort them to the turn-off.'

I often came up with useful ways to improve how we did things. Later, when Palmenter and his mates changed how we ran the operation by collecting the vans themselves and driving off-site to meet the imports, I thought it was because I had suggested it.

'You're a smart boy, Son,' said Palmenter. 'Always thinking ahead. That's the way to do business, think ahead, plan for things.' He looked at me, then to Spanner and Simms. 'Sorry I lost it back there, boys.'

Fuckin' arsehole, I thought. Me and him. Arseholes both.

5

We left Cookie to deal with the muster crew. Soon they would fall comatose at the table or struggle to their rooms to sleep it off. This was just a warm-up for them – the big party was always a day after the import, a few days following the muster. Spanner and I took our sandwiches to the station house and entered the office. No one but Palmenter and his occasional visitors ever came in here. It was like entering a holy place, not quite a tomb, but that was what I was thinking. A tomb. Like in Ancient Egypt we should have buried him with all his wealth, all his stuff, just emptied the office out so he could bribe and trade his way through the afterlife and we could get rid of every last reminder of him.

I had been into the office only a few times and each of those had been when Palmenter was there, times when you couldn't look around because he'd be watching your every move, seeing before you did what your eyes were taking in – and you just didn't want to be seen noticing something you were not supposed to, like the phone on the desk that he said didn't exist. Except once.

One time, Palmenter and Margaret were away and there were no girls at the station and Simms was away on a bore run. Charles was in Melbourne. The place was empty except for Spanner, Cookie and me. I snuck into the house to use the phone.

I wanted to call home but I was never allowed near the phone. I would tell them I was okay even if I wasn't because otherwise they would worry. I was sure Palmenter was not coming back for a while but even so I rehearsed in my head my excuse for being there – I had been doing the books in my office on the back verandah and I needed to call someone. Why did I even need an excuse? But the phone in the office had a lock on it and it was a relief in a way because otherwise I would have to stay in the office for a time trying to talk to my parents. I looked around the rest of the house searching for a second phone, knowing there wouldn't be one.

From the outside, the house doesn't look that big. Deep dark verandahs on three sides, a high tin roof dwarfed by the vast sky. Because the dongas are set up on stumps they look high so the stationhouse roof, although high, doesn't seem it. Also the shed on the opposite side is enormous. It has a grader and a tractor and several vans in it. And the water tower and windmill are huge, so the building looks small even though it is quite a big house. It and the windmill were probably all that was here in the early days.

Inside I discovered six bedrooms. I didn't dare go into Palmenter's bedroom. He had his own lounge and sitting area at the front. The office door was next to that. On the other side, to the left of the front entry, was another large sitting room where the girls must have spent a lot of their time. It felt feminine in some sort of way. Connected to the sitting room was a kitchen and dining area. The dining area had a long table and the kitchen looked more like a laboratory, white benches and glassware and cardboard files that I suppose held recipes. Cookie used to do their meals and send them over so I guess the kitchen here was only used to make coffee and snacks. Two corridors divided the kitchen on one side and Palmenter's rooms on the other, from the girls' rooms: Margaret's room, four big dormitory rooms with eight bunks in each, and at the end, the showers and a clinic-type room with a white covered bed and medical stuff. On a remote station it was important to have some sort of place to treat people who might be sick or injured, but what with the kitchen and this room and the dormitory beds and shower room with three cubicles, the whole place felt more like an infirmary, like a convalescent home or prison rehab clinic, a feeling all the more so for the bolts on the outside of the bunkroom doors.

It was spooky that time, but now with Spanner it seemed as if we were supposed to be there. It was only a small step from pretending to Cookie and the muster crew that Palmenter was away and had left us in charge, to fooling ourselves that we were simply doing our job. I felt like I did when I helped Spanner down at the gene pool, hunting around for what it was we were after. Now, the two of us were going to hunt around in the office for things.

The office was cool and uncluttered and in a way, old-fashioned. A dark oasis in the outback glare. It had the same relaxing pine smell as the interior of the car. There was a bookshelf along one side, books neatly arranged as if more for show than reading. I wondered who he would want to impress. No one that I knew of had ever been into this office other than Palmenter and his heavies. Perhaps earlier he might have lived at the station, a domestic life with neighbours and friends coming for dinner or a weekend. Had there ever been a Mrs Palmenter?

Behind the door there were three filing cabinets. Spanner opened the first and withdrew a file. He knew exactly where the forms were kept.

'Start filling those out.'

They were vehicle licence papers, transfer papers, hire documents and blank international drivers' licences.

'If they get pulled over, this is how they prove who they are and that they own the car. None of them have passports, of course. You don't have photo ID on international licences. Technically, they should have their own ID or driver's licence from their own country but the cops never worry about that so unless they do something stupid this gets them past random stops.'

He came over to the desk with a second file. 'This is their names.'

I looked at him, questioning.

'Not their real names, stupid. But foreign ones, names that are hard to pronounce. We write them in here,' he pointed to the blank licences, 'and some here; each car is different so if they do end up together or pulled over by the same cops they don't see a link. This way, cops can't pronounce their names and they don't twig that they don't react when you say their names. You know that old trick.'

I hadn't realised how well organised this end of the operation had been, or how paranoid Palmenter was. Not until we buried those five out at the pit and I began to get an inkling of what was happening. After that van, after that trouble, Palmenter must have flipped. From sometime around then it became only about the money. Palmenter had a way of telling you what you wanted to hear, but once, in my first weeks, he said to me that these people had no one and it was a moral thing to help them, and I believed him. Then that day standing on the edge of the pit with the flames below he said no one was going to miss them. Funny how Palmenter was now under the sand with them.

'What if Palmenter's family come looking for him?'

'He's got no one.'

'You sure? No one?'

'Even if they do – what? We just gotta not say anything. I don't think anyone's gunna come looking. Not before we do this import and then we get outta here.'

It was true. About the only people who ever visited the station arrived with Palmenter, rough men who kept to themselves. Particularly around muster time it was a place that shunned outsiders and we would be long gone by the time anyone else came visiting.

'What will you do?'

He didn't answer me. Why hadn't he left years ago? He had access to the vans and the fuel. Palmenter seemed to trust him, at least as much as Palmenter trusted anybody. Which was not in the slightest.

We set to filling out the forms. Spanner produced a mix of pens and we used different ones on each document. As he finished a page he might scuff it on the floor, or fold it a few times, things to produce some random wear marks on the paper. We had six vans, so we filled two as transfers from some other address, one in Melbourne and one in Darwin. We made hire documents for three. Three different hire companies, in Adelaide, Brisbane and Alice Springs. The last van we made licence papers for an address in Perth.

'If they get stopped out here, cops can't check any of this, so they just look at it. Lazy buggers, they just ignore it. Too much work for 'em to do much else. In New South Wales cops have computers in their cars but they can't check details across the border, so none of these are in New South Wales,' Spanner explained to me.

'You seem proud of it.'

He sighed. 'I guess it was my idea.'

I waited for him to elaborate.

'I was like you when you first came. Keen to help, show that you were smart, worthwhile to have around.'

I was going to object, like you do when people say things about you that are true, and the more true they are the more you want to object. He was right, but then I think we are all like that, it's natural to want to impress when you first start a new job. Not just a job. Any new place where you want to fit in.

What had led him to this place? Why hadn't he left? Why did he seem, at the same time, so content to spend his days pottering with the various cars and machinery in the shed and yet so discontented, drinking beer steadily from midmorning until by early evening he was grumpy and drunk and best left alone? Obviously he had been, still was, a great mechanic. He would grumble and mutter and sip his beer while he worked some assembly he had dismantled down to dust back up to a complex and wonderful machine. That was when he was proudest, just then when whatever it was came back to life. It lasted about ten minutes, then he would be on to the next thing, pulling it apart, talking in equal measure to us both, idly to me and coaxingly to the machine. Later in the afternoon he would leave his bench and I would follow him out under the trees behind the shed and we'd sit, drinking beer and leafing through his tired magazines until by nightfall I had to leave him. He had girly magazines too but they just made you horny. The better ones, the ones we both enjoyed, were of outback adventure with stories of escape and fishing and camping up the coast.

In all our conversations I had never asked him why he stayed. It seemed to be a taboo topic. Was he just as unable to leave as me? I knew that Palmenter rigged the accounts he had me collate, adjusting the price of beer and other charges so that none of us were ever much in credit but, unlike me, Spanner didn't speak of getting away. Maybe he knew that it was an unobtainable dream.

In that shady spot, reading his out-of-date magazines and talking about nothing became an afternoon ritual for us. The closest we ever came to discussing Spanner and his life was when he told me once, out of the blue, that he dreamed of working on a fishing camp up the Gulf.

He showed me an ad for a wilderness fishing camp that was for sale. Fishing? Over this? I guess I was just not into fishing and being stuck at some remote camp on the coast would be for me the same as how I felt now, imprisoned here on the station.

I had no doubt he could run a tourist lodge, but I wanted to laugh and tell him one prison was the same as another. Then I wanted to tell him he would never be able to buy it if he was thinking he was saving the money working for Palmenter. And I wanted to cry for my own unobtainable dreams, though I did not even know what they were. But instead, because I didn't want to hurt his feelings, we planned and talked of his fishing lodge and a grand free life up the coast.

But now he was reflective. He paused between filling forms.

'You just start out, and, y'know, little by little, things, y'know, and suddenly you are caught up in all sorts of shit, can't see how to get out, then another day goes by, and so on.'

I wanted to ask if he meant now or in the past, but I didn't. I thought it better if I kept quiet and he might just open up, tell me things about himself. We worked in silence for a while and soon he was making his little noises like he did when he was working on an engine part.

'When I first got here you told me you didn't do paperwork,' I said.

He laughed.

'Car parts make more sense,' he said, then continued hunched over the desk, muttering sentences as he wrote. When we finished the paperwork he swivelled in the chair and sat gazing out the window. Normally at this time of day he would have opened a beer, but now he sat thoughtfully by the window without talking.

I went to the filing cabinet and began looking through files. They were full of stuff for the running of the station. Catalogues, windmill service schedules, weather maps, flyers from trucking companies, stuff like that. I knew most of the company names because I had been doing the accounts in that small room off the back verandah. That was my first promotion. No phone or computer or anything, just a small room with a desk and chair and an adding machine. Palmenter called it my office.

'There's no accounts or personnel files.'

'They'll be in the safe.' Spanner pointed to the picture on the wall. It was an aerial photograph of the station taken during the wet. Everything was lush and green and ribbons of blue traced the water courses through the burnt red ochre where the stone country was too steep for things to grow. The roads and tracks were a thin lacework unseen until you looked closely. It looked beautiful and incredibly fertile, not the dusty dry barren it could be for half the year, the half year that we knew it in. Travel was too difficult for us to ever see it in the wet like that but I thought it would have been nice to just once fly over in the chopper and see the station from the air. I didn't see why we couldn't do that after muster one time. Later, we did just that. Rob the pilot flew us down to the waterhole, two trips and a bit of a tour on the way. Cookie brought a picnic and some beers. By then there were eleven of us, including Ingrid and Sally the two English language teachers, and Jill who we called a governess. She looked after the children if ever there were any. You've got to have a certain number if you are going to create a viable community and although eleven wasn't quite enough it was better than before. Without making up jobs I couldn't really justify having any more on the station.

Anyway, we flew into the creek. Spanner drove Bitsy down there. He doesn't like flying, says he doesn't trust machines but we think it was that he didn't trust machines he hadn't taken apart and reassembled himself. Rob parked the chopper in the creek, actually in the creek in ankle-deep water and we got out the sponges and soap, gave her a good wash. It was a good day. So hot. Even splashing around in the creek you couldn't get cool but at least we got to see the station from the air. Everyone enjoyed it. You've got to look after your staff like that. Give them things to do, fun things. Things together.

The picture swung open and behind was a large metal safe door.

'Need a key.'

Neither of us wanted to say what we were thinking. We had buried the keys with Palmenter and there would never be any way of opening the safe.

'Might be a spare hidden someplace.' Spanner looked around the room. Although it was neat, there was an impossible number of places a key might be hidden and we didn't even know if there was one. I was wondering if Spanner might have some powerful tool down in his shed – whatever it was he had used to cut the barbecue plate from a grader blade would cut through anything. But cutting open the safe would throw us into a whole new level: somehow shooting Palmenter was much less than shooting Palmenter and then cutting open the safe. I was sure that was how the authorities would see it.

'Is there anything in there we really need?'

'Guess not.'

I was interested to read the real accounts and see what was in the safe but we were really just snooping around. We began picking out books from the shelves and looking at them, laughing that Palmenter might have such titles. Novels. I guess we didn't know, but we didn't think he was a reader. By now it was late, the house was quiet and everyone had long since gone to bed, and it would be best if we did too and left the office untouched, but as we were about to leave Spanner found a set of keys hidden behind a brass bookend. He opened the safe.

On the top shelf was a bunch of documents in yellow envelopes. These turned out to be passports and personal documents, genuine drivers' licences, birth certificates. I leafed through them. None of them meant much until I came to Arif's. Arif. Palmenter must have taken and hidden Arif's possessions. I wondered why he would have kept these documents hidden rather than bury them out in the pit with the clothes and whatever else Arif had. And these other passports, whose were they? Another envelope had some banknotes in it, several types of strange foreign ones neatly banded with their own type.

The bottom half of the safe was a file cabinet on rollers that slid out to reveal a suitcase that Spanner lifted out onto the desk and opened. There were more banknotes. It was full of tightly bound American dollars, Australian dollars and Euros. Mostly it was just stacks of banknotes but there were also some folded manila envelopes with smaller denomination notes, a few thousand worth in each envelope. In the main bundles there must have been hundreds of thousands of dollars of each currency.

Spanner whistled. 'Jeez!'

He picked up a bundle of fifties and leafed through them, counting.

'Couple of hundred or so. That's, um ...'

'Ten thousand. Ten in each stack, two rows of five, fuck! That's half a million bucks. And there's a bit more in American and Euros. Must be close to two million total.'

'What's he have so much cash for?'

'Who cares? Cash business. Going in and coming out. He wasn't doing it for the charity.'

'How much do you reckon they pay?'

'Word is about five grand for the boat trip. Chopper, renting the vans for the trip south'd be about that and more. My guess is he took as much as he could. Took everything they got.'

Everything they've got. How we treated these people, what we did to them was something known but not talked about, because if you talked about it most likely you would find yourself having to do something about it. None of us was brave enough. Y'know, if you don't talk about something, it either doesn't exist or it goes away, so we ignored the faces we saw and turned a blind eye to Palmenter and his cowboys and how they mistreated these people.

'So this might be from just a few trips.' Despite myself I was calculating how profitable the business was.

Spanner probably didn't know as I did that the legitimate side of Palmenter Station was going broke. Suppliers were never paid unless they asked and letters of demand regularly came from banks and collection agents. Palmenter would bring in a bundle of mail from Darwin and throw it at me. I'd open and sort it all, show him the urgent demands. 'Cunts,' was all he'd say, and scrunch up the letters and throw them in the bin. Sometimes, just to get things paid, I'd forge his signature on a cheque and add it to the pile of outgoing mail. I suppose he posted them.

'Why would he keep it all as cash?' I asked.

'Who knows,' said Spanner. 'Better put it back.'

'Why?'

He looked at me but he didn't answer. I think Spanner would have been happy to continue forever as before and maybe he thought that by putting the cash back, life would go on much the same as ever, only without the occasional appearance of Palmenter.

But that was not going to happen.

'Okay,' I said. 'We wait for the dust to settle. If no one comes for it, then we split it. If someone comes asking about Palmenter, knows his business, the cash had better be here. We leave the office as we found it.'

He seemed happy at that.

'If no one comes for it we take half each,' I added. I was thinking about what I might do next. Surely the next thing, whatever it was, would not be as bad as this.

As bad as this. I had just shot Palmenter. I was stealing two million dollars from a safe and I was getting an innocent man involved. I had shot Palmenter and we had buried him in his 4WD and now I was about to steal all his money. Why did I do it? It was going to look pretty premeditated to the police when they found out. And they would find out eventually. Palmenter couldn't just disappear and no one miss him. Spanner might talk. If someone came asking for Palmenter, how did I know Spanner would not just tell them outright that I had shot him? If Palmenter's thugs arrived – and that would only be a matter of time – they'd pretty soon get the truth out of Spanner. Perhaps I should eliminate Spanner as well. He didn't look very strong, although these wiry types often fooled you. I would have to hit him over the head with something heavy from the shed. Do it in the shed when next we were down there. He was the only one who knew. Hit him over the head and shove him into a van and bury him in the pit and no one would know. More money for me. I looked at Spanner and suddenly I felt sick.

'You okay?' Spanner eased me into the chair. 'You look like you're gunna faint. Pale as a parlour girl.'

I sat down. I couldn't speak. I closed my eyes and all I saw was Palmenter's pale neck, wrinkles and stray grey hairs. I opened my eyes and Spanner was packing the suitcase back into the safe, but it was no good, I was compelled to close them again, to see the film to the end but the end never came, it just played over and over Palmenter's revolting bull neck and then nothing, a slight pause, a blink, then again that reptilian leather skin, his pig grunt, and suddenly he turned to face me and it was Spanner not Palmenter and my hand was holding the gun.

'I could buy my fishing lodge.' Spanner sat opposite me and spoke. I looked at him. 'We go halves. A million each. I could afford to buy that camp up on the Gulf.'

'Be sold long ago,' I said weakly.

'Okay. We go halves.' Spanner either didn't hear or didn't want to hear me. He seemed to be suddenly invigorated. I sat there as he went on, grateful not to have to close my eyes and watch that horror film again. 'Lie low for a couple of weeks, then we split the cash, get outta here. I'll buy that fishing camp. You're welcome to come too, if you want. No more mechanics for me. I can cook, run a few lodges, take people fishing an' show 'em how to catch the big ones. Barramundi, coral trout, barbecues each night, fresh fish cooked on coals right there on the sand. It's what they all want, the doctors, lawyers, city folk stuck at their desks got plenty of cash. Time-poor, that's them.'

'Palmenter is a bit time-poor,' I said. I couldn't help it.

'You done everyone a favour. We all wanted. You just got the balls.' He paused for a moment. 'Half is okay by you? 'Cause, well, just you and me.' Perhaps he thought that I wanted more. 'You and me, only ones that know, we better just act like nothing happened.'

Was he threatening if he didn't get half? It really didn't matter.

'Half is okay.'

'Okay. But not for a few weeks. No one gunna miss him. 'Round here, anyway.'

'Anyone in the city? Business partners? What about Mrs Palmenter? He must have family.'

'Margaret?' he laughed.

The thought was a shock. Palmenter and Margaret.

'Is she ...?'

'No! It was a joke. There's no one.'

'Business partners?'

'I don't think so. He has only ever come in here by himself or with the shooters. Or with Margaret. She just looked after the girls, made sure they were healthy.'

'I meant others. They'll come looking. Put two and two together. Us missing, money gone.'

'If he's got anyone. If there is, they'll be asking within two weeks. Anyone close, that is. We just gotta play it cool, say nothing. That sort of cash,' he indicated the safe, 'isn't legit. Ain't no one gunna know it's here. Or not the amount, anyway. We hide the key, lie low, wait for a couple of weeks.'

We both realised we were talking in circles and stopped. We sat silently. His talk and plans for the fishing lodge had at least got me away from thinking about shooting Palmenter. What could I do with a million dollars? I had been quick in my own mind to assess that Spanner was stuck in his familiar world and yet here was he more prepared than I to set out and do something new. I could travel. I could invest. I thought I had enough business sense to turn a million into a few million. At school our team won the sharemarket game, turning our initial thousand dollars into seven hundred thousand. That was pretend money of course, but the principle was the same. If I could do even a bit of that again I'd turn it into several million. Set me up for life.

I must have dropped off because Spanner was shaking me awake.

'Mate, go get some sleep. The chopper will be here first light. We better be ready to run this import or they might smell a rat. Let them fly everyone in as usual but we'll send them south as soon as we can. Not like he done. We don't tell anyone. Not even Cookie.'

The safe was still open and I swung around in the chair for another look inside. There was nothing of particular interest so I began sifting through the files in the cabinet. I was dog-tired and needed a shower but I couldn't leave the room. The top drawer held accounts, neatly labelled in my own handwriting and I realised why Palmenter had got me doing the books in my back office. Here was my handwriting, my work neatly hidden away in the safe with all the incriminating records.

The bottom was a series of files that I hadn't seen before, each headed with a date that must have related to a particular import, because each file held personal details of thirty or so people. It was incredibly incriminating and I wouldn't do it like that, I thought. Funny how even though you are planning to take the money and disappear, some part of you is calculating better ways to do things.

I pulled several out and took them to the desk. Spanner was idly dreaming of where he was going with his million and not really paying attention to the files, just flicking them over. I was only half listening as he listed names and places he dreamed of, because the files were the records of everyone who had come in via the station. A lot of the files contained just a name, a few details such as age, gender, the country and village they were from. Some had a bit more detail, brothers and sisters, parents. I recognised some recurring names that must have been the people and places along the route they took.

Spanner was by now talking about the Caribbean and luxury yachts and suddenly his voice went quiet.

'Here's a whole bunch of letters for you. From Simon Smart. Is that your brother?'

But I hardly heard him. Lucy's file was trembling in my hands as I opened it to find out what had happened to her.

6

After every muster there was a party of sorts at the homestead and it was at one of these that I met Lucy. Palmenter wasn't what you'd call a party animal. For the most part, life on the station was pretty dull, but with all the hard-drinking people who came in for the muster, a party was bound to happen and it was just something that he had to let alone. The muster crew worked hard, and they played hard too.

I was fresh out of school and quite naive, but I feel stupid that I didn't realise what was going on. My school experience included much, but nothing of girls or sex. Well, nothing practical. There'd been a lot of schoolboy brag and bravado but when we'd see the actual girls from St Mary's down the road, when we stood in the queue at McDonald's and flirted with them, it was as if they were from a parallel world that we had no idea how to get to.

It was much the same at the station in a more reserved sort of way, with none of the skylarking but other more subtle ways to get noticed. The women, girls, sometimes up to ten of them, supposedly worked in the kitchen with Cookie, or did jobs around the house, cleaning and stuff. Palmenter usually arrived with them a few days before the main muster and then he would leave as soon as import was over. Margaret and the girls stayed on longer. They seemed to get a lot more time off than us blokes, and often I'd see Spanner lending Margaret one of his vans so she could drive the girls down to the waterhole or go picnic at a place we called the bluff. That was a limestone ridge along the river. You could sit up on the flat top of it and have a great view down the dry creek, you could follow with your eyes the course of the river by the ribbon of trees from just below where their white trunks contrasted with the light green of the leaves, to far off where the green was darker and was all you could see. The rest of the view was dusty-coloured spinifex or red sand. Lucy showed me all these places when, later, we would sneak off to a picnic, to be alone. I'm talking dry season, Christ, you wouldn't go out there in the wet.

They were like the girls from St Mary's. Of course I was interested. I once asked Spanner about who they were.

'Don't go there,' he said. 'He'd have ya balls.'

'Why? It's a free country. He can't stop me, can he?'

'Maybe wouldn't have to. There'd have to be some of you left after Margaret finished with you.'

'Margaret?'

'Yeah. Last thing she'd want is to have you complicating it all. She's as tough as Palmenter.'

And that was it. I didn't know him well enough back then to ask him more.

The night after that particular muster we had a barbecue in the machinery shed. Spanner parked the grader and vans outside and wheeled out some portable barbecues and tubs of ice. A tinny stereo played both kinds of music and the muster crew and the truck drivers lined up in a sort of circle drinking and carrying on. I can't remember if the chopper crew were there; I thought they were but they never came to any of the parties after that so perhaps I'm wrong. I'm sure Palmenter didn't come, he must have stayed inside the homestead. It was dismal at first. There were about twenty of us blokes and a couple of wives of the muster crew who were later arguing with the men. It is important when you run a party to either have enough girls for everyone, or just none, no wives. They complicate things.

One of the muster crew had a guitar and thankfully he played better than the stereo so things started to warm up. Cookie carried out some steaks and set them on the bench, we began cooking them and drinking and because we had something to do it was soon all right. And then the girls arrived.

There were six of them. I hadn't seen the girls when they arrived at the station but here they were. They walked across carrying plates of salad and stuff, being led by Margaret like a mother duck with her ducklings. Suddenly it went silent, everyone stopped talking or carrying on and watched them. Lucy was one of them. They walked across from the homestead with all eyes on them and an expectant hush, an expectant and almost evil hush, like before you slaughter one of the beasts for meat and despite all the bravado and derring-do just before the bullet, or just after, everyone stops, goes quiet. Big blokes and all, they all feel it but none say it. Then the guitar began again and I swear it was just like at the bus stop when the St Mary's bus pulled up, us all showing off and skylarking, talking louder than we needed to and all the time half looking at those girls.

I'd had a few beers and I didn't usually drink so much. A beer or two with Spanner in the late afternoon was all. I was a bit tipsy. Spanner had said not to go there so I was trying to ignore the girls and all the machismo, raised voices. Some of the guys were dancing, I remember people coming and going, I had a few more beers and went out to where the machinery had been parked to make room for the party. I climbed up and lay on the flat bonnet of the grader, by myself with the machinery and the vast sky and the endless black distance. I watched the stars. The air was so dry and the stars so brilliant and I was thinking that this was not me. I did not belong here. It was so beautiful, it was good fun, everyone was having a good time but I didn't belong. Suddenly I was homesick. I began to cry. I was at a party but I was alone, and instead of enjoying myself I was thinking of home where I had left without saying goodbye. I had not talked to Mum and Dad or had a letter from them and I wondered did I even belong back there. Were they that angry with me?

'Why are you sad?'

Through my quiet tears I saw that someone had come out and was standing near the grader.

It was Lucy.

I didn't answer right away. I dried my eyes and thought about it for a long time.

'It's just so beautiful and it makes me feel so lonely.'

She climbed up next to me.

'Well, you don't have to be by yourself. My name is Lucy.' She lay back beside me. 'You are right, it makes us alone to look at the stars that there are so many and yet all of them are alone too, but it is so beautiful. We ...' but she stopped, didn't finish. She had an accent but I couldn't place where from. Not American or British, an accent from speaking a language that is not your main language.

We lay there side by side and I was wishing I knew what to say to her, was wishing I knew more about the stars and constellations so I could tell her something, impress her that I knew something. All of the years of school and exams and certificates and learning and I could think of nothing at all useful or interesting. Nothing.

'Do you think there are worlds out there too?' she asked. She took a swig of my beer and handed it back to me. I put my lips to it, the place where her lips had been, but didn't drink. I didn't want any more beer.

'Sure,' I said. 'That one,' and I pointed at one of the brighter ones. 'I can see some people looking down at us. One of them is pointing. Shh. Shh, oh, no, be quiet everyone, I can't hear what he's saying.'

She laughed and shuffled closer, put her head right next to mine. I could smell her hair.

'Which one?'

'That one. The one next to that bright one. You can see the people over on the left side. It's too hot if they go too close to the bright star so they have to go on the far side.'

I could feel the heat of her body, her breath as she turned her head slightly to mine.

'How many are there?'

'Just two. A boy and a girl.'

We lay for a while longer, I remember that, my arm was touching hers and it was soft, electric, but then somehow suddenly we were kissing and it was not at all like touching my lips to the can where her lips had been. Her lips were wet and cool and soft and the taste of it I can remember but can't describe. Her breath was hot, and I was forgetting to breathe then wondering how to breathe and where to put my nose but our lips stayed together and our mouths opened and we were one person, one mouth, just a mouth and lips together and my body had evaporated except that suddenly I was aware how hard I was. I wanted to roll our bodies together but didn't know if I should, then Lucy's hands found me, rubbed me through my jeans. Do you know how difficult it is to make love on the bonnet of a giant grader? It was lucky because the difficulty of that hid my inexperience. But she did everything, she lifted her dress and slid me inside her, and I came just about right away and it was the most fantastic thing. We lay together on the tractor looking up at the sky and she finished my beer. I felt soft like I had melted into the hard metal of the tractor, how I had been hard, harder and more urgent than that yellow metal, and then soft, fantastic, spaced out, a little drunk, in love, in touch, a part of the sky and stars and universe and content and I began to cry again because I also felt somehow even more alone and insignificant and also that I had done something I shouldn't have done. Not because of Palmenter, no, because of Lucy. I wanted to be with her forever and yet I knew nothing about her. Only her name. Lucy.

I must have fallen asleep. I woke and she was gone, everyone was gone, the place was quiet; everything was just as it had been except that the stars had moved around the sky a bit and I felt a little better. It was so quiet I could almost hear the stars twinkling, the little crackling noise of their fires across light-years and I knew that not only was I insignificant, but so are we all. I lay for a while, then drifted across to my room, to bed. It hadn't been a dream. I could still taste her and feel her lips on mine. Lucy.

The next few days got back to the routine of station life but for me it felt more like the pointless and futile shuffling of deckchairs. The muster crew left, the canteen was quiet at mealtimes and things were more relaxed. Palmenter drove off before dawn one morning as he usually did and the only difference was his white 4WD missing from the shed and a palpable lack of tension around the place. Margaret must have left with him so I began seeing Lucy more often. Spanner warned me a couple of times.

'Don't go there.' Or, 'If he finds out he'll be furious.' What would he do, sack me? Of course there was also bravado – I don't care look at me I'm not scared of Palmenter – and also a showing off: I got the girl and you blokes didn't. But who was I kidding? Palmenter scared me. When he was away everyone just went about station life and ignored us, so Lucy and I spent most afternoons and evenings together, but always there were Spanner's words in the back of my mind.

After the heat of the day we would walk around the settlement, out around the firebreak that took us on a circuit behind all the buildings. It was like walking around an island, the waves of spinifex and scrub washed the shores of our paradise and we talked of lifeboats and rescue, of many things. I didn't find out much about her but I do know she had lived near the sea because I remember that island thing. The spinifex was an unswimmable ocean and a voyage across would lead to either freedom or certain death. It depended on your state of mind.

The girls weren't allowed to eat in the cafeteria, a rule that for some reason persisted even when Palmenter wasn't around because I don't think anyone would have cared. After dinner Lucy would sneak out to my room and we would make love, or sometimes I would take a blanket and we would go for midnight walks and lie together and talk of stars and other worlds and life and infinity. A few times, we borrowed a car from Spanner and went for a picnic or a swim down at the waterhole but it was difficult to do that because Palmenter strictly rationed the fuel.

Funny how time is. The weeks after I first arrived I was kept busy, the hours passed quickly but the weeks dragged. It seemed like a lifetime but in fact it was only a few months after I first arrived that Lucy and I met. Now, with Lucy, the days dragged but the weeks flew by. I stopped thinking so much of home and I remember Palmenter commenting to me that I seemed to be enjoying the place more. A muster and an import were due. He had arrived: the first sign was his car was in the shed, and suddenly everyone seemed on edge. The tension at mealtimes came back. Spanner drank a few more beers each day and preferred to stay by himself in the shed. No one said anything, but you just knew it was down to Palmenter. Lucy and I kept seeing each other but she didn't stay in my room overnight and we didn't make love anymore. She said it was because she had a lot of work to do but I knew it was something else, something she couldn't talk about. She wasn't herself on our evening walks. Occasionally she would let me hold her hand, but it was fleeting, cautious. I felt we were like misbehaving children.

The last time I saw her was three days before the muster. We all knew a muster was coming. Cookie had to do extra food, Spanner was busy, Charles arrived with the truckload of vans, and Palmenter himself was forever coming and going, roaring into the compound in a cloud of dust. He would make calls on the satellite phone while standing on the verandah and would glare at anyone who dared to come near him. One morning, without warning, Palmenter called me over and told me I was to do a bore run. Spanner would organise a 4WD van for me and a map of the tracks I was to follow. He wanted me to leave that day, after lunch. I tried to find Lucy to tell her but every time I went near the homestead Palmenter was there, he seemed to be watching me. Why was it so urgent to suddenly do a bore run? I'd done them before but now I needed a map, had to go further, all the way out along the eastern boundary. Why? Was this some sort of punishment because of me and Lucy?

The night before, Lucy and I had met by the water tower. It was all innocent enough, I wanted her to spend the night in my room, I missed waking next to her, I said, feeling her warmth and softness during the night, I wanted to lie all night curled together with her. She said soon, not tonight, and then when she saw Palmenter watching us from the verandah she hurried away.

Stupid. I shouldn't have cared. I should have gone after her but Palmenter was watching and in my head I was thinking what Spanner had said and also that if Palmenter found out he would be furious and although Lucy and I might walk together as if we didn't care, in truth I was scared. I busied myself about the base of the tower, pretending to do something with the valves and water outlets. I could say that I was trying to protect her by not being too obviously with her, but that would be a lie.

When I looked up he was gone and so was Lucy.

For the first time since I got to Palmenter Station I drove out that afternoon by myself and it was a freedom I had dreamed and yearned for but now it was all sour because I had gone without saying goodbye to Lucy. I worried she might think it was because I wanted to sleep with her that night and she said no, that she would think I had known I was driving the bore run before I talked to her, that I wanted a tumble with her before I took off. What would we say to each other when I returned in two weeks? I thought about her a lot, but did we love each other? Was this love? Or just sex? Or something to hide our loneliness? After all, what did we really know about each other? We made love and talked of the stars and other worlds, of the sky and planets and we laughed at imaginings and fantasy and we never talked of our own world or family or of our own dreams or what had come before or was to come or of how it was that we both came to be here at the end of the world.

As I drove off I was disappointed I had not said farewell to her but knew I'd be back soon. It didn't occur to me that the girls never stayed beyond a single muster or, if I had noticed, it was one of those things I didn't think about too much. Margaret and the girls were just one of the things that happened at the station and only later did it seem odd, only later when I knew more.

And now here I was alone in the office with Spanner while he went on about cruise liners and romance and I was thinking again about Lucy who I had tried not to think of, and with the twenty-twenty vision of hindsight suddenly saw some things I should have seen before. Like, how the pine smell I found so comforting and vaguely familiar in Palmenter's car was the same as the perfume of Lucy and it was the same clean smell of the homestead. Like how Spanner all along had been my friend. Did he know that Lucy had been arrested and sent to a detention centre? Or did Palmenter drive out with Margaret and all the girls and then deposit Lucy at a police station? I never found out if he did know but if Spanner had not told me to back off I might be with Arif right now.

I had got back from that bore run and Lucy was gone and I knew immediately it was a deliberate plan of Palmenter's. I was furious, but I knew not to confront him. Instead I went to him with a carefully worded speech. I had decided, I said, that station life was not for me. I reminded him that I was promised a ticket home after six months. At first he seemed obliging.

'Sure, have to be after the wet. Roads are all closed, but soon as then, if you still want. We'll see if you want to leave then, Son.'

I asked him if I could use the phone to call home as I hadn't heard from my family for six months. I knew he had a phone in his office and he also had a satellite phone.

'Phone calls are expensive out here. Company doesn't allow private calls, Son.'

'Just a short call,' I pleaded.

He refused, but said I should write them a letter.

'I'll make sure it gets out with the next chopper. Take a bit of time to get delivered, arrive home about the time you do.'

He said it with such derision, as if wanting to contact my family was the thing of a weakling. Despite my carefully worded request and calm forethought I saw red. I called him an arsehole and stormed off. I was so furious that I might have done anything but Spanner told me to play it cool, to take it easy.

'He's right, the roads are all closed. Plus, he's just not worth it.'

He didn't say she's not worth it, but that Palmenter was not worth it.

Of course I didn't leave after the wet and I know now that my letter never got delivered. I think what happened to Arif soon after was a plan by Palmenter to keep me tied into his schemes and make it so that I could never leave. He made a decision who to keep, who should go. I was useful to him. I looked tough but I was a weakling who could do the books and keep the paperwork in order.

I am sure I owe my life to Spanner because he calmed me down.

7

It was the build-up to the wet. Everyone was short-tempered and even the smallest thing irritated. Palmenter and Arif were walking towards one of the vans and Arif was talking and jerking his arms for emphasis. Palmenter was listening, or at least he appeared to be listening, as he motioned towards the car. When he saw me he signalled me to come too.

'Come on, let's take a drive.'

I didn't know what was going on. I could tell that, like me, Palmenter disliked Arif's in-your-face way of talking. Arif would look close at you, stare straight at you as if to challenge. It was annoying.

I knew my way around the station pretty well by now and I couldn't think where we might want to drive to at such short notice. It was three hours to the roadhouse and town was an overnighter. Not that I'd ever done it. Cookie and Charles were the only ones who ever got to leave the station. I thought perhaps Palmenter was going to show us something to do with sacred sites.

Arif had asked about these and we all knew there were sites. Most were so sacred we were not allowed to go near them. Recently, when Spanner said something about sacred sites, I had asked him where they were. He answered that no one knew and I wondered why he had mentioned it.

'They'll let you know if you get too close,' he added.

He was referring to the muster crew, who sometimes made reference to the special places they had charge of in a way that made it clear they were sacred. The crew lived a fairly traditional life on the station somewhere but I had no idea where. From my bore runs I had discovered just how big the station was, and it was no real surprise that after the muster they could disappear as if melting into the land. I wished I could have stumbled upon a group and that they'd take me in, not only to escape Palmenter but so they could show me some of their old ways, share some of their secrets. Because there was something more out there, something spiritual. The longer you were out there the stronger it felt.

Out on the bore runs I would park on a rise and see in every direction: spinifex and grassland and shrubs and the snake path of trees along a watercourse, a shimmering endless view where even the tiniest bit of glass, a car, a movement or smoke from a campfire would have shown up as a beacon. I could never see them, but I was certain they would know where I was. At muster time they appeared as if by magic in their beat-up old cars and descended on the homestead, crowded out the canteen drinking our beer, then disappeared as quickly when it was over. And I knew, even before Spanner said it, that if I had come close to a place I was not supposed to go they would be there to stop me.

Arif was a Moslem. Palmenter called him a raghead.

'Where is that thieving raghead?' he'd ask, as though Spanner or I were supposed to know. Thing was, we usually did, we'd have seen Arif heading someplace a few moments before. Palmenter had given him a job on the station so he could pay off his debt but, like all of us, unless there was a muster going on, his actual tasks were a bit ill-defined.

'Dunno,' one of us would say, and Palmenter would storm off.

Arif prayed several times a day, kneeling down on a special little rug he had. In the canteen he would often talk about God, or Allah, about worship, about how our lives needed to be spiritual. Not in a way that was seeking to convert us, more that he was interested. It was a question. He was a recent immigrant and wanted to know about the dreamtime, the sacred places, and he thought we would know about them. He wanted to be taken to see them and he refused to accept either that we didn't know where they were or that we were not allowed to go there. How could a site be sacred if you couldn't go there? Sacred was where you went with reverence; you paid respect by going there. A place couldn't be sacred if you never saw it.

Of course, I know now that Arif came in on a boat that Palmenter had organised and that he must have come in with a much larger group that landed while I was out on a bore run. He had no family, no one in Australia and if anyone back where he came from knew he was alive, they certainly didn't know where he was. Palmenter had probably given him a job solely because of that, no one would miss him, he could not complain about wages or conditions or anything, but this was a subtlety lost on Arif. He complained about everything.

Arif had been quite vocal from the moment he arrived. About how things were, about how long it was all taking, about money, the food, everything. By then I knew how Palmenter operated and I knew he would make some sort of offer to Arif, put him on the payroll, give him a job. But even that didn't stop him complaining. The food wasn't halal. There was nowhere to pray. We were all godless infidels who would burn in hell. We generally ignored him or avoided him, or sometimes we goaded him if we were bored and feeling like some sport. Mostly that was Cookie, who'd stand at the counter with the hatch open while we were eating and say something like 'all men of god' or 'that halal enough for you?' in a voice of genuine concern.

As we drove off, Arif was talking about the justice of Allah and sacred things. I wondered if perhaps Palmenter was going to show us some lesser site, make up something to keep Arif happy. It was one of Palmenter's things he would do, tell you of bigger things and get you thinking of the greater picture, the greater good. He liked saying things like 'Son, the Great Spirit is watching over you', or he would tell you things about the ancient land and culture, make you feel both insignificant and yet somehow wanting to be important, wanting to play your part. It was all bullshit, of course. It was just his way of getting what he wanted. Other times, it would be 'fuck the land', or 'fuck traditions' or whatever it was that was in his way.

I realised Arif must be leaving because he was haranguing Palmenter about how he was expected to survive in the city now that Palmenter had taken all his money. How much he was owed for working there. Then he was talking more generally, about all of the imports, how Palmenter has been ripping them off. Arif wanted to know why some people had paid several thousand dollars more than others for basically the same thing, to be bundled on a boat with a small amount of rice and a place to sit, then smuggled into the station to be sent off with only a map and a dodgy campervan. I took it from his tone that Arif must have paid a lot more than others. I was pretty sure that Palmenter charged whatever he could: if he thought you had more, you paid more. It was how he operated.

'In business, you charge what you can get away with,' he told me once. 'It's got nothing to do with how much it costs. It's all about how much people will pay.'

'How do we survive in Sydney with no money?' Arif said. 'How we pay for food, for fuel to get us there? Maybe we be better in Villawood, they give us someplace to stay, feed us until we get a visa. They say it's not so good in there but I think maybe it's not so bad. Not so bad as this with no money, no food, you take everything then send us away. You give us some money back,' Arif demanded. 'You pay me for work I do.'

Palmenter shrugged. I got in the back. If Arif could resign, perhaps I could too. But not now. I would have to wait until Palmenter was in a better mood.

'This old van, I think he break down on way. We no get to Sydney, how we gunna fix with no money, eh?' Arif kept talking as he got in the front. 'If we get stopped by police, I must tell all about you.'

'You lucky to get this far, Son. You now in the lucky country. You lucky to come here with me and not one of those leaky boats. Sink on the way. How far can you swim, Son? You keep on like this, you upset everyone. Everyone else is happy to be here and you just making trouble. You talk to the police, you won't even end up in Villawood and everyone knows how bad that is. No, Son, you'll be sent to Maribyrnong. That's right, on the army base, and let me tell you, that is real hell. You'll be left rotting away for years. Throw away the keys, leave you to rot. Don't come running to me for help when that happens.'

Palmenter was driving us out towards the highway.

'You know how bad it is there? People go mad, commit suicide. They die rather than stay there. You don't want to go there, Son. You're best off with me. I do the best for you. You come to a new land because you want the good life and I am the one who got that for you. I got you here. Don't throw it away.' He was speaking in short fragments and I knew underneath he was seething. 'You ragheads all the same. No gratitude.'

But Arif kept on.

'The van is old. You sell us an old car, if he break down maybe someone ask us where we from. I think the police ask us where we from, ask for passport, I no got. No one got.' Arif was looking around the interior of the van as he spoke, pointing to faults. 'This not working. This broken. Look.' He pointed out the interior light, the taped-up side window, holes in the seat.

I kept quiet in the back, wondering where Palmenter was taking us. I knew that Spanner had these vans working reliably and it would be unlikely that any of them would break down. The interiors he did not bother with, but the motors and gearbox, good tyres, they would be reliable. Not worth whatever outrageous price Palmenter charged for them, but then, what was the alternative?

'They not all happy, not like you said. Everyone is complaining, about you, about the boat and the food, about how you take take take, and we have no money left, nothing left. We come here for a better life and now we have nothing, there is nothing.' He gestured at the wide barren sandplain and as Arif made his gesture I could see what he meant. From the homestead the track sloped down towards the highway and we had a grand view. Even the highway was only that in name, and beyond that the land disappeared in a blue haze. 'There is nothing. They ask me to speak for them, they say for me to tell you we don't mind this Villawood, you can't scare us with that. You give us some money back so we can live when we get to Sydney.'

Who Arif had been talking to I don't know. The crew he came in with had all long gone, their vans returned. He had helped out on a second lot a week or so ago but, like me when I first arrived, Palmenter had arranged things so that Arif had minimal contact with them.

We got to the highway and Palmenter paused at the turn-off. I thought he was going to drop Arif here. Tell him to get out and then leave him in the sweltering sun, tell him to wait for a car, a car that would never come because out here along this road there were only about two cars a year. Arif would spend a long freezing night and then walk all the way back along the track the next day, apologetic and appreciative of exactly how isolated we were.

Then Palmenter looked at Arif as if he had just realised something, and drove across the highway and along the track to the rubbish pit.

'That's nonsense, Son. I take a big risk doing this. I don't have to do this. Everyone else is happy to be here, safe, a new life, a new land. This is the lucky country. If you want a better life, you gotta take risks too. Take a chance.'

There was something in the way he said the word 'risks' and 'lucky'. He looked up and our eyes met in the rear-view mirror.

'Ain't that right, Son? This is the lucky country and there ain't no better place to take your chances.'

It was silent in the van for a few seconds. I think Arif was about to start again, but Palmenter began first, talking more to me that Arif.

'We don't want whingers. Complainers. You gotta know your place. That's just the way it is. Anyway, there is nothing wrong with these vans. Ask Spanner. He fixes 'em right up.'

We pulled up at the rubbish pit and Palmenter got out first, walked around the front to Arif's door and was standing with his back to us. I thought he was looking out at the horizon, waiting for us, and I was getting out of the back when a shot rang out and I turned back just in time to see Arif's body slump to the ground.

I'm not sure what happened next, I thought I froze but somehow I was around the front holding onto the roobar feeling giddy and Palmenter was saying something like 'we don't want whingers in this country' or maybe I only imagined that, like I imagined him saying he couldn't take the risk of Arif telling the police and was it then or later that he said that he had found out that Arif was a Taliban spy. Taliban for Christ's sake. Did he think I was stupid?

Arif's body lay on the red sand, dark blood seeping out and soaking into the sand. There was a big hole in his chest but his eyes were open as if he were alive and questioning, staring up at the sky. Those same eyes that had looked around at me in the back seat of the van as if to question, 'Why do you accept it?'

Palmenter kicked a spray of sand over him. 'Be gone in a week. Buzzards and dingoes and ants eat him in no time. That's what happens out here. We don't like dobbers.' He threw the keys at me but I missed them and they fell into the sand. My hands were shaking as I picked them up. 'You drive. Don't go to pieces on me, Son.'

I drove back in a daze. Palmenter had to tell me to slow down, and at some point I think I remember him telling me that Arif was Taliban, but that might have been earlier and we might have driven in silence. I had the taste of vomit in my mouth.

I wondered why he brought me with him. Did he only decide at the last minute? Did I just happen to be walking past at the moment he was taking Arif to the van, or had he deliberately waited until he saw me? Maybe he thought he needed someone with him, and I happened to be the unlucky one. Perhaps initially he was going to leave Arif at the highway and it was only as he went on and on, threatened to tell the police, said he would get the whole group behind him, that Palmenter decided to do what he did.

I never told anyone about Arif. Not until now. I don't know if he was the first but I now know he was not the last. It was from about that time that I thought Palmenter changed but it might have been me that changed. I now knew what he was capable of and feared for my life. His comments were aimed at me. I was the only one with him, and Arif was still warm under a kick of sand and he had said it as if he and I were mates agreeing about something, like simply talking about the footy. 'The Cats will make the finals this year'; 'We don't like dobbers'. He was threatening me. I knew too much, I could never leave, because he didn't trust me. He didn't trust anyone.

'He was Taliban, Son. Infiltrating son-of-a-bitch.'

I doubted it. And anyway, did that matter?

Trust is a funny thing. Some people say you have to give it out before you get it back. I say it is more like the air we breathe and we need it to stay alive, and sometimes a breeze simply blows it all away and some disease of distrust infects everyone and you have to look out for yourself. Suddenly I didn't know who I could trust. Were they all in on it? Charles? Simms? Cookie? Even Spanner?

I hid in my room and slunk between the canteen at mealtimes and my room or my work. I hardly talked to anyone. I couldn't sleep properly. I would wake in the middle of the night, not from a dream, not nightmares as such, just all of a sudden I would wake and lie there terrified, suddenly aware of something I couldn't name, like something more that my subconscious knew and was trying to tell me. I tried smoking some of Cookie's crop but that made it worse. I'd smoke myself to a stupor and then wake hours later gripped by fear.

Palmenter came and went as usual and the times he was gone it was a relief, but I knew he could be back anytime. I didn't trust myself. If I talked with Spanner or Cookie I was sure to blab about Palmenter shooting Arif. I thought if I said anything to anyone, Palmenter was sure to find out and then I'd be out in the pit too. I did the only thing I could do. I busied myself in work.

Despite all the things that happened, life on the station was mostly dull routine. Between the imports or musters we had all the stuff of keeping the place going. I had fences to fix, particularly around the waterholes where we pumped water for the stock up to a trough, and fenced the waterhole to keep the stock out. The pumps were solar-powered and frequently broke down, and it was my job to check them, weekly for the closer ones and monthly out along the boundary. I'd have to arrange with Spanner for a van and Palmenter would release only enough fuel for the trip. Cookie made up a supply pack. I enjoyed those trips away, camping out under the stars. Maybe I could have done a runner, nursed the fuel and got as far as the roadhouse, but that was the only road out and my luck would be I'd run into Palmenter on his way in.

Charles taught me to drive the grader and we used it to fix some of the tracks that had been washed away in the wet. That was fun. I didn't mind being with Charles. He was so difficult to understand and because of that I had to concentrate and that meant I wasn't likely to say anything stupid. I suspect he found me equally as difficult, but we talked anyway, a sort of laughing parallel conversation, him saying stuff and me too back at him, most likely nothing to do with what either of us are talking about, but I think he was mostly laughing at me and my attempts to drive that thing. The grader was too big for the job. I could have put it into gear and driven a complete straight line back to Melbourne, flattening everything in the way. Except maybe Uluru. I would have driven up and over Uluru leaving a scrape mark that would be my legacy in this world. My escape would have been at half a kilometre an hour and would take thirty-five and a half weeks. Don't laugh. I worked it out. It is three thousand kilometres as the crow flies and that is two hundred and fifty days or thirty-five and a half weeks. I imagined Cookie would do the catering. We would all escape. Cookie, Spanner and me. But how do you cover a track like that?

And Palmenter would not need that track to follow us. He seemed to have the ability to appear out of nowhere, to have overheard conversations, to know what you were thinking.

To keep myself busy I did extra things. I repainted some of the dongas. Spanner had Simms repainting the vans so I borrowed some paint and redid my room. Then I did the next, and so on. It was better than thinking about things, although with painting it is easy to start thinking. You have to keep concentrating on the job, all the little details, and make sure you don't start thinking again.

Cookie had his drugs. Spanner his shed and car parts and beer. I became like them and soon I was finding small pleasure in my tasks.

I took over the running of the vegetable garden. I redirected all the pipes from the water tower and made it semi-automatic. There is so much sunlight up there and the soil is fertile, all it needs is water and things grow. Cookie reckoned his herb garden was the best it had ever been and that this was the most potent crop he had ever had. Shame that he was the only one smoking it. Simms or Charles might have had some or maybe he gave some to the girls when they were there. I doubt it. I now understood the joke he had made when I first met him. Community garden. This was no community. This was the hopeless refuge of misfits and unfortunates.

We also had tomatoes, lettuce, pumpkins, eggplant, beans climbing the fences, chilli, capsicum. Lots of stuff. We ate well. Later when I took over, I got some chooks and we had fresh eggs. I planted fruit trees, and the oranges and grapefruit did well. But for now I was hiding in the garden to avoid the others and to not talk about Arif.

Palmenter had given me some admin work that I took to do in the canteen. We quite often got to speak but never of anything other than instructions and answers. A few days after Arif, he told me to do a rubbish run. Out at the pit I scouted around the area, unsure of the exact spot, but there was no sign of Arif's body. He had been swallowed by the red earth. Gone. Buried by someone or eaten by ants and animals – it did not matter. I am sure Palmenter deliberately sent me out there so I'd see there was no trace of Arif and know exactly how much my body would be seen by others if he chose. Not at all.

Soon after that I was given a room at the side of the back verandah where I did some of the bookkeeping and that was the first time he mentioned I could become more useful to him, that he needed someone to take on more responsibility around the place.

Not on your life, I thought.

'Okay,' I said.

My new job was simply sorting invoices and delivery dockets and stuff like that, but at least it put me nearer the girls and I could often hear them inside the house. The floor creaking, a door opening or closing, occasional laughter that was as rare and as cool as rain. I did wonder if Margaret was in some way their Palmenter, if she kept a watchful eye on them and that they could only ever partially relax, and only ever if she were away. If they were sitting on the verandah I would sneak a look out at them through my half open door, or walk past pretending I had to get something from a file, but since Lucy I wasn't interested in anything other than to look and maybe catch a bit of their conversation. Their voices were gentle and soft like dew on a harsh landscape. They seemed muted, half person, half automaton. Suppressed I'd say now. Scared. Like me. Sometimes, if I knew both Palmenter and Margaret were away I'd sit in my office trying to summon up the courage to say something directly to them. Hello. Or a smile. But then I'd remember Arif and my heart would race and I'd get back to work.

Slowly my memories faded. Too soon it was another muster and the place was full and busy again and I didn't have time to remember even if I wanted to. Cars and vans came and went, the chopper flew in and out several times a day. At the cattle yards, trucks loaded and shook the earth as they drove out behind Spanner's shed on one of the roads I had graded. Each time I was fearful that it would collapse, fearful that then Palmenter would notice me again. Then Simms and I went out to shoot a bullock and butcher it to bring home steaks for the end-of-muster party and I found myself a wretched mess, shaking and sweating and Simms had to take over from me. The way the bullock fell, the way it folded under itself and then lay down to rest, eyes open looking out at the big sky, the way the earth stained with blood. I couldn't bear it. I told Simms I was ill and when we got back to the station I hid in my room waiting for the dread to pass.

8

It was about this time that we built the barbecue. I can't remember who first had the idea or even if we discussed it together, perhaps it was Charles who started it by bringing up some bricks. It was difficult to get anything we wanted into the station quickly or officially but we could get Charles to collect building materials from Melbourne. Each time he trucked the vans up, he would pick up things. On trips over several months he got a few bricks or the odd bag of cement, from different building sites each time, so it was all free. He also had a credit card for fuel and food but because I was checking the accounts I allowed him to spend a bit on timber and shadecloth. I knew Palmenter wouldn't notice. This was how we got our brick barbecue.

It was how the bicycle thing started too. One time Charles turned up with an old bike he had picked up from the streetside where it had been left as part of a council clean-up.

'Hey Charles, where you get that old bike from? I hope you didn't pay much. Whatever you paid, I think they seen you coming.'

'No pay nothing. I pick it up from rubbish heap. You want I can get you one?'

'Nah. Where am I gunna ride round here?'

But Spanner fixed it up and gave it a new coat of bright red paint and soon we all wanted one. Next trip Charles returned with several bikes. Most of them ended up on the gene pool but Spanner salvaged bits and turned out three that he repainted. One bright red, one yellow, and one matt black. These three remained ownerless, the only rule being that if you got a flat tyre or if anything broke you took responsibility to get it fixed. I used one to keep fit, riding a circuit around the station houses. Each circuit took a bit over three minutes but the fastest ever circuit was ridden, of all people, by Simms, who clocked one minute thirty-five.

But that was much later. I was telling you about the barbecue. It took almost the whole year to cart up enough material, or rather, we kept adding to it over the year, so it took shape slowly. Everything was trucked up by Charles except what we could scrounge from the gene pool, like the big metal cooking plate that Spanner cut from the steel of a grader blade. The plate had a slight curve to it, enough to drain the fat that would spill over the side and onto the fire. If you wanted the fire to flare up a bit you let the fat drip like that, or you could slide a lever to divert it into a tin. Mostly it was Spanner who did the construction but over the year we all did our share, adding little features and ideas. Spanner had it so the plate could tilt either forward or backward, to give you some temperature control and Cookie loved it. Not only did it barbecue meat exceptionally well but he could do stir-fry and flatbreads and all sorts of things on it.

It was magnificent. We built it under the water tower. We brick-paved an area and built a pergola out from under, so the area had shade if you wanted it. We had tables and chairs and a whole long bench on one side, a sink, running water direct from the tank above, and the barbecue. The barbecue area grew in the same way a garden grows, slowly. Or rather, it evolved. Each muster Charles would arrive with the truck and as we unloaded the vans we would eagerly anticipate what he had managed to find for us. One time he arrived with a Metters No. 1 stove, one of those old wood-fired stoves like my grandma had in her kitchen. We built that into the barbecue, with its own chimney. There was a storage area for wood between, and a curved part of wall running behind that, sort of enclosing between the chimneys, with an alcove and shelf where we had a statue.

The statue was life-size, as tall as a real person, and was of a naked woman holding a jug. It was solid cement and arrived, as usual, with Charles.

'How did you get that?'

'Oh, I was driving along, and it, how they say? It fell off a truck.'

'Then how did you lift it onto your truck? And why isn't it damaged? I think if it fell off a truck it would be broken.'

'Oh, I think it was landing on something. Lifting it on by myself was very difficult, but I am strong,' he said evasively. Charles was developing the larrikin Aussie sense of humour. He stood a little Van Damme pose and flexed his biceps. Ripples. He was not as thin as Simms but he was no weightlifter and there was no way someone didn't help him to steal it. We were all very proud of this statue and it was given centre place in the barbecue back piece.

The barbecue area only stopped growing when Charles arrived one time with some beanbags. Somehow, we discovered that these fitted perfectly on the tray of Bitsy so we would load up with beer and food and head out to the river flats where the bloodwoods were old and dry, because with the brick barbecue came the need to collect firewood. So we had a great excuse to spend the day out – Simms, Charles, Cookie, Spanner and I. Once Cookie even persuaded Margaret to let the girls come with us.

There was an area of woodlands to the east, beyond the creekbed and past the bluff, flood plains where bloodwood trees grew quickly and died just as quickly each wet season. We drove Bitsy around, smashing over sticks and dead trees, and breaking them into fire-sized pieces by driving back and forth over them. As we drank more beer our enthusiasm for destruction grew and we would knock over a few extra 'for next time'. We would stack the branches up over the top of Bitsy and tie the lot down with a long rope that went up over and then back to itself underneath the car. Often on the way back the rope would snag on something and we'd have to retie the lot. But efficiency wasn't our aim.

The after-muster parties became centred around the barbecue. There was no way Palmenter did not notice the slow build of that thing. I think it must have been about six months before the main part was done and we could start using it, but we kept adding and adding and it was the second Christmas when the statue came. Palmenter never said a thing. Never. Early on we thought he would ask what we were doing and tell us to tear it down. Later, when it was obvious what it was, he might have said something. Like he liked it. Or well done. Or even that he didn't like it. Nothing.

He was always interfering in work around the place, asking what we were doing or watching from his place where he often stood on the verandah. Although he let stuff arrive on the truck without commenting I was smart enough to know that Charles and the truck was not a way of escape. I didn't even dare ask Charles to take a message out for me. But it was like the barbecue was invisible. It became a sort of shrine, a special place for us all. This massive brick and metal barbecue with stove and sink and statue was never going anywhere yet it was our symbol of freedom. Of escape.

To a casual observer the station seemed to be running well and that was exactly as Palmenter wanted it. We all knew, to varying degrees, what was going on. Although Simms noticed very little about anything and Cookie rarely knew what day it was, I am sure we were all aware that the station was a front for smuggling people into the country. Charles must have known and approved because at each import he collected and returned the vans to us. Exactly how much of it Palmenter owned or organised directly I didn't know, but he had something to do with everything, of that I was sure. When the boats reached the coast, the chopper, under cover of the muster going on, flew into the station where the people were put up in the dongas for a few days. This got them away from the coast and out of the areas where authorities might be looking for them. Later on we used this same basic system but I improved it quite a bit.

They were divided into groups of three, or four, maybe five for one of the bigger vans, and sent south to either Melbourne or Sydney. Only one van would leave in a day, and we gave them each a different route. We had several routes marked out on maps. When they got to the city, the vans were returned to the station ready for the next import. I suspected Palmenter had eyes and ears all along the way, tracking their progress and reporting any problems, and people in the city ready to take back the vans as they arrived.

Although I was doing the bookwork I had little idea about the import side of things. That was all handled by Palmenter and it was all done in cash, but I did discover that the station was losing money and that Palmenter was feeding just enough cash back in to keep it afloat. At least, that's what I thought was happening. One time, I added up the amount of musters and the number of cattle supposedly shipped out and sold. I joked with Spanner.

'Must be something in the grass out there, 'cause they sure are fertile cattle.'

Spanner was the only person I could talk to. He was my friend but I didn't want to come right out and say what I suspected. I wanted to see if Spanner would volunteer anything, how much he knew or was prepared to divulge to me.

'Best if you didn't notice that one, I think,' was what he said.

Earlier on, before Arif, before leaving became so urgent, I was out on a bore run and I noticed the road out along the east boundary was well used. At the time I idly thought it must lead somewhere. Later I calculated that if I drove carefully on my runs I might siphon off some small amounts of fuel, store it in containers some place, and I could leave the station via this back way without Palmenter knowing. So I had followed the road for a way and was surprised when I came back to the cattle yards: this wide road did a big circuit around the property and came right back to where it started. Except for a few very sandy 4WD tracks, the only way onto and off the station was via the homestead so the purpose of this well-formed loop of road was a bit of a mystery.

Sometimes Arif was only a memory and I could spend content afternoons with Spanner looking through his fishing magazines. Life was as near to normal as it could be. But other times we would sit together and I'd leaf through the magazines angered at how old they were, that Spanner could be entertained by something he had seen or read thousands of times. Or, worse, I'd have something I wanted to know or understand and I would struggle with how to broach the subject.

It was like that one day when I had been doing some accounts and suddenly it dawned on me. Close to the time of each muster there was a cash deposit, barely enough to keep the place solvent. There was no other income and the amounts varied considerably. I didn't think cattle prices fluctuated that much and I doubted buyers paid cash. Plus, we were running a muster every month now and there simply couldn't be that many cattle or I'd have seen them while out on the bore runs. The cattle were mustered up, loaded on trucks, driven around the property, then unloaded again.

'It's all a front, isn't it, to cover the choppers coming and going? The noise and dust and traffic. It hides what he's really doing.'

'Best if you don't go there,' Spanner said.

Obviously the truck drivers knew what was going on. Probably the whole muster crew did too. Anyone who knew anything about how to run a cattle station would know that you couldn't run a muster every month. Perhaps they all started out like me, innocent, doing odd jobs and legitimate business, slowly being drip-fed more about the real nature of it and by acceptance becoming complicit, or being threatened and being too weak to act, slowly in deeper until too far gone to get out. Perhaps that is how they all got involved.

Must be that everyone was in on it at some level. The cops, too. The cops had come to tell Palmenter about the five who had perished out on the south track and I'd seen them take money and steaks from him. And some of Cookie's dope.

The imports paid thousands of dollars each and there were twenty or thirty each month. This was more than a few dollars earned as a bus stop along a people-smuggling route, it was a big business, a hundred grand or more a month, and we were the central point. Even if Palmenter himself was not the king pin, what happened at Palmenter Station was integral to the whole operation and now that I was doing the accounts I was becoming integral too. I had helped to bury bodies and I had witnessed a murder and I felt the real threat that if I tried to leave I would end in the pit next to Arif. I had to get away. Far away. I couldn't trust any of them, not even Spanner who had been here with Palmenter from the beginning and was warning me, gently, to back off.

It was about then that I decided that I had to leave no matter what. Palmenter was slowly giving me more office work to do and Simms was being sent on more of the bore runs. I realised that eventually I would not be sent on any bore runs so I'd have to act soon. I figured if I drove to the south boundary along the cattle road I'd only have to cross two creeks and some dune country to make one of the old desert tracks. They would be soft sand, but should be possible if I let the tyres down. Once I got to the main road I would drive slowly until a roadhouse where I would pump them up again. If I did it on a bore run I would be in Sydney by the time they noticed I was gone. I siphoned off small amounts of fuel whenever I could. It would have been easy to bleed diesel from the generator tank, or from the dozer or grader, but the vans were petrol so I had to take a little each time I went out on the bore run. If I drove very carefully I could eke out the ration I was given, siphon off a few litres each time.

I started a collection of two-litre milk containers that were easy to hide each time I did a rubbish run. I hid the full ones under the laundry where no one would ever look. Although Spanner was my friend I didn't tell him. When I left I'd take one of the vans and he'd work it out. I told Cookie, saying I was heading off on a two-week bore run and needed extra food. I probably shouldn't have done that.

I was nearly ready to go when Palmenter came to me.

'Come for a drive,' he said, 'I've got something to show you.'

He drove me in one of the vans towards the main road and I wondered what we were going to see. He was so casual and disarming that I didn't suspect a thing until about halfway there.

'So you wanna leave, Son. Wish you'd told me. We could have talked about this.'

I was stunned. I didn't know what to say. I nearly panicked. If he had discovered my plan or found my secret fuel stash I would be about to join Arif. But of course he knew I wanted to leave. When I first asked he had said, 'Okay, but work out to the end of the month.' By the end of the month, another muster: 'Not while the muster is on, Son, don't leave us in the lurch.' There was always a reason to stay a little longer and he either preyed on my sense of responsibility – 'You did sign on for the year, Son, and we've spent a lot of effort getting you up to speed, to be useful round here.' – or he'd offer some incentive.

'Son, if you stay the six months, that gets you to the bonus, well worth it, Son. I know you're only up here for the cash so it would be silly to pass up the chance of the bonus.' He was sort of right, and then there was the wet, another muster, another year gone by.

'I look after my people, but if they don't want, well, what can you do. You just gotta let them go.'

Had he found the stuff? I was trying to form words, wondering whether to deny that I had planned to leave without telling him, but he didn't seem to want me to talk and I think he was saying something but I couldn't hear anything but the rush of blood in my ears. We were approaching the road and beyond that the track up to the pit and the rifle was sitting there on the dash as it always was and perhaps as we slowed for the corner I could grab the gun and run. I tried to still my breathing, calm my heartbeat.

I was much younger than him. I could move a whole lot faster. If I jumped as we turned to the right I could roll with the momentum and grab the gun as I went. I'd be out before he moved. I moved my hand onto the door handle, but instead of turning he stopped at the road, left the engine running and sat looking straight ahead.

'Out ya get. Off you go, don't come back until you're ready to be on the team.'

Dumbly, numb, and without grabbing the gun I got out. He wouldn't do it here on the road, but just in case, I stood back a bit, behind the door pillar where I could see him but he would have to turn to see me. He simply drove off, away up the road as if he had dropped me at the highway to catch a bus. I watched dumbfounded as the van sped off and I hadn't moved when it slowed, turned around, and gathered speed as it came back towards me. I felt hunted. Was he playing with me? Was he going to run me down or worse, was he going to shoot at me for some sporting fun?

I ran. I took off into the desert as quickly as I could across the soft sand and tried to put some scrub between me and him. I heard the van continue up the road. I kept running, jogging, fearful he might come back. I ran from the road until suddenly I was on the long downhill that leads towards the pit. I would have heard the van if he'd come along that way, but even so I turned and jogged to my left, parallel to the road, until I could jog no more. I walked. I meandered, at first towards the pit where I knew that eventually someone would come when they did a rubbish run, and then away, deeper into the desert, because it might have been Palmenter who came. I collapsed near a tree and cried. I moved closer to the highway, close enough to hear any cars. I hid as best I could. It was too far for me to walk anywhere but back to the station. Perhaps a car would come.

9

During the day I burned in the sun. I had no hat and the tree offered little shade. I had nothing with me. No money. None of my stuff. I had no water, no food, nothing other than what I had been wearing when he said come for a drive. I spent two freezing desert nights and then walked to the station. Of course he knew and I knew that no cars would come and that the only thing for me to do was walk back to the homestead. I went straight to the water tower and gulped cool water and splashed it over my aching head and blistered skin. I saw him watching me from the homestead verandah. Bastard, I thought. I went to my room and lay down, I wanted to cry but couldn't. I couldn't stop shaking. The moment I began to feel just a little under control that terror would come back. Of being out in front of a loaded gun, of being unknown, alone, insignificant and invisible to the world but enormous in the great wide land full from horizon to horizon of nothing but that bullet with my name on it.

I thought of Arif and his body out there, that there was no one to miss him, and then I thought of my family. Why hadn't they replied to my letters? Because, stupid, he never posted them.

Maybe my father or Simon would come looking for me. How many years would have to go by? When I left home I hadn't given an address because all I knew was it was a place called Wingate Station. But they could find it. You can't hide ten thousand square kilometers of land. But the name had been changed, and I had been told to ask at the roadhouse and suddenly I realised that the roadhouse must be in on it somehow.

'Wingate Station?' At the roadhouse when I asked, the manager had wandered to the door and checked out my van. Satisfied, he continued, 'Yeah, mate. That's Palmenter's place now,' and he gave me directions.

How much was the roadhouse a part of it? Probably only enough to let Palmenter know if anyone ever came asking. He must have known the police were coming that time, that was why they waited for him as he walked casually over to their car. Maybe the roadhouse only did it to keep the lucrative avgas contract and didn't know much else, but I felt sure if someone turned up asking for directions to Wingate Station Palmenter would get to hear about it well before any maps to Palmenter Station were handed out.

I must have become delirious because I remember hearing my father talking to me. He told me he was driving up to find me. He was going to confront Palmenter. And then there was a fight, my father and Palmenter outside my room, and my father was being beaten, but I was at school again, caught in the classroom at lunchtime and it was not my father and Palmenter but me and Dan Taylor and Dan tripped me and I fell, and there was no Dan, I was walking, stumbling, alone in the scrub, and my father told me again he was looking for me, and in all that I realised my father was exactly like me, he would no more confront Palmenter than I would. I cried. I went to sleep crying because I was just like my father and as I cried, in my self-pity, I understood what the recruitment agent had seen. That I was the perfect candidate for this job.

Cookie brought me something to eat later. He tapped gently at the door and came in.

'Thought you might be hungry.' He set a fresh roll with salad and meats on my dresser and waited, apologetically.

With the fresh bread smell I was suddenly ravenous. As I ate I wondered if my fuel stash was safe. Between mouthfuls I asked.

'One of your containers leaked. He smelt it. Came into the kitchen in a fury, saw the food I had packaged up for you.' Cookie seemed to wish I had got away with it. 'Sorry mate.'

'Not your fault.' I ate some more. 'You know what's going on. Can't you leave? Why do you stay? Maybe if we all left.'

Cookie didn't answer right away. He took out some leaf and concentrated on rolling a joint.

'Some of my finest. You probably need one of these and I'm just the person to share it with.' He was that. Cookie the space cadet. Was he a part of it all? Was it for the drugs that he stayed or were they simply how he coped?

'Spanner and I were here before he was. It was okay then. Still can be okay, y'know, if you just keep to yourself, don't get involved in the shit. Here we got freedom you don't get most places, wide open space, clean air, no one to hassle you. At some point you gotta give up caring about the rest of the world anyway, might as well be before you die.' He made a little gesture of smoking the joint that he hadn't yet lit. 'I know, I know, I smoke too much of the ganja but when it comes down to it, what else is life? What else is there?'

It was the longest and most coherent speech I had ever heard from him. Indeed, what else was there?

'Girls,' I suggested. 'And travel, people, art, music, culture, restaurants.'

'There is that. But what else? What is there that is important?'

'That is all important.'

He shrugged. 'Maybe.'

He lit the joint and took a long toke then passed it to me.

'Thing is I don't disagree with any of it. Give people a chance, these people have nothing, have nowhere to go. He's a bastard and a bully and an arsehole but, hey?' He shrugged again.

The dope was strong. I closed my eyes for a moment before I handed the joint back to him and watched the end glow as he drew on it. He closed his eyes and tilted his head back.

'If you want to leave you'll have to be a bit clever about it. He's totally paranoid someone is going to talk, dob him in.'

I watched Cookie, motionless except for the subtle roll of his wrist to prevent ash falling. His eyes were still closed.

'But he can't make people stay. He can't keep me here as a prisoner for the rest of my life. You can't give freedom to some people if it means imprisoning others. He ...' I was about to tell Cookie about Arif, but I didn't. 'I feel like I am trapped here until he decides I can go.'

'Walls are in your head, mate.'

'Bullshit. If there are no walls, why do you smoke so much shit?'

He considered that. He looked at the joint in his hand, thought for a while then relit it, took a long drag and held his breath. As he let it out he leaned back. 'I'm just putting windows in the walls in my head.'

But I knew he agreed with me. We were two prisoners discussing the outside world and the walls were a thousand kilometres of desert and scrub and land only a nomad could live in.

'Don't you think we have a duty to ourselves to always strive, to fight to escape whatever it is that holds us and that this is all the more imperative when we find ourselves in a situation we don't agree with,' I said, rather than asked.

Bullshit, I thought. I had walked from the road to here, right back into the situation I didn't agree with rather than die in the struggle to escape.

'We are all trapped on planet Earth. Do you check out if you don't like it?' he asked.

'I notice you check out most of the time.' I couldn't help myself, but then added, to make it less of an accusation, 'Philosophers trapped in their mortal coils.'

'That's deep shit that is,' he said.

He passed the joint to me again and I drew on it slowly and deeply. Bloody drug-addled, brain-dead idiot, I thought. Me too, I wished. You had to like Cookie. He was harmless and kind-hearted and he had a good laugh, always saw the funny side of things. He had brought me food. But he would never amount to anything. Why did that matter?

'So how come you stay here? What was it like here before?'

'It was a proper cattle station. Called Wingate. Went broke. Run by the McArthur family, you woulda read about it. South Pacific Pastoral Company. They went belly-up and all the stations were sold off and Palmenter bought this one. This is the last cattle station in this area, all the rest been turned into national park or private nature reserves. Run tourists instead of cattle.'

I began to laugh. Something about that seemed funny. He relit the joint and we passed it between us a few more times.

'We sort of run tourists,' I said.

He laughed.

'Yeah. Tourists. You have to admire them. Their guts. To leave their home and all their friends, all that is familiar. To make a better life. Meanwhile ...' he waved his arms to encompass the room, the homestead, the station and himself.

He leaned back and closed his eyes as if exhausted by the effort of speaking and I thought how some of our most lucid thoughts are immediately before we go to sleep. He was right and had obviously thought about this before, and I wanted him to keep going but I couldn't think what to say. The dope was strong and it might have been some time before we began talking again. We might have both dozed for a while and someone coming into the room would have seen two grinning dimwits incapable of clear thought.

'I stayed on as cook,' he said, answering my question from a while ago. 'Spanner too, although his missus didn't last too long, she took off after a year or so.'

'Spanner is married?'

He considered the question slowly. Was it his speech or my hearing that was slurring?

'I guess so. No, I don't think they was married. They was just travelling around together, picking up work here and there. They had been over on the mines, decided it was time to see something else. He and his missus came only about six months before the place was sold. I guess he likes it. He's all right, is Spanner.'

I suppose it shouldn't have come as such a shock that there would have been a woman in Spanner's life. He was self-contained and content in a way and I had only ever known him like this, but why not? As Cookie spoke I pictured Spanner and his woman, the two of them. She would have the same laconic outlook. Whatever happened to her probably didn't involve Palmenter because Spanner didn't seem to hold any strong hatred for Palmenter. He drank, all day and slowly, not the fast and fall-down drinking of the muster crew. It was the same as Cookie who smoked and drugged himself daily as if to avoid thinking about his discontent. Cookie smoked to escape and Spanner drank to escape. I need a hobby, I thought.

Cookie told me about how the place was under the former owners and how when Palmenter first arrived nothing much changed. There were a lot more workers, all the muster and cattle crew were on staff and lived at the homestead. Often the dongas were full because as well as the staff there were frequent visits from other stations, or they would all have a few days off and go the few hundred kilometres to have a rodeo with the neighbouring station. One by one they closed down and were taken over by Parks and Wildlife and let back to nature. Now, apart from the rare lost tourist, no one ever came out this way.

'Do you think Palmenter bought it with what he is doing in mind?'

'Who knows? I think we all, him included, just little by little get into things. Like boiling frogs, you know.'

I knew what he was referring to, about that thing that they say if you put frogs into cold water and then slowly heat it they won't get out because they don't notice the temperature rising and eventually you boil them alive. The way he said it was as if he had done it, as if he was talking about how to make hard-boiled eggs and I couldn't get the thought out of my head of Cookie boiling up some frogs and serving them to us for dinner. I thought he was capable of it when he was all herbed up. Then I thought instead of frogs he'd boil up cane toads and serve us and we'd all die like one of those strange religious cults. At least it would get rid of vermin, I thought, and couldn't decide if toads or humans were the vermin. I started laughing again and soon we were both lying back on the bed giggling. None of it was important.

'Sometimes I feel sorry for Palmenter,' he said after a long silence.

'He's an arsehole.'

Cookie laughed. 'You're right. He's an arsehole.'

And we were both laughing as if that was riotously funny. Palmenter had driven me out to the road and left me. He knew no one would come along, he knew I would walk back to camp or if I didn't, I would perish out there. How did he know I wouldn't decide to walk, struggle for a few days along the road until I had gone too far to turn back, was too far gone? I would have died out there and he didn't care. No one but he knew I was out there. Would he have come to get me in a few days? How many days would he wait? I'd spent two days hiding under a spindly tree near the road and there had been no cars. He hadn't come back. No, he was prepared to have me die out there and I was sure he would not even come to get my body. I wouldn't even get the careless burial those five blokes got. Birds and dingoes and insects would gnaw at me until I was nothing but sun-bleached scattered bones or, if my body were found, he would say I was some foolish city boy who knew no better. By walking back I had accepted the inevitable, his ultimatum, my entrapment. I didn't want to die and so I had agreed to his conditions. He held total power over me. And here were Cookie and I laughing ourselves silly over it.

Simms was given the job of the bore runs permanently and these were done far less often. At muster time, I was put with one of the truck crew, someone I was sure was a spy for Palmenter. Other times, I was left to my duties around the camp, the garden and my small room on the verandah.

I kept my head down and got back to work. It must have been weeks later that Palmenter said something to me, it might even have been the first thing he said to me after that time. He said I seemed to be getting on a bit better, and that maybe I could start to play a more important role.

'I need people I can trust around here, Son, because I can't be here all the time. There is a lot to organise in the business. Perhaps you could think about taking on a bit more responsibility.'

I said yes, I was ready for that. I agreed, but not so enthusiastically as to arouse suspicion, because not only did I have the sense it was in fact a sort of threat in the same way that he had said I was free to leave when he left me out at the road, I was also thinking that here was my chance to find another way out. I would have to be careful. He had shot Arif in front of me in cold blood and I knew that I would be next if I got caught a second time.

As it turned out it was a year later that I left the station for the first time, and that was when I drove down to visit Lucy.

10

I decided I would go to Melbourne in one of the campervans. I could easily hitch a ride with one of the last groups and by the time they were ready to go it would be ten days since the previous one and that was long enough to wait. When I was in Melbourne I would abandon the van and there would be nothing to link me to Palmenter Station. Except the million dollars in my backpack. If we departed early then Simms and Charles would be less likely to see me go, Spanner could take his half and head his own way and I'd go mine and we'd be well away by the time anyone started looking for us.

The idea came that first day, when Spanner and I were in the office doing the false papers and I found the file on Lucy. But I didn't say anything then. The idea grew, however, as we were loading that first lot into their vans and sending them south. Why wasn't I going too? They were so happy. Well, not happy: relieved, thankful. We had forgotten this part of it because recently, well for at least the last year, Palmenter had been meeting the imports somewhere in the bush and we never got to see them at the homestead. Now, as I handed them false documents with a new identity and explained as best I could that this was now who they were, I had two thoughts. The first was that Palmenter had not been doing this and that any of them who arrived in the cities would have to start with nothing. And secondly, that Lucy was one of those. She would have nothing. I had seen Palmenter's handwritten note on her file: *Handed to Trent. Sent to Maribyrnong.*

Palmenter had kept me away from this part of the operation, at first by sending me out on bore runs and then by keeping me busy with accounts. Their faces and smiles of gratitude were new to me. Whatever your politics or religion, whatever you think about what we were doing, it felt great to be helping people. Finally they had made it: survived floods or famine or religious persecution, they had crossed war zones or deserts or mountains and at least one ocean to get this far. Now, they faced a whole new life in a new land and we were the ones who were sending them off on the final leg of their journey.

I determined I would go too, find Lucy, find out what happened. Until I read her file I hadn't realised that Lucy was a refugee, that she was one of them, that all the girls were. I thought Margaret and the girls came up from Melbourne to work with the muster.

I didn't tell anyone my plan. First, we had to finalise what we thought would be the final muster and import.

Normally we would spread out the departure of the vans but, without discussing it, Spanner and I had understood we wanted to get everyone away as quickly as possible. Charles and Simms, Cookie, they all accepted it as going back to the old way and agreed it was a good idea. None of us had liked the new way. Spanner and I watched as Charles led the last of the imports to their van. I was thinking that this was it, it was over. There would be no more 'musters' or imports. I would lie low for a while, then take the money and run. It didn't occur to me that we might have to cancel anything, that there might be something like a standing order, a regularity to the whole system. We were the end point of something that began far away and if at the station we said 'no more', it would be someone else's problem. We – I – never dreamed the entire outfit was not Palmenter's brainchild. But it was like a massive pipeline of people flowing towards us. Now they came twice a month, twenty or thirty a time, with boats and choppers and other businesses and people all relying on it and we were the main point in that pipeline. We couldn't just stop. Perhaps Spanner knew this. I never asked. It became a moot point.

I was thinking of this and nothing much, waiting with Spanner in the shade, watching Charles teaching the last lot to drive. The van spluttered and jolted down the driveway and stalled. I didn't think they would get far and that suited me because my plan was to grab my half of the money and leave with them.

'Beer tonight to celebrate,' I said.

'Not waiting till tonight,' answered Spanner. He walked across to refuel Charles's truck.

The chopper crew came over to me and the one I knew as Newman spoke.

'Where's Palmenter?'

My heart jumped. 'Dunno.'

'Whaddya mean? Where is he? He didn't come to the collection.'

'He's not here. He left. Yesterday.'

'Is he coming back? What about the money? We can't wait around for him.'

It had been too easy. I knew it. Of course, that was what all the cash was for, and I remembered now that after every import Palmenter would disappear into the house with Newman and Rob. I had assumed they had a beer or something, that Palmenter would overcome his grumpy nature for long enough to have a drink with them to keep them happy. Station country runs on a beer at the end of a job. Wouldn't matter how good a deal you made outta someone, if they didn't share a beer with you after you wouldn't want to work with them again.

'Sure. He's left me in charge. I'm the station manager now.'

The chopper crew looked at me quizzically but I didn't introduce myself. Newman had met me, they had all seen me over the last few musters taking a more pivotal role in the running of the place. Still, I wouldn't trust them as far as I could spit, so I didn't want them to know my name.

'You want a beer?' I asked.

'Jeez, fuck, we just gotta sort the fuckin' cash so we can get outta here.'

'Okay. Wait a minute.'

He looked at me funny as I walked off to the office.

Was it the whole amount, two million? Surely not, but I could hardly ask them how much. Did they even count it? Perhaps I should give them the suitcase? They hadn't followed me so I thought that meant it was either not that much or they took the payment without counting. That would be the stuff of movies where the payoff is a high-tension stand-off and the cash expert sniffs and counts and hold samples up to the light while trigger-happy bodyguards face off across the room. I went through the desk. Perhaps Palmenter had a bundle of cash ready for them. He wouldn't open the safe and count out a lesser amount from the suitcase in front of the crew. But of course, there was nothing. I had interrupted his day.

I wondered if Spanner knew. He had been here for years, from the beginning, and I was finding out he knew more than he let on. How could I talk to him without the chopper crew seeing me?

I stood at the window and saw several things as if in a dream. I saw Spanner had finished refuelling Charles's truck and he looked up and saw me. I signalled him to come over and as I did, I was realising I was free to go anytime because we had unlimited access to the fuel. I saw the last van bunny-hopping away down the drive and I calmly thought, not 'there goes my lift', but that the driver had several thousand kilometres to learn to drive before he got to the city. I saw Charles climb up into his cab and follow the last van down the road and I knew I would not see him again – by the time he returned with a load of vans we would be gone, because for us it was all over.

Spanner and I talked through the open window.

'Newman wants to be paid. I don't know how much. They're all waiting out the front.'

'Ask 'im.'

'Can't do that, they might smell a rat. They wanted Palmenter. I told them I was station manager now.' He raised his eyebrows at that. 'He did offer that. That was why, y'know, it happened.' I didn't want to say 'I shot him'.

Spanner was looking at me funny, like I had made some monumental fuck-up.

'Is it the whole lot? Do you know?' I asked.

Spanner hadn't even looked at me like that when I ran over to get him after I shot Palmenter. He simply looked at me and asked if he was dead. Then he asked if I was all right like you might ask if someone was okay after a minor car accident. Then he said, 'We'd better get rid of the body before any of the crew gets here.'

'Manager?'

'Yeah. He said I was the only one he could trust. He wanted to get rid of Newman. He told me to shoot him, take him out to the pit and bury his body.'

'Arsehole.' Who did he mean? Me, Palmenter or Newman?

'He said Newman was not happy about things. Had been complaining about the way we've been doing things and was going to set up a rival operation. I was to go with him after the last chopper load and then I was supposed to kill him and bury his body out there. Palmenter said Newman was demanding money,' I added, realising as I spoke it that none of it made sense.

Exactly what Newman thought was wrong with the way we had being doing things, I wasn't sure. The old way, the way Spanner and I were doing it now, made the homestead a very busy and chaotic place and all of us were frantically at work until the last of the vans left.

We didn't know the exact reason for the change but sometime – it was about the time of Arif – Palmenter did all the handovers. He would drive out with them on the first part of the trip and we began waiting up to a week between departures. Although the homestead was crowded while they waited, it was altogether more relaxed for us. We were supposed to have nothing to do with the imports, but sometimes they would give little gifts of gold or jewellery or buy food and clothing off us. I presumed that Palmenter thought if we got our hands on cash or some of these gifts that we could sell, it would be a way of escape, so eventually the imports didn't even come to the homestead. I couldn't think where they went instead. Probably someplace in the scrub where the chopper would land. A variety of places. Maybe that was what Newman objected to, although I thought it made good sense to mix it up a bit.

Newman came and went with the chopper and normally had nothing to do with anything at this end. If Palmenter was supposed to be paying him, that proved Palmenter was in charge of the whole thing. But the way Newman had asked to be paid didn't seem like extortion. He simply said we had to sort out the money. Like a contractor wants to be paid. As usual, Palmenter had fed me bullshit. It was only much later, when I understood more about the real nature of it, did I realise that Palmenter had set up Newman and I, that both of us were expendable. For now, I thought Newman must have realised what was going on and objected, and that was when Palmenter came to me and called Newman a double-crossing bastard. He gave me a test; if I passed I would be manager.

I think everyone thought I knew a whole lot more than I did, that working from my little office I talked with Palmenter more than I did and that I helped plan things. But in reality, after I had tried to escape, Palmenter didn't trust me and I spent my days sorting the paperwork and files and handwriting neat labels on everything.

'He said I was the only one he could trust to do the job and that then I would be station manager.'

Spanner continued to look at me as if he couldn't decide whether he was pissed because I was offered the opportunity to be manager over the top of him who had been there so much longer, or at Palmenter for wanting me to do his dirty work and kill someone, or at Newman for threatening the whole operation, or himself at being so stupid and being stuck in this backwater when all he had to do was demand cash for silence but do it in a smarter way than Newman.

'That's our answer, then. Tell him Palmenter wants him dead and he'd best get outta here and lie real low for a very long time. Without the cash.'

'Don't you get it? It's all bullshit. Palmenter made it all up. Or most of it.'

'So don't give them anything.'

I shook my head. Newman had asked about the money with no sense of threat or extortion. A payment would normally be taken care of by Palmenter and if I was now station manager, it was something I ought to know about.

'Must be one of those brown envelopes. They've got about fifty grand in them.'

'Okay. Give him one of those. No more.' Spanner looked away to the midday glare. 'Fuck. Well, I'm not giving up my money.'

Funny how we get to own things after such a short time. All he had done was help me shift a body. Bury a car. But I agreed with him because half of the money was mine and I had decided that a million was enough for me. So what if I had come about it illegally? Wasn't that exactly how Palmenter got it? I felt no lesser attachment to that money than if I had worked years and years in this godforsaken place and saved the pennies out of each pay.

'You're better with words than me,' said Spanner. 'I'll go get him, bring him in there. We threaten him, give him fifty grand for the work with the chopper. Let's hope that's the end of it. Better fuckin' be, 'cause I'm outta here next week.'

So that is what we did, and it went about how you'd expect, that is, not at all. Firstly the pilot was in on it and the two of them must have had wind of something, that Palmenter was going to do the nasty to them, because while the pilot stood guard over the chopper, Newman and a new guy who looked like a tattooed Viking came into the office together. The Viking stood by the door like a statue with his arms folded and a duffel bag at his feet with the handles rolled open like he might want to get something out quickly. Two things occurred to me. One was that Palmenter didn't expect me to succeed and that he would not have minded if I had been shot instead. The second thing was that he had probably planned to coerce Spanner to knobble the chopper so it went down somewhere over the Gulf country. Private mustering choppers went down all the time and this one, flying low and unseen by coastal surveillance radar, would crash unnoticed. The crew would perish, if not in the crash, shortly after of thirst, or hunger, or crocodiles.

'Palmenter wanted you dead,' I said, 'but I talked him out of it.' Newman raised his eyebrows at that. Nobody ever talked Palmenter out of anything. 'He's left me in charge now, gone to look after other things. I promised him I'd sort things here. You wanna set up your own operation, fine. You wanna go to the Feds, fine. We've got things pretty well organised here and you can do what you like. But just so you know what you're dealing with.'

It was all bluff. I was thinking all I've gotta do is get them to leave, then we are outta here. If the statue went for the gun I thought he had in the bag I'd rugby-tackle him and we stood half a chance. I wished we hadn't buried Palmenter's pistol with him.

The Viking statue didn't move but they exchanged the smallest of looks, or rather, Newman glanced across. In that glance was my confirmation that they were in on something.

'Like fuck,' said Newman. 'Anyone gunna be dead it'll be that arsehole Palmenter.' He looked at me, into me. Like he knew. 'Why did you send these ones south again? I thought that was over.'

Before I could answer Spanner spoke. Did he know what was going on? I sure didn't.

'New policy,' said Spanner. 'They are people too and we just want to give them a chance. He's in charge now,' he pointed at me, 'so that's the new policy.'

'What about the hunters?' asked Newman.

Recently after each of the musters Palmenter had been bringing in groups of hunters and using the chopper to fly them out to far reaches of the station where they could hunt wild boar, water buffalo, or even feral camels. I knew how poorly the station finances were and this seemed a reasonable way to earn a bit of extra income. That Newman was thinking about that meant he had already accepted the new way with the imports.

'Hunting is off for now,' said Spanner. 'So we won't be needing the chopper again. We can pay you for the cancellation.'

Newman made a dismissive gesture. He glanced again at the statue and there was a barely perceptible change, as if the statue was now of softer granite.

'They won't be happy. This Palmenter's idea?' he asked.

'Not your problem,' I said. 'We'll deal with it at this end.' The groups that came hunting with Palmenter were tough-looking men but I was trying to appear tougher. Didn't matter. Soon we would be gone.

'So it's back to the old way,' Newman said. 'Well, I don't disagree. That was what we argued about.'

When Newman said this it was like he pulled the pressure switch. The room defused. Suddenly I knew what this was all about. Palmenter, as usual, had only told what he wanted to tell. This was not about a rival operation or going to the cops or even about the money, this was about the chopper becoming redundant now that Palmenter met the imports somewhere near the coast with the vans. This was Palmenter finding out that Newman disagreed with him over something trivial and then realising that he no longer depended on Newman, so deciding to remove him.

From the way that he dismissed Spanner's offer of payment for the cancellation, I saw that this was not about money for Newman. For Palmenter it was about the money. Whatever way he could maximise the profit was fine by him and the human cargo was just that. Cargo. The vans hadn't been going to the city because supplying the vans and maps and the trip to the city and then collecting and redelivering them to the station was a cost Palmenter saw as unnecessary. It was years later standing with Spanner above a tidal creek that he told me what had actually been happening, but for now I thought I understood. Newman and Palmenter had argued, and nobody won arguments with Palmenter. It was me who was supposed to deliver Palmenter's final say. I never wondered how he planned to continue without Newman because I didn't know then about the boats. I found out later that there are plenty of people willing to bring in boatloads but for now that wasn't my problem and it wasn't going to be.

At Newman's signal the Viking handed the bag over to me. It was full of cash. He and the Viking shook my hand.

'Welcome on board. We'll see you in ten days.'

'What?'

'Next lot from Timor in ten days, then another coming from Indo already on the water.'

'Oh. Sure. Okay.'

After the chopper had left and before we went to join the others in the canteen, Spanner and I discussed what to do. Abscond with the cash immediately? How far would we get before someone came looking? There was a new chopper crew perhaps already in the area waiting for Palmenter's signal. A new delivery in less than two weeks.

'Fuck, what the fuck's going on? Newman is paying Palmenter, yet Palmenter wanted me to get rid of Newman. And he's got two more boats coming in. I can't see how he'd do it without Newman or the chopper.'

'Might have been a plan to remove you. You know he'd never make you manager.'

The room went cold. Why did he say that? Did Spanner know Palmenter planned to send me out to the pit thinking I was armed when in fact I was going to my own death? Was that why Newman turned up with a bodyguard? Had someone told him something? No. Not Spanner. Spanner knew nothing about it, and anyway, the gun was loaded. Palmenter meant for me to shoot Newman and bury him at the pit and then run the thing without a chopper. Save money. It was no more than a test. A test that if I passed would bury me even deeper in Palmenter's world. And if I failed?

'You still think we need to wait around a while? We could take off now. Have a big party tonight. Get everyone drunk. Roll up some of Cookie's finest. By the time they wake up we'll be well gone.'

'There's no vans left. You can take Bitsy, but I'm waiting for Charles to bring back something decent,' Spanner said. He turned to leave. 'I need a beer.'

'Then we can take off just before the next lot, when the vans come back but before anyone comes asking for Palmenter.'

'Nup. If we do that someone will come looking for us. Place crowded and no Palmenter, no one to run the thing and you and me gone, having just told Newman you are in charge. Chopper in the air and us only a day ahead? They can hardly go to the police, but if they come looking for us, you know what will happen.'

'You think we have to run this next one? Get the vans back, do the whole deal?'

'No one else can do it. Charles is already on his way. Plus, we can't abandon them out here. And if we do one, we'll have to do both. If the second boat's already on the water it will be less than a week later.'

'You can drive a long way in a week.'

'Not far enough.'

He was right. We would have to deal with this next lot and then after that, or the same problem would arise. To not do so would have made a lie of all our talk of being the new managers and the plan to revert to the old way of business. Maybe we could have worked a way to get an extra serviceable vehicle but as soon as Spanner and I absconded with our cash we left the whole operation high and dry. We would be implicated as soon as it was discovered Palmenter had disappeared.

One boat had left Timor and another was on its way from Indonesia. Spanner and I would hang around as the refugees on these boats landed and Newman flew all seventy-eight of them in from the coast. We didn't know yet how much we could trust Newman. After all, Palmenter had said that they – Newman and his pilot Rob and now this Viking character – had threatened to set up a rival operation and although I'd believe anything over something Palmenter said, we had to be careful.

Also, if we didn't do these two imports, what would happen to the refugees? At best, they would wind up under arrest and in a detention centre where it would take years to process their claim. At worst? I thought of those five who had perished in the desert. None of them had any idea how harsh and remote it was and if they tried to get somewhere on their own they were sure to die. We owed it to them to get these last two boatloads to a new life.

That was how Spanner and I became business partners. We would stay and run these next two arrivals.

11

It probably sounds to you now as you read my story that life at the station was pretty bad. But much of the time Palmenter was not there and we just got on with living and working and making our own fun.

With Palmenter away, the place wasn't too bad. You know, how the day to day can keep you busy and you don't have to think about all the big stuff, all that is going on in the world that, of course, you'd rather not be happening, you'd rather there wasn't war and famine and murder and rape and all the other stuff that humans do to each other. And all the stuff that the world throws at us. Floods, disease, drought. Earthquake. Isolated as we were, it was as if none of that stuff was happening and we were simply working on a remote cattle station that did a few more musters than usual. The bits when Palmenter arrived and strutted around, when Margaret and the girls were hidden in the homestead, they were a quirky sideline business of a difficult boss. And things like Arif, or those five dead men out on the track: if you didn't think about it you could cope with it. It wasn't as if we could do anything about it.

Only Spanner and I knew that Palmenter was never coming back. We waited a nervous ten days for something to happen, each day a little less tense than the one before. We, I, had got away with it. The phone rang a couple of times but I didn't answer it. Unless Palmenter was here it wouldn't have been answered anyway because he never let anyone into the office.

We told Cookie to get ready for another lot. I was pretending I was in charge so I tried to get Simms to help with the paperwork but he was hopeless, so I left him to clean the rooms and wander about.

I couldn't even send him on a bore run, unless we sent him in Bitsy and we didn't want to do that. Spanner and I were keeping Bitsy fuelled and ready out behind the gene pool. We figured if it came to it we could escape overland, although that was something I didn't want to think about because it brought back the terror of that time out on the road, with Palmenter roaring towards me in the car with a loaded gun on the dash, and that led to scenes of us in Bitsy being hunted down and shot at from the chopper.

Spanner spent those ten days trying to do something with a gearbox. He had in mind some way of making Bitsy a bit faster. Quite often I'd go down to see him, to chat. I noticed he wasn't drinking and it seemed odd, he had engine parts on his bench and no beer, and instead of muttering to himself or the metal he worked quietly on it. I told him that the reason he couldn't fix it was that he didn't have a beer.

To maintain the charade of being in charge – who for, Cookie and Simms? – I spent the days in the office marking up the false papers and drawing sets of maps and directions for the trip south. I didn't like to be in the office. I felt trapped. We would hear if a chopper or a car arrived but not with enough warning to escape. Spanner would get away from the shed but if I was in the office there was only the window to escape through if someone came in the front. Despite the midday heat I worked with the window open and planned to run and hide under the laundry if anybody came.

But no one did. The phone rang out a few times, and then Charles arrived after a whirlwind trip to Melbourne. He had collected six vans on the truck. He told me the people at the warehouse had run out of money and had not heard from Palmenter. Until they got more cash there would be no further vans. I gave him the duffel bag with twenty thousand in it and told him to leave as soon as he could to collect another load, because the next import was hot on the heels of this lot and we would need transport for them all.

Early next morning the chopper came in and then every two hours until the last trip late in the day. Newman arrived on that last trip and handed me another duffel bag. This one had a hundred and twenty thousand in it. He almost ran over to me where I was directing the imports to their rooms.

'Getting late, gotta fly back before it gets dark. See you in two weeks. Tell Palmenter he better sort out his boys.'

I had no idea who Palmenter's boys were and I didn't care. All we had to do was get through the next two weeks.

Rather than send the whole lot off in a convoy that was sure to arouse suspicion, we sent them off over three days, one each morning and evening. There were thirty-two of them, so we filled all six vans. I put six in the first five and then chose four for the last van. I was going to go with them.

Spanner was aghast when I told him I was heading to Melbourne to see my family and that I'd make sure I was back in time for the next, and final, muster.

'You can't do that! What if you get picked up?'

'I'll just say I'm hitching.' I'd already thought about that. 'Or I'll drive and say I picked them up hitching, didn't realise they were illegal.'

He threw his hands in the air. 'What are you going to do there anyway? She's gone. Been sent home. You won't be able to see her. Forget her, mate, she was just a holiday fling.'

Spanner never called people 'mate'. I was angry at him for saying she was just a holiday fling but his calling me mate distracted me. He had seen straight through me when I said I wanted to see my family. It was Lucy. But him calling me mate, there was something else. Spanner was furious. He thought I was doing a runner, that I was abandoning him and was never going to return. He'd be left alone on the station and eventually, when either the police or Palmenter's 'boys' arrived, he would have to tell them that a bloke named Nick Smart had shot and buried Palmenter. When I left there would again only be Bitsy or the grader, or the dozer out at the pit. He would be trapped.

'I will come back,' I promised. 'I'm not taking the money.'

He looked at me angrily.

'I wasn't going to take it anyway. I can't risk carrying that amount with a bunch of refugees. I will come back and we will run this last one, then we take off. You go your way, I go mine. Charles will be back in a week. I gave him money to buy good vans. When he gets back, send him south straight away because he won't fit enough on in one trip.'

'Think you're fuckin' in charge.' He was short. Then, calming down somewhat, 'I guess I'll have to go buy my fishing camp now.'

Maybe that was the real thing. Spanner didn't actually think I'd do the dirty on him. It was that I was forcing him to act. Without Palmenter and if you didn't think too deeply, life was pretty good.

We left early the next morning. I took a leaf out of Palmenter's book by going quietly, before anyone was up. They would all soon learn I was gone, but only after the fact. I drove the east track, out across the spinifex country to Morgan's Well, then south along the boundary. There were five of us. Their names were Zahra, Tariq, Noroz and Emma. They did not know each other before the boat trip and I have no idea if they have stayed in touch, but I will never forget them.

We didn't talk much, not at first. I thought perhaps they didn't speak English. I drove for seven hours, eating Cookie's sandwiches as we went and only stopping when I needed a toilet break. I made a joke about girls to the left, boys to the right. They looked at me puzzled.

'Toilet,' I said, pointing to the wide red plain in front of us. We were a few hours from the Stuart Highway. It was midafternoon but not too hot. The sky was cloudless blue. I mimicked peeing. There is nothing so glorious as peeing under the wide open sky, the beautiful relief of letting go out in the open like somehow that's how it's supposed to be. I miss that.

I drove a little further and found a sandy creekbed to camp near. Spanner had given us the best van and some good camping gear, a gas stove, swags and canvas chairs. If we had to we could cram into the back of the van but it was so calm and beautiful I rolled my swag out and lay down on it to show them how to do it. I was still thinking they didn't speak English.

I opened the esky to look through what was there and Zahra come over, found ingredients and rice and began to cook while we sat in the chairs and watched. We had left early and I had driven all day with only a sandwich for lunch, and I was about to say 'I'm starving', but I didn't because it suddenly occurred to me that maybe I didn't know what starving was. Zahra took a lot of care in her cooking and it was beautiful to watch, and I was proud of the fact we had fed them well at the station. We put on a big barbecue and a party. You could tell that these people had become used to hiding, of being inconspicuous. And if you thought about it, that was what they would have to do in the city. But for now we got them all out in the open, cooked up lots of food and fed them well.

You do things and it is only afterwards you realise the subtle ways things have been, like Palmenter used to rush them to the dongas and we never fed them, they only ate what they had brought for themselves, or if they had money or gold or jewellery, Palmenter would sell them food. And they accepted that. They hid meekly in the dongas until it was time to go. Palmenter would lead them out in groups of five.

'So,' I spoke slowly, 'tell me your story.' I asked no one in particular although I expected Zahra would be the one to speak. I felt as if we had to speak, say something, and I did want to know how they had come to be one of Palmenter's imports.

None of them spoke.

'I am Charles,' I said, pointing to myself. 'Charles.'

Zahra looked up from the stove.

'Charles. Hello.'

The others looked at me but didn't speak, avoided my eyes. I waited.

'They don't know if to trust you yet.'

I shrugged, as an apology, but also to imply I didn't care if they trusted me. They could trust me, for although I had just given them a false name, that was just in case we were picked up, or if they were caught sometime in the future I didn't want anyone to know my real name.

'We have a long drive. I think you have to trust me.'

It was her turn to shrug.

'We come, we leave everything, then we have nothing, we pay everything we have to people who say they will help. Then the police come, or maybe they just leave us anyway, take our money and say wait here and then we wait for days and they do not come back. We hear stories. Bad stories. People say of rape, of slavery, of never being free or if they try to come they are taken away never to be seen again. But we cannot go back so we keep on going. But we do not trust. We do not trust too easily.'

I didn't know what to say. Was she thinking I was going to ask for more money? Were they scared I was going to abandon them in the desert? Bad stories? How bad would it have to be at home to run away into rumours of rape or murder or slavery?

I looked at each of them and saw them for the first time: people, individual people. Up until then, over all the imports and the musters, the choppers and the vans and the girls and all of it, all I had seen was people and cattle and there was not much difference between them. Crowds of each coming and going, groups of each that behaved in ways sometimes so similar. Milling around collection points, not sure where to go, what direction, if it was safe, talking, scuffling, mooing and circling, waiting for the leader to emerge.

I thought I knew that they had nothing left. No money, no spirit, no hope. Or rather, they had long ago lost the desire to hope after it had been resurrected and then dashed so many times. Not just on the journey, but from before, from the very first when war or famine or politics or terror began to erode their lives, when they first began to realise the only hope was to flee. And now I knew with an organic jolt, that here were four people who had nothing left. I saw it in their faces.

Tariq looked as if he might have been a nobleman. Noroz was no more than a scared little boy. Emma was ageless. She could have been a grandmother or much younger in years and prematurely aged. Zahra would have once been quite attractive but she was only my age and yet already worn out.

'How old are you?' I asked.

She continued to stir the pot.

'I am the oldest.' As if that were enough or answered the question.

'In my town I am head man,' said Tariq proudly, as though this had some relevance. He spoke thickly, slowly. He probably only partly understood what we were saying. So far on the trip he had barely spoken, and when he did it was in fragments.

He didn't continue, even when we all looked at him and waited. I wanted to know more. Why would a chief need to run away, become a refugee? His failure to continue speaking made me suspicious of him. Everyone knows that the best way for the guilty not to incriminate themselves is to not say much. Perhaps he was not a genuine refugee, perhaps he was one of the queue jumpers. Perhaps they all were. How do you tell? People say the wealthy would just fly into our country and abscond and why would they risk a long boat journey when they could buy an airticket and fly in on a tourist visa? Miss the flight home, no one would ever find you. But looking at Tariq now I realised that he might have been a rich man in his home village, a man of some power, but he was nothing here. The very rich in most places would be a pauper in Australia. He sat there proudly, not speaking; you could tell he had nothing but that. Nothing but his pride.

'Where are you from?' I asked.

He looked at me but did not answer. Zahra said something to him in her own language and he turned his gaze from me to her.

'Where are you from? Are you two from the same place?' I asked.

'No! Look at us!' she said curtly.

Of course I recognised they looked different but who knows what people look like from these places? Australians don't all look the same. Tariq had a high forehead and a big nose. His skin was dark, almost black, blacker than his hair that was in dirty short curls against his head. Zahra's hair was black and straight and long, and she held it back with a coloured scarf. Her nose was a button, small and cute, sitting like it was hiding between her big cheeks on a round face. Her eyes were wide too, large and angry, she looked nothing like Tariq but she was pretty in her own way and seemed ready to take on the world.

Noroz said something in another language that Zahra must have understood.

'True,' she said, and then something directly to Noroz who listened carefully and answered.

Their conversation was slow and I understood they were using what little of some common language they had including the occasional English word but I understood nothing of what they were saying.

'Do you speak English?' I asked Noroz.

'A little,' he said.

'He says he must also send money back for his family,' explained Zahra. 'Like me, he is the oldest. We only had money for me. My sister is ten. When I make enough money in Australia I will go back to get her.'

'Oh,' I said. I thought it was odd that she would make this trip with the plan already in place to do it a second time with her sister. To leave her family, to spend years away simply to save enough money to do it all again. It didn't seem like the plan of a genuine refugee. 'What about your parents?'

'They kill our parents. My brother is twelve when they take him. They don't kill him but they kill our parents. My sister and I hide in the house, look after ourselves. People give us food. We sell mother's jewellery, I carry water to houses of the old people and they give some food. Then the foreign workers find us, move us to camp and give us food but we run away, go back home. But it is gone. Burned. Chickens and goats gone, all gone. But the money we hide under a rock in the chicken pen is still there. We take it and go to the refugee camp where some people tell me about this trip, how they find a way to go to Australia. I ask if we can go with them to Australia, but it costs money, they say. I don't want anyone to know we have money, but they tell me it is one of the workers at the refugee camp who knows how to get a bus, then the boat, then to here. I only have enough money for me, so my sister will wait there for me. It takes all the money for the bus and the boat, but now I am here I will get good job and money for my sister.'

She spoke the whole story without emotion, as if she were describing the plot of a movie, and I wondered if someone had put her up to it.

'Where are the people you travelled with? You know you just can't come and go from Australia like that.'

She looked at me for a moment as if to say, 'Well, you are driving us to Melbourne, aren't you, so it's working so far?' and she was right, except that Palmenter Station was now closing down. I suppose that with enough money people can do what they want. Same the world over.

She had said she would go back to get her sister. I idly wondered if there might be a need for an exit trip soon. All these illegals who make good and then desire to leave, go back home wealthy. Full boats both ways. Or maybe, more likely, they discover Australia is not so good after all and want to leave.

'They go with another boat,' she said eventually, in answer to the first part of my question.

She served the food. Although by her story I guessed she must only be fourteen or fifteen she showed all the signs of having been the homemaker for some time.

'Where is home?' I asked.

'Home is gone. Burned.' She said it as if clarifying something for the inattentive listener to a story.

As she spooned the rice and beef onto plastic plates I handed them around and looked carefully at each of them. I saw again that they were quite different, that they were obviously from different places. Up until then, despite all the groups of imports I had seen come across the dirt into the homestead, all the vans leaving full of expectant faces, they all looked the same because I never looked at them. I never, or rarely, spoke to any of them. What country were they from? Did they all leave loved ones back home? What horrors had they fled? Or were they just well-scripted players in some queue-jumping system that Palmenter had orchestrated? Up until then they were all from some unnamed war-torn country like Iran or Afghanistan, or from Africa, itself just a single starving country full of black-skinned refugees fleeing violent war lords or famine.

The food was good. I was about to say so when Noroz spoke again. Zahra translated for us.

'He says that his father sold their last cow to get the money for this trip, to send him, and he must send money back to them.' Noroz spoke again, pausing long enough for Zahra to translate. 'His mother cannot walk and it is too far to the refugee camp. His father walks for two days there and then two days back with whatever he can carry, whatever they can give him. He walks there and back once a week so he can feed her. They have no milk now. The rains don't come so there are no crops.'

We ate in silence. It just didn't seem right to say that the food was good, but it was. Cookie had done us proud. The beef was from our own cattle. The tomatoes and garlic and capsicums, chilli, eggplant, were from the vegetable patch under the water tower. It's easy to grow stuff in the desert, all you need is water and sunshine. I wondered if all their stories were bullshit and if they thought I was some sort of underground immigration worker whose evidence would be used to verify their story later on or, if true, I wondered how they felt about eating big delicious meals under a star-clustered outback sky while Noroz's mother and father huddled starving under a rainless African sky.

I finished and noticed that Emma was eating slowly, picking at the food and eating only the rice.

Noroz looked at me and shook his head.

'Emma doesn't talk much,' Zahra said to me, then said something to Emma, who looked up at me, then the others one by one.

'I'm not supposed to eat beef.'

Sometimes it takes just some simple action like the slow eating of plain rice when hungry for you to realise that what people are telling you is the truth. She didn't have to act this out. There was no point in any of them continuing any act for my benefit.

'Sorry,' was all I could say. Cookie had provided us ample food, steaks, stews, cold meats. All beef. Tomorrow at the roadhouse I would buy something else.

I let them sleep in the back of the van that night. I rolled my swag out but didn't sleep. I lay awake thinking of stars and destiny and what it took to change the course of things. These were the same stars Lucy and I had seen that night on the grader bonnet. Each of the stars was different in just the way each person was different, and they didn't shine or fall because of the place they were in, they carried it within them and the more you looked the more those differences showed, until, like Tariq, you saw that one of them is a chief and will always be a chief and then you began to wonder which star you were and then you know that if you were in a different place you would not shine any brighter. If I were in their place and they in mine I could not have made their journey. They were made of better stuff than I. Perhaps if we had been in each other's places they would have succeeded in escaping from Palmenter Station and Palmenter would be alive and not lying dead and buried under this selfsame field of stars.

All through the night I lay as the stars wheeled around the sky and the longer I thought about it the more everything seemed to be in the right place. Humans have no more say over the flow of destiny than they do over the arc of the stars. As bad as their life had been there was nothing I could do about it. We each have our own journey to travel, our own destiny, and if I could help a little and offer kindness that was all it was. It was right that I was here looking after Tariq the chief, just as it was right that Palmenter was gone.

12

I guess it was a bit much to expect that Lucy would rush to meet me, that she would throw her arms around me and we would hug and kiss and make up. In truth, we only knew each other for a few weeks. I had recently arrived at the station, I was naive; she was on the run from something, desperate and vulnerable. And a long time had passed, three years. Three long years or three very short years. Looking back, it seemed as if those three years had dissolved into nothing and along the way I had come so far. I was now a rough and ready outback jock who knew more about some things and almost nothing about other things that I should have. I had seen and done things that people should just not do but it had all happened so gradually, incrementally, with each next step no big remove from the last. When you stand at the end of those three years and look back, you think, 'My God, what have I become?'

Lucy too had her own three years. Of life in detention. A long slow wait while unknown, unseen people decided her future. A wait that weighed on her and those around her as they tried to forget their stories – but that, and the food, the small attempt at a garden, the English lessons, that was all there was to talk about. So there was no forgetting, no new life, and no identity other than a case number.

We are all who we are because of our history and if we forget one part of it we lose our sense of self. It was years later when I visited Sierra Leone and Guinea that I understood how we absorb our homeland and why the Aborigines say they get sick if they cannot live on their country. They say they belong to the country, not the country belongs to them. But on that day sitting with Lucy I thought that it would be necessary to lose both history and country in order to start again and that they could be as easy to shed as dirty clothes.

She didn't rush to meet me. She didn't know how hard it had been to get permission to see her. Funny how hard it was to get into a place where all those inside wanted to do was get out.

'Hello,' she said, suspiciously.

'Hello.'

I was standing near the table and she was holding onto the door as if deciding whether to come in or go out of the room. For a while I thought she was about to turn away but suddenly she came in and sat at the table. That was all there was in the room, a table and two chairs arranged as if it was an interview. I sat down opposite. We didn't speak for some time.

'How are you?' I tried to soften my voice. 'Are you okay?'

It was a mistake to come. Unlike here, there was no time limit on visits and now I was going to have to talk and make conversation and then make some reason to leave and it was going to be awkward.

'Did HE send you? I haven't said anything. Please leave me alone. Is this because I come up for review next week? If you do anything to stop that –' she was getting angry, demanding, but then she changed, began pleading. 'Please, please, I didn't say anything. I promise, I not say anything. Never. Please, please,' she sobbed.

'Whoa, slow down, Lucy, Lucy.' I remained seated. I had an overwhelming desire to rush around and hug her. But I thought she might hit me, or scream, or something. She seemed to be blaming me for something. 'What's the matter? I won't hurt you. I promise. Never.'

She sat quietly sobbing. What had this place done to her? She was different than I remembered. She spoke differently. Was it possible she didn't remember me?

'It's Nick. Remember? Nick.'

She nodded.

'Yes. I remember. Did he send you?'

'Who? Palmenter?'

She nodded again.

'Why would he send me? I came to see you. I came myself, I wanted to see you. I didn't know what had happened to you, you left without saying goodbye, no note or letter or anything. You had gone and until, well, until now I didn't know you were here.

I thought you had ... I dunno.' Truth was until I read that file with Palmenter's handwritten note I didn't know how or why she left. Had Palmenter removed her? How? Perhaps Arif had not been the first. Perhaps those five who perished on the south perimeter track were not the first. A little fearful thought that I refused to let out niggled at me sometimes. But thinking it would have made me insane and there was some small part of me that knew that if it were the case, the best thing for me was not to know and not to think down those lines. But now I could admit to it: I had been afraid that Palmenter had shot her and buried her out at the pit and that was why it was so important to see her again. To verify that Palmenter was a bastard who deserved what he got. What I gave him.

Lucy stopped sobbing and looked at me. 'My case is being considered next week.'

I'm not sure if she fully trusted me, but she looked at me longer and I must have been looking entirely confused because she began to talk. 'My family is waiting for me to get them out, to bring them here. I must get out of here next week so I can do that. Palmenter said if I spoke anything about him he would hurt my family. I think he could do that.'

I looked around the room. It was bare. Plain gyprock walls, no pictures or mirrored walls or phones or fancy light fittings to hide a secret microphone. If Immigration recorded conversations and then used the information word of that would run around the camp like wildfire. But I couldn't help myself from checking.

'Why would he say that? Why would he hurt your family?' I didn't doubt that Palmenter's net extended all the way back and that if someone did the dirty on him he could, and would, extract revenge. It was a risk to the operation that one of our imports might say something – reveal even by accident the name of the station, how it all worked, the boats, the chopper. In case of that, I was sure Palmenter would have made it known his network stretched far back into the countries these people had come from. If caught and if ever tempted to cut a deal – information about the people-smuggling operation in return for guaranteed residency – Palmenter's threats would have been remembered. I didn't think Immigration worked like that but it might not stop someone from trying it and I wouldn't trust Immigration not to string someone along.

Spanner and I had the philosophy that people would not kill the golden goose, that if we did the right thing by people they would do the right thing by us. Most people had someone back where they had fled from who they wanted to bring out later. The story told by Zahra and Noroz, and Lucy, was one we would hear time and time again. We knew that they would require our services again and that closing us down would not be in their interests. That is an important lesson in business. Look after your customers and you will get repeat business. Hell, until we were running the operation, no one had any desire for anybody to actually succeed in getting to Australia. We changed that. But something always in the back of our minds was that if caught, when desperate, people would do anything to survive.

Obviously Palmenter had been a bit more upfront about prevention, it would be his style to threaten people so they would not reveal anything when put under pressure or offered a deal. His deal was worse.

'I ... I say I not want to do it no more.' She was crying again but she looked up and saw I didn't understand.

'Sex. We were supposed to give sex to the people.' I must have looked stupid. 'Even you, Nick.'

Did she say that to hurt me? I sat there open-mouthed, gutted. All we had been was nothing. She was told by Palmenter to screw me, that was why she had come out to me and found me on the grader bonnet and she fucked me. But all the other times? After? Was it all done because she was told to, because she lived in fear of Palmenter?

'But ...' The brain knows something but the voice still has to act out, come running along behind like a dimwitted cousin trying to catch up with what the brain has been hiding, what it knew all along but didn't reveal. The body is even further behind.

'He raped us, Nick. He makes all the girls work in brothels in the cities but before that he takes us off the boats and away from any people we know and puts us at that house. Girls who are healthy. She made sure we are healthy, gives us health checks and then sees if we can work, first on the people there.' And the brain showed a little more of what it knew all along, of Lucy when Palmenter was home and how she was different than other times.

'Palmenter?'

'Whatever he wanted. Whenever he wanted. The more you

fought the more he wanted it. Him, then everyone else. You too. Margaret told me to go to you.'

'You and I ...'

'I said I was not going to do it any more and he said I had to pay. He demanded more money. I said I haven't got any. He said I already owe him too much and that I would have to pay it off working in his house in Melbourne. That is where all the girls go. He sends them all there or to other houses, he and Margaret would discuss it in front of us. But I say I no want to do that, that I had paid for the trip already and could leave anytime. He was very angry. I say I go, and if he not let me, I tell about what he doing. I meant with the girls, not the boats, I never meant the boats but he got even more angry and hit me, rape me, lock me in room. Then I hear Sami screaming, screaming. I know it was her. He was hurting her so I could hear, so we could all hear. Then nothing.

'Next day the police came and took me away, took me to here, but before they came he told me he was letting me live so I could be a lesson to others. He told me if ever I say anything my whole family dead. He said he knew everyone everywhere and the police were his friends and even if I did speak they wouldn't believe me but he'd still kill my family and then he would kill me.'

'Palmenter is dead. I shot him,' I said.

She looked at me in disbelief. Her dark eyes held mine. 'You don't have to say that.'

'It's true. He's gone. You don't have to think about him anymore. He can't hurt you anymore.'

There was not much to say after that. When I left she was crying. I was too, but we were two different people and we had to cry alone in our own way. Our love wasn't real and there was nothing I could do to help her. Kindness, that was all there was. I could have offered that but I was also struggling to cope with my own world. I had shot Palmenter. I was a murderer. It was a relief to discover that Lucy was alive and yet I found myself wondering why he had not shot her and buried her in the pit, and as I thought that, I knew that it was I who should be locked up and she who should be free and, in the face of that, I ran because denial is the easiest form of freedom.

Palmenter had been supplying girls into brothels in Melbourne and everyone knew the brothels of Melbourne were the front for the big crime gangs, front door to the underworld. I wondered if he owned the brothels and if that might complicate or simplify his going missing. The deeper you live in the underworld, if you live and die in the underworld, that same underworld is not likely to come to the surface looking for you. There might be some serious shit to go down or Palmenter's disappearance might cause not a whisper. I prayed it was the latter.

I did toy with the idea of not going back. I had promised Spanner I would return in time for the final muster but if I didn't turn up what could he do? I could make myself impossible to find. I wouldn't go home, but I could drive out west, get a job on the mines. Problem was, except for a small amount of cash, I had nothing. No job, no money, no home. I had never been paid for any of my time at Palmenter. Bastard had never paid anyone. 'Sort it out when you leave, Son. Too difficult up here to bother with weekly pay and you don't need cash while you are here. You'll save a packet, Son. I'll look after you.' Bastard.

Also, all that money was in the safe at the station and I wanted my share.

On the day I left Melbourne I drove to my parents' home. It was early and the street was quiet. The garden wasn't as lush as I remembered and the lawn was overgrown. Dad was always so proud of the garden. I had forgotten the weekly suburban ritual of rubbish day, wheeling the bins out, three bins each house – rubbish, greenwaste, recyclables – and these stood in clusters waiting for collection. Nothing had changed, but it was not as I had remembered.

I parked outside and watched the house. I knew Lucy and I had no future but inside me something was hollow. Now, after meeting with her and realising my youthful foolishness and then seeing this small crowded street where I grew up and remembering the childish way I left, the emptiness inside me grew. I saw that this was not my world. This small crowded street was empty. I began to long for the healthy space of the outback, where you can sit on a bluff and see the distance, the red-yellow earth and ivory sky and for as far as you can see, so far, you see both everything and nothing. You are an invisible speck on a timeless landscape but somehow, you are important. Here in the city, in this street and all other streets exactly the same, there was clutter filling up the meaninglessness of lives lived trapped on a lonely planet.

I couldn't go in. If I had, I would have broken down and cried and told everything including about Palmenter and eventually that I shot him and I would have not been able to leave, and what with the rubbish truck clattering by and its arm lifting and rolling and then burying all within, it reminded me of the pit, of rolling that van in with five poor men in it, or us rolling Palmenter's car in and Spanner pushing loads of sand over it. Of Palmenter contemptuously kicking sand over Arif as he lay still warm and I regretted not for a moment that I had shot Palmenter.

I didn't go in. I sat there in the van for a while and the forlornness of the early morning street must have rubbed off on me because then I began to think of Cookie and how he had said, 'We are all trapped on this planet.' Kind-hearted Cookie, the only one who had risked the wrath of Palmenter to visit me, bring me food. I at least had to say goodbye to him.

The funny thing is that, at that moment, with that choice, I felt the most in charge of my life that I had ever been.

Anyway, I would be back with the cash in a couple of weeks and it would all be over. I would stay at home for a week or so and my mum and dad would forgive me. I would tell them about the money, some of it. I would explain that I had been paid well and then I would take off overseas for the backpacking holiday I had always wanted. But right now I was on my way back to Palmenter Station and I was a murderer and I had to lie low and sort out this final muster and get my share of the cash. When I came back things would be different. I could relax and be myself, myself with a secret million dollars that I could never tell anybody about.

I started to write them a note. What could I say? *Dear* ... I wrote, and then sat staring at the paper. What could I say? I could not even work out how to start, and as I sat in the van I thought about all that had happened and how I came to be sitting in a van outside my parents' home, writing a note that said I would be home soon, but that I must first go back to a place that had effectively kidnapped me.

Why? To collect a million. And why were they giving me a million dollars? They weren't. I was taking it. I had shot Palmenter, a thug with underworld connections. I had shot an underworld figure and was stealing his million dollars.

With sudden cold certainty I knew someone was going to come looking for me. Palmenter must have friends or associates who would come looking. What did Newman say? Sort out Palmenter's boys. Already they were asking and Newman had told them to talk to me. And when I wasn't at the station they would search the office and not only find all the money but they would find all the letters from my family. Foolishly I had left them on the desk. I had been reading them all the night before I left but I left them because I did not want to have anything personal on me if we were picked up in the van on the trip to Melbourne.

It was such a sudden and real thought I began to look around up and down the street to see if any other cars were casing the place. I really expected to see someone, but the street was empty. I had to go back to the station and destroy all the letters and all the paperwork with my handwriting on it.

By the time I had driven across town I had calmed down and I decided I could at least visit Simon. It was sort of on the way.

This street was busier. People were up and about, some schoolkids walking as a group with their parents behind. It was such simple, happy, suburban life that I wanted to cry. I wondered if Simon had any kids yet, if he still worked the mines, what his wife did.

I had determined that I would go in and the way to do it was to not stop outside and think. I'd park and get out and walk straight up to the door. So that's what I did. I parked and got out and walked straight to the door, and froze. I waited an age and was about to leave when the door opened.

A woman in her late twenties stood looking at me. When she opened the door I had turned to go but now I was half turned on the front step and she was in the door looking at me and we stayed like that for a very long time. I had not met her before but she was looking at me like she knew me.

'Simon?' was all I could say.

'Nick? Is it Nick. Oh my God, it is you!'

'Are you Michelle? Is Simon here?' I must have sounded so formal.

She shook her head. 'He's at work. But come in.'

She came out to greet me and take me inside, but her friendliness, the fact she recognised me, the fact that obviously I had been talked about and missed and that she knew me – something in me cracked and I began to cry. Not the quiet sobs of before as I hurried from the detention centre, this was full-blown, out of control crying. She put her arms around me and hugged me and that made it worse. She dragged me inside.

'Where have you been? Simon's been trying to find you. What is the matter? Are you all right?' She talked and talked, asked questions, made me coffee, made me breakfast, and I do not recall saying very much at all. She let me take my time.

Eventually I recovered enough to tell her things had been tough but that I was on my way home. I had a few more things to sort out before I was back in the city for good.

'What sort of things? Where have you been? Everyone's been looking for you. Last they heard was Alice Springs, then nothing. You didn't answer letters. Simon's been trying to find your station. Police up there didn't want to know. Are you all right?'

'I've been on Wingate Station. It's very remote. No phone or anything.' If Simon had been there I might have said more, told the truth, admitted to him about Palmenter. 'Tell him not to worry, I'll be back soon.'

'He's home in a few days. Where are you staying? You can stay here if you want.'

'No, I've got to drive back, finish off some things. I've promised the guys to come back and run one more muster, then I'm coming home.'

She looked at me kindly, concerned. I felt I had to explain my outburst. Grown men don't break down like that even if they have been missing for a few years.

'It's about a girl. I had to come to Melbourne to see a girl. But that's all over now.' I gave a shrug. Maybe she believed me.

'Oh.'

'Sorry to ... you know.'

'You okay now? Do you want to talk about it?'

'Yeah. No. I'm all right. I'll be okay.'

'Simon is at a camp near Port Augusta. If you're driving north why don't you visit? I can email him and tell him you are coming. You should go see him.'

'I might not have time.'

'You should go see him. I'll email him, he'll be expecting you.'

I left with the address of Simon's camp but I only half promised to go there, it was a relief to be back on the road. Michelle had promised to call my parents for me and tell them I would be back in a month. That was enough for now, I thought.

It takes two full days when driving alone to get from Melbourne to Port Augusta, and by that time I had decided I would drive right past the turn-off to Simon's camp. I justified it to myself as that I didn't have much spare time and anyway I would soon be back. I'd go there on my way south in a couple of weeks. One more muster, collect my cash and keep the van I was driving to go home in.

But before I knew it I was driving the wide gravel road that led west off the Stuart Highway. If you had asked me, I might have pretended I was not stopping but the road goes nowhere else and the outback is the same all over. Same as on Palmenter Station: if a car drives anywhere on our roads we feel it, so Simon would sense I was arriving even as I turned off the main road.

Anywhere along that hundred kilometres I could have turned around. But I didn't. I arrived, and immediately felt the need to leave. Simon and two others were lounging in the shade next to a caravan that served as the camp office. As I drove up he came to greet me. I was expected.

'Don't you blokes do any work out here?' I put on a brave face. Seeing Simon now I suddenly realised how much he looked like my father. This was going to be hard.

'Nick!' He shook my hand, pulled me in to hug me. 'How've you been?'

'Long time.' I was trying to be casual. No big deal.

'Too long. We were worried. Folks have been really concerned.'

'Yeah. Sorry. It just got, y'know, a week, a month, a year.' I shrugged, tried to be dismissive. I had to maintain composure in front of these other two who I didn't know. I had nearly blabbered the whole story to Michelle. 'We don't have a phone on the station. It's really remote out there.'

'You can't have been that remote.' He knew something else was up. 'Everyone has sat phones now. How do you operate? No one can run a place without a phone. I tried to find Wingate. I wrote to you. Did you get my letters? They never came back. You should have answered them.' He grabbed my bag from the front seat and headed towards the caravan. 'Stay the night. No one else here. Drill rig is due tomorrow.'

'The boss was a bit funny about, it was a bit, well, I only just got your letters.'

'Michelle says you were upset. She says –'

'Girl trouble,' I said, interrupting him. The two other blokes were watching us so I forced a laugh. 'I'm okay now.'

Simon put my bag on the table and introduced me to the two whose names I don't remember. At my mentioning 'girl trouble' they tutted in sympathy.

'Look, really, I can't stay. I have to get back to Wingate. I was driving this way so thought I'd drop by.'

He looked at me and knew I was serious, and that despite the years apart we knew as brothers do when to ask questions and when not to. I shared a beer with them and we talked about stuff and then, because I at least owed him something, as we walked to the van I explained.

'I have to go back and sort some things out. I'm in charge now and they are relying on me to be back soon. We have some serious shit to deal with but it's no biggie. Life's tough in the outback.' I tried to sound cavalier, as if serious shit was something I was used to dealing with, as if perhaps this particular serious shit was only a little bigger than what I was used to. 'Soon as it's sorted, a month or so, I'll be back.'

'What sort of shit?'

'I can't say. Look, can you let Mum and Dad know? I asked Michelle to but if you talk to them as well.' And then, to distract the conversation away from me, I added, 'Married! She seems great.'

But it didn't work. It had taken him no time at all to know this was not about a girl and now he thought I was in trouble. We were alone by the van so we could have talked a bit more openly. What would have happened if I had confessed then and there?

'Don't try to deal with it by yourself. What's really happening?'

'It's financial. Place is losing money and I'm trying to sort it out. I've been in charge of the books so I've known for some time. They rely on me to keep the place going.'

'You are getting paid, are you?'

I tried to laugh that off. No one got paid. Palmenter kept all the money to himself and as I now knew, kept most of it in a suitcase in the office.

'I've negotiated a deal. I'm due over a million bucks. That's why I have to get back, make sure this deal goes through and I get my share.'

White lies. It is a lot easier to bend the truth than to ignore it. And once bent, it is a path easier to follow. When I enrolled at Charles Darwin University I wrote down that the success of Palmenter Station was because of my financial and business planning. I had to, because the MBA is reserved for postgraduates or businesspeople of some experience and I could hardly write *I drove the bore run and kept the paperwork neat*. Or that I had shot and killed the boss. Maybe that conversation with Simon was where it all began, with me pretending I was something more than I was.

Things have a habit of not going how you plan them and having already said too much to Simon I got out of there as quickly as I could.

13

During the long days driving back to Palmenter Station I decided that I would try to find Lucy's family and bring them in. It seemed like a good idea at the time. I guess it was that trip, bringing in Lucy's family, that set Spanner and I on the road to being people smugglers ourselves. You sit by yourself driving the van and the road is dull and long and you get sick of singing along to the CDs so eventually you just sit and drive and the world outside rushes up and under and away behind and you start thinking, and while you are thinking the sun comes up on the right and then it swings overhead then it falls a slow decline to the left. Ever noticed how it takes longer to fall down from the top than getting up there in the morning? You stop and refuel and have fleeting words with other travellers or a truck driver. You buy food and pay the attendant who has the same conversation she has had with every other customer with that faraway look of those who are going nowhere.

The real world rushed up with the tarmac and retreated behind and in my little world inside the van I thought of Lucy and what she meant. Had I loved her or used her? Had we used each other? Do we all use love to battle against loneliness? I don't know. What I did know was it was because of me she was in that place and I had the power to help.

And then I thought of Zahra, the way she took so much care cooking the food, about how you could tell from that that she cared about everything she did. I wondered how could that be, to continue to care for the smallest thing when all around is war and destruction and poverty and hunger and people living by whatever means they could.

Then Tariq, his noble pride, his reserve. And Noroz. All of them. How we hadn't shown any regard for them in catering their food. You are refugees, you are hungry, you will eat anything. Emma prematurely aged, her young eyes weary but clear, at once hopeful and afraid. What would the rest of her life be?

Arif. Annoying as he had been, he deserved better. While Emma waited for what life would deliver to her, Arif had set out to find, to demand and demand until he got what he wanted. Or not – as Palmenter delivered it to him.

All the girls who had come into the station, separated from the rest of the import and sent south to work until they paid off the cost of their passage. How much would that be? How long? Would they ever be free? They had no choice but to place their trust in others and hope for the goodness in people, a goodness denied to them in their home land. By bad luck they came across Palmenter.

It seemed to me I had a duty to help, and the least I could do was find Lucy's family and bring them to her. Because of me, she was in prison, a detention centre, while her family waited helplessly.

But it wasn't me. It was Palmenter. Palmenter who had killed and casually kicked sand, who had watched the van and those five bodies burn and said no one would miss them. It was Palmenter who took their money and then their freedom and at some point started taking their lives. Was Arif the first? I had thought so, but Lucy said she heard someone named Sami being beaten. Screaming. And then it went quiet. Who was Sami? A girl or a woman who was maybe dead and did not even have me to remember her. She was one of the many girls who came and left the station, most of whom did not even get a name.

Everyone should have at least a name. I tried but could not remember her. I did not recall Lucy having any particular friends. In my mind all the girls became one crowded memory of people who came and went with the musters, people who would all have someone somewhere. If Sami were dead – or alive and working in a brothel with all the others – there was nothing I could do about it. But what I could do was help Lucy and her family.

As I tried to find individual faces all I saw was the looks of the men and older women, the mix of fear and hope as they climbed into the vans with their new names and new friends, the strangers we sent them off with. And I remembered then the recent looks on the faces of Spanner and Cookie, Charles and even Simms as we sent people off with new hope. For that was what it was: we supplied not food or vans or maps or driving lessons. We supplied new hope. What had Newman said to me? 'Can't say that I disagree.' These blokes I worked with were not bad people.

I must have crossed in the Northern Territory but I didn't notice when. At some point it got dark and I must have turned the lights on but I couldn't remember doing it. I kept driving, and then later I woke up and the car was still driving itself. Luckily there was no other traffic and I had slowed to a crawl before the roar of the gravel shoulder woke me. I pulled off the tarmac and crawled into the back but I lay there unable to sleep. In my confusion of leaving Melbourne I hadn't thought to buy any food. I wasn't hungry anyway. I made black coffee and drank it sitting on top of a collection of boulders. The moon was rising over the far-off ranges and spreading its soft light over the desert and far far away to the north I could see the lonely lights of another car. It was cold and I pulled the sleeping bag around myself and lay down on the rock to watch the stars. I felt sad and happy at the same time. I remembered all the good times we had at the station and, for what it was, these people were my friends. As I fell asleep I decided that a feel-good delivery such as Lucy's family would be a good way to end it.

I might make it sound as if it was all bad all the time, but in reality when Palmenter was there we learned to be invisible and we did our jobs and kept out of his way as much as we could. When he was away we entertained ourselves with picnics and barbecues, waterhole swims, drinking beer and smoking Cookie's power weed or munching on his magic biscuits. I got good at table tennis but I could never beat Spanner at pool.

'My misspent youth got me something useful,' he'd say. Because we had no cash, and none of us ever got paid by Palmenter, we would bet stupid things. Cleaning roster for a week, or to wash the grader, a task as pointless as it was impossible. Simms collected a group of small rocks and called them his pets, and he would bet with them. Funny thing is we all began to covet his pets even to the extent of having favourites. You could simply walk out beyond the perimeter and pick up as many as you liked, but they were all wild, feral, not house-trained. Eric was the favourite. He was a rounded grey riverstone with flecks of white quartz across his back. He was the perfect size and shape to fit in your palm where he would lie sleeping.

Usual thing was, I'd win Eric from Simms in table tennis, Charles would win him from me and then Spanner would win him off anybody in pool, then after making Simms stew for a while Spanner'd let him win again. Then, the whole thing would start again.

During the windy season, the time after the wet when the east wind blows relentlessly from far across the desert, we went land yachting.

Spanner had welded some old car wheels together onto a triangular frame, a single at the front and two sets of doubles at the back so it would not bog in the sand. It was steered with a big tiller, a length of pipe that ran back from the front wheel, although steering is not an accurate word to describe what it actually did.

He had welded a long mast to the frame just behind the front wheel, and made a sail from tarpaulin. This was stitched with a hollow hem that slid down over the tapered mast and a rope that led from the rear corner of the sail overhead and around a second shorter mast at the very back. In the shed it was easy to roll the sail around the mast and this was the theoretical way it would be done in the field. For a seat he had welded one of the kitchen benches across the back and then laid an old mattress so that you sat on the mattress leaning back against the bench and holding the tiller in one hand and the sheet rope in the other.

I had seen him building something in his shed. He was often constructing things and I hadn't asked him what it was for. One day – Palmenter had just left and was unlikely to return for a day or two – Spanner came and got me. It was a cold morning but by later in the day it would be hot, and a strong wind blowing. The tamarisks around the garden echoed and haunted, doors slammed and swirls of dust rose and fell across the compound.

'Wanna see my new girl?'

'Yeah?' I was doubtful. 'What is it?'

We stood in the shed admiring it. The thing was ridiculous. It must have weighed a ton. Once rolling, not much would stop it. I wanted to laugh but I knew not to laugh at anything Spanner made, not because he would be angry or upset but because I would be proven wrong. Whatever it was would turn out to be magnificent. Perhaps not elegant or stylish, but more than capable of doing whatever Spanner had set out to do. In this case it was to sail across the sandplain powered by the wind. Harmless fun.

We towed it out to the disused landing strip that was behind the helipad. Helipad is a nice way of saying bare bit of ground. Disused landing strip is a nice way of saying the scrub here was marginally smaller, but we needn't have bothered. As soon as Spanner rolled out the sail, the thing started moving, slowly at first, slow enough that we could walk beside it, then run, then he jumped onboard and I couldn't keep up. I followed in the grader as he bounced across the sand, over shrubs, up and down small gullies trying desperately to steer away from the bigger trees and holes. Trouble was, the front wheel bounced and dug in in equal measure. Steering was so erratic. I should say it was hit and miss. Mostly miss. One hit. He hit a tree. It was a small tree that sort of folded over in slow motion as he drove over it, bent under the frame and then stood up again from underneath. The land yacht was snagged. Spanner rolled up the sail.

'I was aiming for it,' he explained. 'It wasn't going to stop.'

'Yeah, sure. Why not just let go the sail?'

'Well, you try it.'

He reached in under the seat and pulled out the chainsaw. Spanner thought of everything.

As he cut down the tree I was calculating how far and how fast the wind was blowing. About thirty kph, all the way to the Gulf. Then into the sea. Be sort of funny to escape this place and end up drowned in the sea. Pass the refugee boats on their way in. If we could veer a bit to the left we might miss the Gulf, end up in Broome. We'd have to jump off onto Cable Beach as we went past. Camels and sunbathers jumping aside as this rumbling shuddering rolling monster tore past. They'd hear it well before it arrived. I had an image of Cable Beach, serene, midmorning, tide out, and people slowly sitting up, saying, 'What's that noise?'

'Forget it,' said Spanner after my attempt, as if he was reading my mind. 'But let's go get Charles. He can grade the landing strip for us.'

The land yacht was christened *Matilda, King of the Desert*. I forget how the name came about but *Matilda* was a she, despite being a king. We spent afternoons when we could, towing her to the upwind end of the old airstrip and then sailing it back. We set up drums as an obstacle course, then as a demolition derby. If you hit the drum a glancing blow with the rear wheels you could set the drum flying, or spinning across the sand. Each time when we had finished we would tow it up to the top and park it ready for the next session that might be in a week, a month.

One time we all crowded onboard and sailed at no diminished speed across the spinifex until we found the creek, and we picnicked on the sand in the shelter of trees growing in the creekbed.

We dreamed of using it in the wet, sliding and slewing our way across the mudflats, but it needed the strong trade winds to move it and they only came in the midyear. In the wet, wind came in short sudden bursts before the rain. The day would be full of wet heat, clouds gathering in the north and rolling around the sky until out of somewhere came a wind, cool, strong, sweet, and then the sudden hard din of relentless rain that left mud puddles and impassable roads.

I think Palmenter only ever asked what it was once, and I heard Charles tell him it was a wind indicator. From the homestead all you could see was the mast of it when it was parked out on the airstrip. Cookie had tied a bra to the masthead so it looked a little like a wind sock.

One of the funniest times was when we had been at the waterhole all one afternoon, smoking some of Cookie's finest, and swimming, relaxing. Simms might not have been so bright but he was a great swimmer and, as we were to discover, he had a talent for mimicry. Palmenter used to bully Simms around a lot, he was his lapdog, so I guess Simms had a lot to imitate. Simms was a decent bloke. So was Charles.

I was lying in the shade and Spanner was next to me drinking a beer. Charles had made a small fire and Cookie was barbecuing meat on it, slowly, the way he used to get this fabulous smoky flavour into the meat.

The conversation, sporadic though it was in the late-afternoon cannabis haze, always turned to Palmenter. Palmenter had been away for a few weeks now, hence the relaxed picnic. We were wondering why he had been gone for so long.

'I reckon he's been arrested. He's never coming back. Cops locked him up and have thrown away the key,' said Spanner.

'Nah. He's found a girl. Shacked up with her over on the Gold Coast.' Cookie didn't raise his head from where he was resting as he said this. He giggled at his own joke.

'Girl! Why would he want one of them when he can have all the ones he wants. For free.'

Something in the way he said this compelled me to look up. Simms stood up on the flat rock at the edge of the waterhole. He walked up and down exactly as Palmenter did, that strutting busy self-important way that Palmenter had of walking, as though everything he did was urgent and you were in his way, distracting him.

'Madam, line the girls up.'

Simms paused, pretended to be choosing. Despite Simms being thin and Palmenter fat the imitation was uncanny. He stood as Palmenter would have stood.

'Mmm, this one. Come!' Simms pretended to lead her away, still walking exactly as Palmenter did. 'Now, suck my cock.' He stood thrusting his hips out, hands on hips and looking across at something in the distance. It was the posture that Palmenter had whenever he stood on the verandah watching the goings-on of the camp. Gazing into the distance but seeing everything that was happening nearby. Simms was hilarious.

'Palmenter's cock is too big,' said Spanner.

'You know, do you?'

'Well you suck his cock more than any of us. How big is it?'

It was true, Simms was browbeaten and bullied more than any of us by Palmenter. It was when Spanner said this that Simms became even funnier. He stood up as if he was Palmenter angry, advanced threateningly towards Spanner, not far, but enough to show the walk, then he turned back and dismissed the girl with a wave of his hand.

'It's this big!' Simms was Palmenter boasting of his massive size in that exact tone that Palmenter had that could say something as both a boast and a threat. 'You're no good, go back to where you came from. Simms, suck my dick.' Then, 'Simms, wipe my arse, what am I supposed to do, do it myself?' Simms danced and gyrated, swapping between being himself kneeling at Palmenter's feet or bent over wiping his arse, and Palmenter standing and bending over to receive.

We were all giggling and laughing in that infectious dope way. I had tears in my eyes and couldn't see properly. Spanner too. Cookie was laughing out loud, crying and wheezing and asking them to stop.

'Yes-men. You are all just yes-men. Why can't I get people who can think for themselves?'

Charles stood up and joined Simms, and their posing and gyrating became a dance.

'Not like that. Like this.' Simms was Palmenter insisting Charles move his way.

'Yes boss.'

It wasn't at all funny. It was too real. But how we laughed. I was aching, could hardly breathe.

Charles followed Simms in the dance, chanting in time with the beatbox, 'Yes boss, yes boss, yes boss.' Then he suddenly stopped, stood up hands on hips and arched back and yelled, at the top of his voice, out at the trees and the sky and the birds and whatever else was listening.

'You can go fuck yourself, Palmenter!'

It was as if something had shattered. The spell had been broken, both the drug-induced hilarity of the moment, and the long, slow, oppressive spell that Palmenter had cast over us. Things would not change, but Charles had spoken the truth. Palmenter could go fuck himself and we all wanted rid of him. There was suddenly a silent understanding between us.

Cookie served up lunch of the barbecued meat and salad. We ate in silence. Or near silence with the occasional comment.

'Is good, Cookie.'

'Yeah, good stuff as usual. You are wasted on us.'

We settled back quietly to our own thoughts.

I wanted to ask Spanner about his missus, the woman Cookie had told me about. But I didn't. I didn't think that Palmenter had something directly to do with her not being there but I suspected his name would come up somehow. And as quickly as we had been laughing at Palmenter and quick to abuse him, we were now suddenly fearful of being overheard by the trees, the rocks, the lizards and the wide open sky. They all had ears, nothing but ears. It doesn't make sense now, but back then it was exactly as it was.

The next few days I half expected to find Simms bashed and bruised and remorseful and Palmenter standing on the verandah watching him with a know-it-all self-satisfied grin. But that didn't happen. Things carried on as before.

On that long drive, five days by myself and totally unlike the last time I drove to Palmenter Station, I was thinking about that and also thinking about Lucy and her family, and I was thinking of the stories Zahra and Noroz and the others had told me. It seemed so unfair that we could lie around a waterhole smoking dope and laughing, complaining about Palmenter and his temper, while in the world real people like these were suffering real threats, death and torture and starvation. These people had nothing, they travelled across hostile lands on the last of what little they did have in the hope that someone somewhere along the way would hold out a helping hand. That could be me. Us. At the least I could help Lucy by finding her family for her because, because of me, Palmenter had turned her in and she had now spent three years in Maribyrnong. When she got out, if they accepted her refugee claim, she would still have nothing and it would be many more years before she would save enough money to help her family. If I didn't help them now, would they survive that long?

When I told Spanner that I wanted to bring in Lucy's family, he tried his best to dissuade me.

'You're mad. Why would you want to do that? You hardly even know her.'

'We agreed to hang around, we've got this next import anyway. It just means one more, two more weeks. If we can find them. One more, then we're done.'

Eventually he agreed. He didn't have much choice. I knew he wouldn't take off without me, he was too decent for that and anyway, he owed me, because while in Melbourne I had looked up the business broker with the fishing camp for sale.

The agency had hushed modern offices with wall-to-wall carpet and wood panelling and framed awards along the walls. The agent advanced at me with his arm out to shake my hand and offered me a coffee or tea that a girl in a tight dress made for us. I took an immediate dislike to him.

The camp had been on the market for several years and I gathered there had been little interest because the broker hinted that an offer could start well below the asking. He showed me files and pictures of the camp and played a short video. It looked idyllic, the leafy camp area, fishing boats on a sparkling ocean, warm sunshine and long golden beaches, rocky headlands sheltering isolated coves, pictures of smiling men holding up big barramundi. I was suspicious as to why there had been no sale for so long and it didn't take too long to discover that the problem was that there was no lease or title over the land. The camp had been set up illegally and was squatting on Aboriginal land. Given the remoteness, even the gear was pretty well worthless as it would cost more to move it than it was worth.

'What can you do with a few dinghies and some tents up there if they throw you off? Just have to walk away from it. Waste of money.' I thrust the files back at him. I guess I looked the part. It was only when I had arrived in Melbourne that I realised how tanned and tough I had become. I wasn't yet leathery like an old-timer from the Territory, but I was getting there. If he wanted to rip off some redneck from the outback it wasn't going to be me. Or Spanner.

How we did end up with the camp is that Newman and I, with two of the muster crew, flew up to the Gulf and got introduced to the people there. See, the thing in business is you have to get the locals on side. The further you are from your home the more important that is. Palmenter never understood that. He flew all over the place, drove thousands of miles between all his operations in Melbourne and Sydney and up the coast, Indonesia too I guess, going all over intimidating everyone to keep them in line. Waste of effort. Far better to get everyone on side and working in the same direction. Matter of aligning goals. In the books they call it win-win.

I told the locals that there was this illegal camp operating on their land, but that if they would give us a lease we would take it over and expand it, provide jobs and income, a percentage of the profits. Of course I didn't mention about the importing, but you have to be a little bit discreet. Can't be stupid about it.

We ended up buying the fishing camp. Sort of stole it. But that was a lot later, several years. Right now Spanner owed me because I had saved him from doing his dough.

14

When I arrived at the station after that trip to Melbourne to see Lucy it was only two days before the import was scheduled to arrive. The place was busy. Charles had managed somehow to fit in two trips to Melbourne and on one of them he had even picked up a minibus. Spanner had done a great job of organising. As soon as Charles arrived with the first truckload, Spanner sent Cookie off to buy supplies. He gave Cookie a few thousand dollars and told him to go overboard.

'I told him things were getting bigger,' Spanner said to me. 'That way, when we leave, he'll pass on to anyone that asks that he expects us back soon.'

Spanner had also forged all the paperwork. He had contacted the muster crew and the truck drivers somehow and sent Simms out in Bitsy to shoot a beast. It was amazing, because underneath all this activity you could tell it was a happier place.

We had no way of contacting Newman so we had to assume he would fly in as arranged: the first delivery would begin as soon after dawn as the chopper could fly and then every two hours until they were all done. The first surprise was when the girls arrived. The girls had been taken off the boats first and brought in a day early. The chopper arrived with Rob the pilot and eight girls but without Newman. Nine in a chopper designed for six. Rob just shrugged.

'They don't weigh much.'

Indeed they didn't. Thin girls, ageless but young. Too young. They gathered confused and nervous, bewildered, like cattle are before you force them up the loading ramp. Simms took them to the stationhouse and showed them the showers, told them to settle in, to wash, and then come to the canteen. I was thankful that Margaret hadn't showed up but wished we had a girl on staff to help. They either didn't speak English or were too shy to talk to us.

They were frightened and I now know why, because at the coast when the boat landed they had been forced apart from their families. Rob had then flown them in the chopper but they had no idea where to. As soon as he turned up with that load of girls I began to worry about Margaret, although I wasn't too concerned because I doubted Rob was in direct contact. Even if she did find out about the new shipment of girls somehow and arrived unannounced I would simply tell her to contact Palmenter and feign ignorance when she asked where he was. Anyway, I had my van hidden out behind *Matilda* with my million dollars buried nearby. The van had fuel and food and I was ready to go at short notice. A couple of years later when I was doing the MBA I remembered this. In business, they call this your parachute. Always have an exit plan.

We decided to send them out immediately so that if Margaret did arrive we could tell her that Palmenter and the girls had already left. Charles drove the minibus with the girls to Brisbane and dropped them at the train station. We gave each of them some Aussie dollars. We had no idea exactly who was on the payroll or when and how people would be paid for their services or for their silence so I had bundled up various amounts in plain envelopes and kept this in the office in case anybody should turn up demanding to be paid. I took some of this, a thousand, and gave some to each of the girls. I'm sure Spanner would have agreed.

The men came the next day with Rob flying and Newman back on board. If Rob noticed that the girls had already gone he didn't say anything. Simms greeted them as they landed and checked them in. If they were sick or weak he put them in a donga and they could rest, otherwise he sent them to me. After they had all their false documents he took them to the canteen where Cookie fed them. As soon as the first lot were done Spanner set them off in the campervan we gave them. With each group he gave them a driving test; they had to drive around the compound and if they successfully negotiated the gate, the cattle grid, the sand patch behind the dongas, that was good enough for him. If a group of five didn't have at least one driver he would swap the groups around. He had printed some maps to guide them to the Stuart Highway and we gave each van five hundred dollars, enough for fuel and extra food.

The last chopper load arrived after four.

'That's twenty-five,' said Newman, who no longer had the Viking with him. 'Palmenter didn't come to the collection so I've brought it along with me. Less two and a half for the chopper is one twenty-two and a half. It's all there.' He gave me the duffel bag and waited, as if it might need it explaining or I would want to count it. We were in the office where I had spent most of the day issuing false papers and cash. I put the bag uncounted into the bottom drawer of the filing cabinet and decided the best thing would be to say nothing about Palmenter or the cash.

'How would we go about bringing in a particular family? Would we be able to find them, bring them all the way?'

'Who?'

I showed him Lucy's file with the details of her family.

'I can take it back, pass it up the line, see if anyone knows.' He scratched his head. Obviously he wanted to ask more but I wasn't going to volunteer.

'I'll pay for it.' He gave me an odd look. 'I mean we don't charge them. This one is gratis.'

'Okay,' he said doubtfully. 'It is unusual. Why?'

'Don't know. It's from up high,' I lied. 'How long?'

'Shit. Dunno. Palmenter's gone crazy. We might not even find them. They could be anywhere along the way, gone someplace else. Dead. Who knows? If we ask anyone direct they won't say. Scared why we ask, they don't trust anybody. Even us.'

I nodded as if I understood. I certainly wasn't going to correct him on Palmenter. Invoking a higher authority is a good way to get what you want. Churches have been doing it forever.

'So can you do it in two weeks? It's kind of important.'

'Two weeks or not at all. I can let you know when we arrive with this next lot. They're on Yamdena waiting for our say-so. Soon as we got something happening at Ashmore, we go. I reckon could be less than a week.'

'What? Shit.'

'What?'

'Oh. Nothing. We got nothing left here. No food. No vans. Why so many all of a sudden?'

'Word is out,' he said simply, looking at me.

He was waiting for some reaction from me. Word is out. About what? That I shot Palmenter? Had Spanner said something? A moment of panic but Newman was watching me closely for some sort of reaction, to say something. Surely if he knew and hadn't done anything already he was not about to do anything now.

'We'll cope. You'll have to do the collection again, bring us the cash, okay? Same as this time.' I pretended my panic was merely about the logistics of this next lot. 'But bring them in mixed loads. Men and women together, okay? How many?'

'Forty-five.' He said this as though he expected me to object. Nearly twice the usual run. Even with Charles's two truckloads of vans and the extra food Cookie had bought we would not cope. But, if all went well, in two weeks Lucy's family would arrive and I could send them to join her in Melbourne. Spanner and I had agreed to do that. We would have to run this intermediate lot of forty-five. The timing didn't change. Spanner and I would still be able to escape in a couple of weeks. Before the wet.

'Word is out,' I said to Newman, and he smiled.

Spanner and I discussed what we would do. Allowing a van for each of us when we left, we had only four for the refugees and for forty-five people we would need at least another nine. And another one for Lucy's family, but as we didn't know how many in her family maybe we should make that two. The truck could carry six vans on the back so it needed two trips to the city and back. To get that many vans back from Melbourne would take all of two weeks and we had sent others off to Brisbane and Adelaide, as well as Sydney and Melbourne, with no system for returning them. We hadn't thought we would need to.

No matter how we shuffled it, we knew this next lot would arrive and we would have no transport for them. We had agreed to lie low for two weeks although it seemed an incredibly long time to sit idle with the threat of Margaret reappearing, or worse, one of Palmenter's cowboy mates. I remembered the fierce looks they had. We called them the cowboys. The muster crew laughed at that. And yet, it was such a short time because it would take all that time and more to get things organised. I wished if we found Lucy's family we could fly them in and forget about the boats and choppers and all the carry on. You can fly to London in less than a day. But Newman had made it clear that two weeks was the absolute minimum he would need and of course we had to do it as we always had done.

In a way we were lucky for this intervening lot. Without them and all the work they made for us I think we would have sat around on edge and eventually our resolve to bring in Lucy's family would have faltered.

But as it was, the next group would arrive with no transport and we had to do something. The bus was a twelve-seater but needed a competent driver. Charles could take a busload to Darwin and be back in four days but we needed him to drive the truck. We could move them all by bus to closer towns, three trips plus the four vans. But you can't drop twelve refugees in the centre of a small outback community without it being obvious. Even in Katherine or Alice the chance of getting caught was pretty high and if anyone got caught Spanner and I would lose our chance to get away. Plus, if we changed the method too radically, Charles or Simms or Cookie would wonder what was going on. Our plan had to remain something believable under the pretence that Palmenter was still running the business. We talked around and around with all these ways of dealing with this next mob but it all came back to doing as much of it as we could in the same way as it had always been done.

Spanner thought he might be able to resurrect one or two vans from the gene pool but no more. He didn't say anything about the one I had parked over behind the landyacht.

'They'd go, but not much else.'

'And Bitsy?'

'You're joking. Get picked up first patrol car. We need more.'

'Can you drive the truck?'

Spanner looked at me. Of course he could.

'What you got in mind?'

'You take the truck up to Darwin. Take Cookie and Simms too.

Buy eight more campervans from wherever you can and bring them back. Take you a week, ten days. Do the shopping too because we're going to need a heap of extra food. I'll wait here for Charles and the bus. And in case Margaret or anyone comes.'

Already I was planning a week by myself. I'd camp away from the homestead, up on the ridge where I could see the dust of any comings or goings, and I'd get my escape van properly equipped and well hidden, somewhere along the river under the trees where it couldn't be seen from the air. It had occurred to me while talking to Newman that from the chopper on the way in he would have had a great view of the old landing strip and my escape van.

And that was what I did. I also re-buried my million under some rocks away from the van. Just in case. I hid Spanner's million too. At first I put it inside an old oven out on the gene pool but then it occurred to me that if we were ever raided, having it hidden near the homestead wasn't such a good idea, so I took it out about ten kilometres in the other direction and buried it near a tree.

I kept about two hundred and fifty thousand dollars in the office, plus all the strange foreign notes that we would need to exchange somehow at a bank in the city. In the office I went through all the files. I burned nearly all of them, keeping only Lucy's. In the end I burned that too.

The import went really well. It was hard to believe this was not what had been planned all along. Despite what I had asked, eight girls arrived on the first load with Rob. All of them looked frightened and very young but fortunately we hadn't heard anything from Margaret. We mixed them with the men and older women who arrived on the next run two hours later. We set them off as quickly as we could, a girl, a woman and three men in each van, with maps taking them to Brisbane, Sydney, Adelaide and two to Melbourne. I gave them each some cash and told them to sell the van when they arrived and to split the money.

It took two whole days for all forty-five to fly in. It was organised chaos, but at the end of it there was a satisfied feeling about the place.

Newman gave me a calico bag of cash this time. I wondered if I was supposed to be giving him back the empty duffel bags.

'Eighty-two and a half. We had to buy them out of Kupang. Plus the free trip that I've paid for out of this lot.'

'Expensive!' I had to play the part.

'Tell Palmenter he's getting soft. We've filled the rest of the boat, though, so's there'll be another hundred or so as it lands.'

'I'm not telling him he's soft.'

That was the first time I ever heard Newman laugh, a little laugh of derision and understanding. He was the only person I ever knew who had argued with Palmenter. Except Arif. It was this moment that I realised he was also someone I could trust. When you first meet him he is stern, serious and businesslike, but you come to see he is solid and self-confident, someone who knows who he is and what he expects from the world, and he is not afraid. People like that are rare.

'Me neither. But I agree with this now. Like when we first started. That other way wasn't good.'

He seemed about to say more but stopped. It was after five and the chopper would have to leave soon to allow them to get back to the coast before dark. I walked with him to the pad. He didn't seem to be caught up in all of this as Spanner and Cookie and all of us were. It felt that while all of us had become slowly enmeshed in Palmenter's web, Newman stayed because he wanted to. It suddenly occurred to me that Newman might in fact have been in charge all along. Perhaps Palmenter had been working for Newman and, when he asked me to 'take care of that double-crossing cunt Newman', he had been attempting to take over the whole operation. Why else was Newman now paying us? It made more sense. A station near the coast struggling to pay its bills was hardly likely to instigate people smuggling but when offered some good money for simply hiding and transferring a few people there was no reason to refuse.

'Why do you do it?' I asked. I had nothing to lose. One last import, then Lucy's family, and then I was out of there with over a million bucks cash.

He thought for a while.

'Starting out I worked for GAP Oil, driving the service tugs for the rigs in the Timor Sea. We used to go back and forth all the time, between Timor and Darwin and all the rigs, it was no problem to drop a few of them on the way. Money for jam.'

'So it's just for the money?'

'Oh, no. Started out, sometimes we found bodies, stuff, bits of wreckage. This once we pulled a bunch of them from the water barely alive. Fishermen had sold them an old leaky boat, they had no chance and it was lucky that we came along. We took them back to the south coast of Timor but they kept asking us to take them to Australia. Offered us money, jewellery. We said no at first but hell, why not? If we were caught we'd just say we found them floating. Which was true. Then, on weeks off we used to go surfing up off the south coast of Roti and they'd paddle out to us. So that's how we started.'

'Who is we?'

'My people.' He looked at me hard. 'Was only meant to be once. Then another. And so on. You hear their stories and it seems so selfish to be up there surfing and earning enough each week between times to buy entire villages, shunting drillers and stuff for the rig when here are these people just over the horizon, starving and homeless. Then you find that you are being ripped off, that some of them have money and gold and just want a backdoor entry and that you are just a little fish in a very big sea. Or that they are paying money onshore to others just for the chance to come on our boat. Our boat. Other people are selling trips onto our boat without us knowing about it. And then along comes Palmenter. Solves a few problems until he is the problem.' He shrugged. 'Where is Palmenter?'

It was a direct question and he looked straight at me.

'Gone.'

He shrugged again. 'Good riddance.'

Rob was waiting by the chopper. He signalled impatiently then climbed up and started the engine. We could not talk against the roar, but Newman mouthed to me and held up his fingers.

'See you in ten days.'

I remember when Lucy's family arrived it was the same as any other import. I was standing on the verandah as I usually did when the chopper came in. It takes about an hour to fly from the coast and then an hour back, so every two hours on import day I would find myself standing at the back near my old office. I did this even later, years later, but Lucy's family was soon after we were running it without Palmenter so I hadn't seen so many. I never tired of watching the arrivals.

All day the chopper would be coming and going. It was not until later, after we had the fishing camps and could store them safely at the coast, that we could spread the imports out over several days and restrict the chopper to a few flights a day. That was when we could bring in bigger boats too. Using the choppers was a big bottleneck in the whole operation because choppers can't fly at night. They are expensive too and I wish I could have worked out some other way.

Newman would help them down off the chopper and point them towards the dongas where Simms was waiting to show them to their room. They would climb down and despite his urging to move away, to move quickly over to Simms, they invariably stood like six lost sheep with Newman behind them and Simms near the buildings waving his arms, gesticulating and urging them to move.

What they would see was a collection of eight low buildings around the compound and behind them a horizon full of sky and sun, a few spare trees and spinifex scrub. This, after how long fleeing their homeland? Travelling by whatever means across Asia, past rice fields and fish farms and through village after village and over mountains or through tropical jungles. Then crowded onto a small boat with strangers, with little or no food for days, because this was before we began running the boats ourselves and making sure there was food for everyone for the trip, after the noise and rush of the ground below, the chopper ride where they would see how big and barren and impossible this country was, after all this it would take more than Newman or Simms waving and yelling to hurry them.

As they stood looking at our oasis I remembered when I first arrived. How my first impression of a wide land of nothing had slowly opened to reveal hidden wonders. Secret waterholes, creekbeds, rocky breakaways and escarpments with ochre paintings of giant lizards, kangaroos, snakes, crocodiles, animals that still wandered here and gave the impression it was they who posed for their portrait tens of thousands of years ago. The silence.

The noise. Flocks of birds, rain in the wet, thunder and lightning. And insects. Thousands and thousands of insects. More insects than there were stars at night. This was not a dead and barren land, this was a land made alive by the oppressive heat, the wet season rain, the floods and winds and insects and the space.

But it took me years to find that out. What they would have seen was no paddy fields, no food crops, no village, just a lace of roads and a stationhouse compound. I wondered whether they saw safety here, salvation or hidden threats. If they were farmers did they look and see untamed pasture, a place they could work into productive land away from the tyranny of war or the vagaries of climate? Did they wonder why no one was already here or did they know, unlike our forebears, that this was a harsh land and worthless for farming, either too dry or too wet and in any case certainly too far from markets?

The confused and bewildered look on their faces told of hope but not realisation that the journey was over. The way they trooped dejected and defeated to the dongas spoke more of retreat. What small rising of hope they might have felt must have been lost when they saw this tiny outpost from the air. They had come all the way from Indonesia or Timor with little idea of exactly where they were going, and it would take someone to tell them when they finally arrived because there would be no welcome mat. No friendly greeting. If they made it, it was another place to hide. No wonder Palmenter could abuse and confuse and enslave until he had taken all they had.

But Australia was a land of new hope, of new opportunity, a land they had been told about that they could hope to live a life free from persecution, where food was guaranteed, where there was no war, so after a good look round they would shuffle over to Simms who would lead them into a donga that would be theirs for a few nights. What they knew was little. What they expected, less. It was a better place than where they had come from but what they knew of Australia was not seen on television or in a documentary, it was not from glossy brochures and it was not returning holidaymakers or businessmen who told of a great land over the sea. It was word of mouth, rumour, of someone who knew or heard of someone else who had made it, made a new life.

They had handed over whatever they had – money, gold, precious stones, anything easy to carry that was of value would buy them a trip on one of our boats. Others were less honest than we were. I made sure prices were fixed, a standard price for a standard of trip that included food and water. Some other operators would take as much as people had and then demand that they find their own food and water for the trip.

We also standardised the exchange rate for gold and jewellery. Sure, we took a bit extra for the commission but it was the same rate for everyone. The funny thing is, in business, if you standardise and charge everyone the same, then if you do a good job, that is, deliver what you promise and just a tiny bit more, people are so appreciative. I don't care if it is a refugee on a crowded boat or someone buying high street fashion. Give a little bit extra. Gift-wrapping. Bottled water on the boat. Cost us next to nothing but our people appreciated it so much.

And when customers appreciate they will often tip. Americans tip money. Refugees tip what they have, which was usually gold or jewellery that they had managed to hide. We made a lot extra like that, because the wealthy, those who were not really refugees, they had been prepared to pay a lot more than we charged.

I didn't recognise them at first, Lucy's family. They looked like any other refugee family and they didn't look, to me at least, like Lucy. Mum, grandma and an aged uncle. A typical family. The remains of a family, the bits left over after famine or war, attrition by disasters both human and natural until they could take no more. Grandma, a tough shrunken case who shuffled rather than walked. Mum, dare-I-hope eyes, weary of charity, watchful for opportunity. Uncle, the leftovers of another family, as if he was not supposed to be there at all and looking confused, as if all the recent months have been too much.

The message had gone back up the line to find them, bring them to Palmenter Station, letting them know that they could pay later. Better to say that than to complicate things by saying I wanted to give them a free trip to reunite them with Lucy. I didn't want anyone to know why. I didn't want anyone to think I was a softie.

My idea was they could have a free trip but charity like that is hard to give. The more desperate they are, the less people seem to be willing to take. They seem compelled to give something back in exchange.

I had wanted to remain anonymous, to watch them quietly disembark and see them okay to their new van, wave goodbye as they headed off armed with Lucy's address and a tourist map of Australia. But someone must have said something. Lucy's mum led the way over to me.

She nodded, a sort of half bow of respect and thanks like to a priest or to the Queen.

'You must take this.'

She took both my hands in hers and slipped into my grasp a small brass object. It was cold to the touch but I didn't look immediately at it as she was looking into my eyes, a look that reminded me of Lucy, a look full of inner strength and thanks and pity. It was the look Lucy had given me at Maribyrnong when I left, after I had said I had been trapped on the station and Palmenter had abused me. A whole world of emotions were in her look but mostly it was pride, a pride that she knew who she was and that I had no idea what being trapped meant.

Lucy's mother let go of my hand and I looked down for a moment to see what she had given me. The object was a cast statuette of Buddha, small enough to wrap my hand around and beautifully pleasing to hold. It was plain enough but it exuded calm. I looked up to thank her but she was leading them away. Lucy's mother, the shuffling grandmother and the stooped uncle. The Buddha was solid gold, not brass, but I knew its value was far more than anything it was made of, and the thought came into my head that we can all be far more than what we are made of. We can all be worth more than our weight.

15

I never planned to be the Mr Big of people smuggling. That's what they call me. The Mr Big of People Smuggling. Trafficker in human misery. Well, my father always told me if you are going to do something, do it well. No point going at something half-arsed.

After Newman dropped off Lucy's family and gave us another bag of cash with over a hundred grand in it, he told us he had two more boats of twenty-five coming in. We could hardly say no and not arouse suspicion. Let them turn up and not find us. Spanner would go find his fishing camp and I was going to drive Lucy's family to Melbourne and then, well, who knows. It would all be over. The best-laid plans and all that.

We had money coming out of our ears. There was our original million plus all the foreign notes, and now over three hundred thousand Newman had given us. I said goodbye to Spanner and took my share and set off to drive Lucy's family to Melbourne. It was a quiet trip, mostly because they didn't speak much English. Along the way I realised how hard it was going to be for them because, although there are plenty of non–English speaking people in Australia legitimately, if you were illegal and didn't speak the language what could you do? What work can you do? Where do you stay? How do you avoid attracting attention?

I tried to give them some words as we drove along – car, tree, road, sky, clouds – but these are disjointed and make no sense, are no use when you are trying to understand what is going on in the city, when you are looking for a job or wondering if the policeman on the corner is about to arrest you. The uncle, whose name was Kayeb or Kaheb, was pretty sharp and would nod and repeat what I said, then translate to the others, but when we tried to play I Spy I realised how hopeless it was. I thought I Spy was a universal game. Kids everywhere must play it. But just getting the idea across was impossible.

I'm not a teacher either. Teachers learn ways to say things, how to graduate the learning and build on what is already there. We'd be barrelling along the highway and I'd see something, something we hadn't seen before.

'Kangaroo.'

'Ah. Kagarro.'

'No, Kang-gar-roo.'

'Ah, yes. No kagarro.' And a chorus of nokagarros would echo around the van.

Or a cow. At least they would be familiar with a cow.

'Cow.'

'Ah. Cow. No kagarro. Cow.'

'Yes, good. It's not a kangaroo but a cow. And those are cattle. All of them together are called cattle.'

'Ah, cow cattle no kagarro.'

I held up one finger 'cow' and five fingers 'cattle'. I think he understood. He babbled to the others and they spoke back to him but I didn't hear the word cow or cattle or anything recognisable. And what use is the word cow in the city? Perhaps beef. Or beefburger.

At the roadhouses I bought takeaway food after I stood at the counter with Kayeb pointing to the pictures, saying the words. 'Hamburger.' 'Chicken.' 'Coke.' How do you explain the relationship between a cow and cattle and then beef and hamburger, and why is there no ham in a hamburger? I saw why English was so confusing to them. I wanted to sit at a table in the dining area and practise words with them but I thought we might attract too much attention. Perhaps it would be all right on a busier road during tourist season but we were usually the only customers, so we'd sit back in the van and say 'chicken' or 'hamburger' to each other as we ate. At least in the city they'd be able to buy chicken and Coke.

Once we arrived in the city, I didn't want to go anywhere near a migrant detention centre with them in the van so I took them to a park in Fitzroy where they could wait until I returned. That was pretty scary because they thought I was dumping them and there was a bit of a scene and people were looking and I was tempted to leave them and drive off. I tried to say to them to wait, I would be back, but they looked terrified and confused and they wanted to take their bags from the van. They must have thought I was trying to steal the bags or something. Lucy's mother thrust some more money into my hands and grabbed her bag, talking continuously at me, not yelling, but not friendly. Angry. You can sort of tell.

I gave up and bundled them back into the van. They could stay in the van at Maribyrnong while I went to see Lucy and after that I didn't know. I'd have to find somewhere for them to stay so I could tell Lucy where they were. It was fate then that on the way to Maribyrnong I saw a sign in a window *House for rent, enquiries next door*. It was handwritten, not from an agent or anything, and the area was mostly migrant families so I figured they'd blend in pretty well. On the spur of the moment I parked and went in. I took it for three months and I paid the cash the mother had given me as rent and bond and indicated to Kayeb they would have to pay the rent themselves after that.

At Maribyrnong I discovered Lucy had been accepted as a refugee and had been released. As she was now an Australian resident she could go wherever she wanted, and it was the law that they were not allowed to keep track of her. They said it like that, not that they didn't keep track of her but that they were not allowed to and I got the impression they knew exactly where she was. Anyway, they wouldn't tell me. I got a leaflet with the phone numbers of some migrant centres but no one I talked to had ever heard of a Lucy. I began to realise how easy it was to disappear in the city.

My dream of reuniting Lucy and her family was looking impossible. I'd had visions of them coming together at last, rushing in with hugs and tears, and the flow of their garbled words like water over dry rocks at the start of the wet. Them speaking all at once. And then their thanks to me: finally the family would realise what I had done for them and her mother would forgive me. They would thank me and hug me and then we'd all sit down together to a decent meal, with Lucy interpreting and all of us getting along, so much to discuss. No more pointing at cow and chicken and kagarro, but at last a chance to understand where they had come from, what they had been through, and by that, perhaps, a chance to understand Lucy.

I drove back to the house and showed the landlady the picture of Lucy from Palmenter's file. She shook her head but pointed across the street to another house and at that house they must have trusted me because they led me through the dark front rooms to a large skylit back room where ten or so women sat at sewing machines. A few men too, who came and went with piles of cloth cut into shape, or carried out bundles of the finished shirts. Two young girls – they couldn't have been older than ten – were running the shirts through a machine that ironed and then wrapped them. An even younger girl was stacking them into boxes that, when full, one of the men would carry to a stack out the back. Despite the hectic pace of the place it had a friendly atmosphere and they all stopped when I entered.

I showed the picture of Lucy to them one by one. There was much headshaking and discussion and laughter but no one could help. None of them spoke more than a few words of English and I realised it was pointless, but that at least here there was work, some income for her family. I would tell the landlady to show them across the road to ask for work.

Have they found each other? I don't know. I think there is a pretty good chance that they have. You can only do so much for people.

After that I was alone. I was free. But the city was so noisy, so rushed, so crowded. People and traffic everywhere. I felt anything but free. At least my parents would be happy to see me. What news did they have? Maybe I should ring them first. I had found it difficult to read the letters Spanner had discovered hidden in the safe but I had them all in my bag. Maybe I should stop and re-read them first but then how would I explain the fact that I had not written? What would I tell them? What had Simon said to them? As I drove I rehearsed what I would say: that the station was remote, that it was very busy, that the boss was difficult. The more I went over this in my mind, the more I knew I was not ready. I needed to calm myself and get my story straight. The shooting of Palmenter did not happen. But what did?

I was stopped at some traffic lights and two young women in short skirts walked by, looked long at me. I smiled at them and they walked towards me. In a flash of realisation I panicked. What if I was recognised by one of the girls who had been shipped south to work in the brothels? Or maybe Margaret. What would happen if she happened to walk by? Or one of Palmenter's cowboy mates. The graffiti-painted campervan was distinctive. Suppose someone recognised it?

I had burnt all the files and records at the homestead but I didn't know what else there might be, and the more I thought of it the more I knew there must be some connection between the recruitment agent and Palmenter. I was pretty sure the recruitment agent had my parents' address; I didn't remember but I must have filled out some sort of application form. If someone came looking for me – the recruitment agent, or more likely, one of the cowboys – if they arrived at my parents' and saw the van, or worse, found me, or if they searched and found the million dollars, then my parents would be involved. I decided that before I visited my parents I had to get out of town and dump the van and hide the cash.

I drove west along the Princes Highway and suddenly it felt as if behind me Melbourne was one big trap full of Palmenter henchmen. The cowboys, Margaret, the recruitment agent were all in Melbourne somewhere looking for me. Before I knew it I was in Geelong. The warehouse was in Geelong. On his last two trips Charles had simply paid cash for campervans being sold outside backpacker lodges because the warehouse was locked up and no one was about, but I didn't want to take the risk. I'd go a bit further before I dumped the van.

I kept going towards the coast and then past Anglesea and although it was summer it drizzled all day. I slept in the van and it was still drizzling the next day, that horrible, not quite enough to wet you, but enough to chill and make you miserable type of rain. I was lonely. Empty. It was cold outside but warm in the van. I wanted to head home but I had over a million dollars in my bag that

I wanted to hide somewhere. I couldn't work out where else to put it. I couldn't put it in my own bank account. Not that amount. I was terrified someone was going to steal it.

From Anglesea I continued along the coast, worrying about all the money and the distinctive van. I had in mind to buy another car but each small town I came to was little more than a holiday stop. I would have to wait until I got to a bigger place. I promised myself I would ring my parents, but every time there was an excuse, mostly that I could not ring them until I had ditched the camper and was ready to head home. As I went, I realised the van was pretty functional. I felt I could travel forever with it.

I kept driving, taking it easy and playing the tourist, stopping at all the sights. At Cape Otway I decided to camp in the forest so I drove back to Apollo Bay and bought some food and some warmer clothes. I parked in the forest and slept uncomfortably in the van. I found the forest oppressively dark and cold and full of strange noises. I missed the desert.

The next morning where the Great Ocean Road meets the Princes Highway it was time to decide: turn back to Melbourne or keep going? I drove into Warrnambool and sat in McDonald's with the duffel bag of cash at my feet. I wondered what Spanner was doing. How far he had got. Up until then he hadn't even crossed my mind but now I was wondering if I could visit him on his fishing camp. How would I find him?

It made sense from Warrnambool to go visit Simon as I was already a good part of the way out to the mine camp. From there I could ring home and have plenty of time to sort out a new car, ditch this one someplace remote where it wouldn't get found. Or if it did get found, it would look as if I had been on the way to Adelaide or Perth.

Outside of Port Augusta I picked up two hitchhikers, Ingrid and Sally. They had been backpacking down the east coast and now they were on their way to Darwin to fly out to Bali and the rest of their world tour, but as soon as I picked them up there was something between Ingrid and me. We argued like fury. She looked at me as Lucy did, right through me, and I took that out on her. If she chose a Johnny Cash CD I'd hate Johnny Cash. If the news said a carbon tax was coming and she would tell me about Germany's carbon tax,

I'd say global warming was a lie even though I had no idea. She had recently graduated as a teacher and so I told her you didn't learn anything from books or classrooms, all the real stuff was learned on the land.

But there was no way I was getting rid of them, for they were company I needed, and talking and arguing with them let me avoid having to think. For them I was a free ride to Darwin with stops at Uluru and Kings Canyon. While Sally sat between us shielding herself from the sparks Ingrid and I made, I forgot the difficulty of going home. I told them I was going to Darwin and could give them a lift all the way.

I took them to visit Simon's camp. We arrived late afternoon and sat outside sharing a barbecue dinner and some beers and then stayed the night. His buddies remembered me and my 'girl trouble' and ragged me when the girls left to have showers. They watched them walking away and then offered to help me in the way that blokes do.

'Doesn't look like it, but if you are still having trouble, maybe we can give you a hand.'

'Sucker for punishment, some people. One's bad enough, eh, Simon?'

But Simon wasn't interested in joining in. I think it was not that he and Michelle had only recently married but that I had again turned up out of the blue with no explanation of where I had been or what I had been up to. He wanted to know more, about why I had been missing for so long, where I had been. When I left the camp last time I had said I would be back soon, I had some 'serious shit' to sort out. I think he could tell I was not completely free from whatever it was, that there was something weighing on my mind.

'Time to take charge of your own life,' he said as we walked to the van the next morning.

'We'll talk next time,' I told him. 'I'm having a break now, a well-deserved holiday. Girls and I are going to Darwin, then I'll be back home.'

We stopped at a roadhouse for lunch. As usual, Ingrid and I were debating about something. On the wall a television played with the sound turned down. Ingrid was speaking but I lost track of her words, because I saw a refugee boat in a wild storm. Up until then, I had always imagined the boat trip they took as a fairly simple calm-water crossing. The footage showed the boat rear up and surf into a cliff, and people on the rocks above, throwing lifejackets and floats down to people in the water who were clinging to bits of timber. Waves were smashing into the jagged cliffs and I did not think anybody would be able to survive it. Ingrid and Sally turned around to watch. We sat silent while women and children clung to bits of debris and the waves smashed into the sharp rocks only metres away. Someone threw a rescue rope but it was useless.

'How can your country do this?' asked Ingrid.

I would have argued with her. It was not my country, it was some other country. It was someone who put these people on an old boat with only enough fuel to get to Christmas Island. It was some war lord in a far-off place who had burned their crops. But twenty-seven people drowned and I could not answer her because those twenty-seven were Lucy, or Tariq, or Noroz.

16

You know we didn't go to Darwin. We went to Palmenter Station. By the time we got there it was coming up to the wet, and the build-up is never a time for making good decisions. We drove in and Spanner was there trying to organise things with Cookie and Simms and Charles because Newman was about to arrive with the next import. Except there wasn't a muster. No one had contacted the muster crew so although it was chaos it was a different sort of chaos to the usual muster.

There were forty-seven in the group. Newman was expanding. He said it was because two of the boats ended up landing at the same time but that was nonsense, he was wanting to bring in more. It took four days of chopper flights to get them all to the station but there was no raucous crowd and trucks weren't coming and going and there was less dust and it was altogether a better time.

We were completely unprepared for this. Every room was full. There were young kids in this lot too, something we hadn't had before. Simms put the women and girls and all the kids in the stationhouse but Sally insisted we put the families together. She crowded them into the two-bed dongas and moved some of the men across to share a dormitory in the stationhouse. It felt wrong to have men staying in the stationhouse. There were people everywhere, milling and moping around. Waiting. Waiting for us to do something, whatever it was that was next. Cookie was short of food to feed them all and we had only three vans that were working, and one of them was mine. Charles had returned from Melbourne with only one because the warehouse was locked up with no one around. He had spent several days visiting backpacker lodges but it was out of tourist season and he only managed to find one van for sale, so finally, not knowing what else to do, he came home to Palmenter Station. Whoever had been running the warehouse part of the operation had gone. Presumably they had given up waiting for either Palmenter or the money to arrive. What I hoped, at least, was that after a while they had simply locked up and gone and there would be no questions or difficulties because of it. However I told Charles there had been a problem and that was why I had gone to Melbourne, and I was sorry there wasn't time to tell him before he left on the collection run, but in future he was to go nowhere near the warehouse. I might have given him the impression that some heavy shit went down, that I had sorted it, that I was big-time and Palmenter's right-hand man.

I was running the thing from the office. As fast as I could produce papers, more people would arrive. All the time it was people wanting something. It was so noisy, women in the kitchen and kids running up and down the hall, shouting, crying, or men sitting in the lounges, waiting. Waiting. That was the thing underneath all the noise and talk, people just sitting and waiting.

Hardly any of them spoke English. Once, a couple of years before this I had suggested to Palmenter that we could print them a list of useful words and I even suggested some English lessons.

'Waste of time and effort, Son. Ship 'em in, ship 'em out. One thing you gotta learn is that these are low priority people,' he said. He said 'low priority' as if he was describing a sick dog.

I got Ingrid and Sally to look after groups of them in the canteen. Ingrid taught them English and Sally helped her with the kids. With everyone in the canteen, that got them all out of my hair and gave me time to think.

I went to see Spanner.

'What we gunna do?'

'Fuckin' chaos all right. Two vans and the bus, we could send some off and bus the rest, several trips.'

'Put 'em on a cattle truck and ship 'em south.'

He laughed. He thought I was joking. I probably was, but I am sure we could have got one of the cattle trucks back to do it.

'Three vans. There's my one.'

'Why did you come back?'

I shrugged. Why did I come back? Compassion? To hide the money? Because I was cold and lonely? To show off to Ingrid? Because I had nothing else to do? Because I missed Spanner? No simple answer.

'Why'd you stay?' I asked.

'Same reason.'

I laughed. At least we understood each other.

'We could just piss off,' I said.

'Can't do that. You seen 'em. Poor sods. And if we don't get them outta here soon the wet will break, be stuck here for a couple of months. Cookie's already short of food.'

These people needed our help. We couldn't abandon them here and to hand them in would condemn them to years in detention, and instead of being two weeks ahead of anybody looking for us, we would be right in the thick of it. I took charge.

'Tell Simms to go out and shoot a beast. Two, a pig or goat as well. Least we can put on a barbecue and feed them well. Then Charles can go to Darwin to pick up some more vans. Give him some cash.'

'Can't send him by himself. And he can only fit six on the truck, he'd have to do several trips.'

'Well, we gotta get 'em away from here. It'll take a month to get enough vans in and by then it will be pissing down, so looks like we'll be stuck with at least some of them for a while. We could set up a couple of camps away a bit so if anyone comes the station doesn't look too much like a refugee centre. One up on the ridge and another down south, away from the river, like say down at Morgan's Well.'

I had thought about this before, the time when I was camped by myself and I had thought what a great place to set up a camp, have people stay. Right now it was the best plan I could think of. With ten refugees on the back of Bitsy we towed one of the old van bodies out to Morgan's Well. We took tools and timber and tarpaulins and rope and they knew exactly how to set up a camp. It took a bit of explaining and persuading but eventually they seemed to accept what was happening. We left them to it. Hopefully we would be back with extra food before the roads got too muddy. Cookie and Charles drove to Darwin to get supplies and as many vans as they could fit on the truck. We offered work to two of the refugees, two who could drive and had reasonable English, so they went with Charles and would return with empty vans. If all went well we would have enough food and transport for everyone within two weeks and in the meantime hide as many as we could away at other camps.

It might sound as if this all happened quickly and easily, but in truth it was an uncoordinated shambles. We kept my van at the station and sent five south in another. Our third van had a bit of a mishap during driving lessons and became unroadworthy. We put up a second camp for another ten people, up on the ridge behind a large rock with great views across the riverflats. It was one of our more popular campsites. We called it Coffeehouse because we set up a stove inside an old van body we towed there, and there were table and chairs so it was a great place to chill with a view. Except that more beer got drunk there than coffee.

Spanner welded two extra sets of wheels onto Bitsy so she became an all-weather mud-loving crawler. There were six wheels side-by-side at the back and the diff had been welded so it was a bit unwieldy, but it would crawl anywhere. On hard ground it was just about impossible to turn and you had to be careful of trees and narrow gaps or big boulders or uneven ground, but to get out to Morgan's Well in the wet she was perfect. Later, Spanner bolted two couches to the back platform and it became our most popular tour. We didn't have to go anywhere particular because driving around in her was such a thrill.

The other popular activity was *Matilda* the land yacht, but I'm getting a bit ahead of myself here because all this happened a lot later and I was telling you about that muster. Non-muster.

I decided that we should stop calling them musters or imports and use the word tourists, but old habits die hard and, anyway, with what happened later it got too confusing to call everyone tourists, so imports it was. People used that as some sort of proof that we were treating them poorly, like cattle or goods, referring to them as imports, but that wasn't the case. Tour operators have always referred to their customers as 'pax', an abbreviation surely just as inhuman. Some even joke amongst themselves about 'cattle' or refer to their coaches as 'cattle trucks'.

That wet was one of the wettest ever. Charles and Cookie made it back in time but then the rains came and nothing would be coming or going for eight weeks. We were isolated but safe, and it was a happy place. We had thirty imports at the homestead. Ingrid and Sally ran English lessons every day in the canteen and some of them were real smart and learned quickly. Every second day Charles would drive Bitsy on a tour out to one of the camps, take ten from the homestead out to change places with the ten at the camp. Spanner worked on getting the vans ready. Charles had bought eight old vans in Darwin that Spanner wasn't happy with, fussy bugger that he was. He had plenty of time to check them over and fix any faults because we had decided it was too risky to send loaded vans south in the wet. Once on the tarmac they would be all right but there were several hundred kilometres of outback highway to cover before they got there. We all remembered those five who didn't make it.

Funny time was when we taught them Aussie Rules. They kept wanting to soccer the ball, or if they picked it up they would then throw it back like in rugby. Couldn't kick or handball for nuts. We played a continuous championship with four mixed teams and Spanner, Cookie, Simms and Charles as captains. Most afternoons there was a game. The team that lost got to change two of their players with the winning team so it was always a fairly close competition. After the match there was a barbecue dinner, or if it was raining too much we would crowd into the canteen and play pool and table tennis or some of them tried to teach us their card games.

By the end of the wet we were having a pretty good time and it was a shame to send them off, but we had to. I kept back Joseph and Chad, the two I had employed to go with Charles to Darwin. They were happy enough to stay and we needed more hands around the place. Also there was a young mother, Judy, who stayed on with her three-year-old boy. She helped out Cookie and later when there were more kids coming in we called her the governess and put her in charge of the homestead.

Of course during that wet I spent a lot of time in the office going over the books. I didn't play the games so much, I preferred to let the others do that so I had a lot of time looking through the accounts and records, searching the entire house and destroying anything incriminating. I couldn't think of anything else we should be doing.

We had so much money. I had spent some but not much of my million and I think Spanner had all of his, plus we had over half a million more that had come in since. I paid cash to everyone, to buy vans and food and fuel, and I gave ten grand to Cookie and Charles and five grand to Simms. Still the money kept piling up. I kept no records, but on the last trip alone, Newman had given me a bag with over two hundred thousand in it. I counted the money into envelopes holding fifty grand and some with smaller amounts. I hid these around the office. I didn't let people come into the office but even so I thought it was best to have the money in different hiding spots.

Ingrid and I moved in together. We needed all the donga rooms for arrivals and I could not explain to her why Palmenter's old bedroom was not being used. My excuse was that Palmenter might be coming back anytime, but she argued that it was unfair to leave the biggest room empty and if he did return we could simply move out for a few days. She did not know Palmenter. But then Spanner and I were the only ones who knew the truth. Palmenter was dead under the sand and never coming back.

Ingrid and I repainted and completely redecorated the room. Sally helped, and she moved into Margaret's room. We agreed it would be easier for one person to move out for a short time if ever Palmenter did return so we shifted all of his stuff in with Sally. The thought of Palmenter returning and happily accepting Margaret's room made me smile. Slowly I began to feel more comfortable in the house. Sometimes, with Sally in Margaret's old room and when there were no refugees, we were almost like a family.

It all seemed too simple. We waited at the station for Newman to rock up after the wet. He'd give us some people and a bag of cash and say see you next time. We'd put them in vans with a map and say see you later. There had to be more to it but I couldn't find it, and given that Palmenter had kept records and files of every import, neatly labelled by date, whatever extra there was couldn't have been run from the station. Perhaps it was that simple. I think that is the thing in business. The best systems are simple and they run themselves and you sit back and count cash and wonder what else is it you are supposed to be doing.

After that wet Newman turned up with no people. He came straight to me and left Rob at the chopper and I was panicked into thinking he was planning a quick getaway, that perhaps he knew of or had guessed about Palmenter and I was in trouble. I was pretty sure that there was no love lost between Newman and Palmenter but you can never tell. I mentally planned my escape, but I didn't need to because Newman didn't ask after Palmenter or when he was due back or anything. He came straight to me like I was the man. He wasted no time in pleasantries other than looking at me hard, as if to say hello and can I trust you.

'I've got a biggie. Hundred and fifty on their way.' He said it as if he had a big problem and I would be helping him out. You know, if you ask things like you are vulnerable, people can't help themselves. Clever.

'Hundred and fifty!'

'Yep. Women, children, oldies, the whole thing. Full rate. Can you deal with that many?'

What the hell. Here we go again, I thought. Spanner and I would say yes, then quietly disappear during the night. I laughed at the thought of Charles and Simms, of Cookie, trying to deal with, what would that be, six, seven days continuous chopper flights, a hundred and fifty people and no food and no vans. I would take Ingrid and Sally with me. Spanner could come as far as the roadhouse because there was only my van working. I'd drop him off with his million dollars in his backpack and I pictured him waving goodbye as Ingrid and Sally and I drove off: a thin potbellied man hitching a ride with a backpack full of cash and not much else.

'When?'

'They're on Sumba. Be here in a week from when I say go. I thought I might land them and leave half someplace hidden up the coast and bring half here. Spread the rush out a bit.'

I got up and walked to the window and stood looking out to the water tower. Cookie was playing with the three-year-old while Judy looked on laughing. She looked so happy. Cookie was laughing too, and I realised how much he had changed from the first time I saw him. Ingrid and Sally were lounging on the back of Bitsy without a care in the world. Over behind, in the distance, I could see Spanner in his shed tinkering with some machine part. Would he ever be happy not doing that? Probably not. Unless he was fishing. Had I really done him a favour by discovering his fishing camp was not worth buying?

'Give us three weeks,' I told Newman. 'Can you fly us up the coast now?'

17

Spanner got his fishing camps and left me to run the station. That first import was a bit rough but after that he got things well organised. He set up two outcamps and had a total of sixty-five beds. Eventually each camp had four or five boats, a big centre console and smaller dinghies, so everyone could go fishing at the same time. Between times he took genuine fishing groups and he was doing so well I realised that tourism was the future, a much better cover for the importing than mustering had ever been. It gave us a legitimate reason to fly at anytime between coast and station, also to own boats, have camps at different places in the wilderness. Graffiti-painted vans full of non-English speaking people would be only another set of backpackers visiting our tourist camps.

We had made the camps at Morgan's Well and Coffeehouse as temporary places to hide away the imports. I sent Joseph and Chad out to set them up as permanent camps and to build two others at different scenic spots. Eventually we ended up with eight outcamps as well as the three on the coast. On the station they were constructed around the shell of an old bus or campervan. That was our theme. You have to have some sort of theme running through your operation, something that links it all together and gives you a point of difference from the others, because the thing is no matter what business you are in you have competitors.

With these outcamps we could easily bring in a hundred and fifty at once. Three quarters of a million dollars each time. It was extremely profitable because of course the only better thing than running bigger numbers less often is running bigger numbers just as often. We made nearly ten million that first year.

It was only later that other operators started to see how well we were doing things and asked for our help. We were full up with our own people and couldn't take anybody extra and maybe I could have given some advice, or perhaps I should have said yes and got rid of the risky part of the business, let others do the boat trips and leave us to deal with the land side of things. After all, we owned the real estate, we were untouchable in that area. In business, you have to own the real estate or whatever the thing is that makes you solid. I don't care what they say about intellectual property or virtual systems: when it boils down to it, the physical thing is what sets you apart.

But at the time I didn't see the need to cooperate with anybody. It's not as if you can go to a people smugglers' convention and share ideas, or buy a magazine and study what others are doing. *People Smuggler's Weekly* or something. But there is an underground network, word gets around, you meet people, things are said, comments, ideas pass up and down the chain of command and I guess a lot of the people on the ground in the villages were working for whoever they could. But like I said, at the time I didn't see the need to cooperate and as you know, we never had a boat stopped or caught. In part that was because of the custom-designed carbon fibre boats that don't show up on radar. Other operators were so afraid of their boats being caught and seized that they used leaky old things that they didn't mind losing. They would send them off with only enough fuel to get part way. When they ran out they could call for rescue. If there was crew at all it would be a couple of kids because the United Nations says kids can't be prosecuted. Half the time the boats sank before they even got to the coast. Boat would sink, everybody would drown. But our competitors didn't care because they already had the money. How silly is that? Drowning your customers is not good for business, although other operators drowning a few was certainly good for my business. Our reputation was good, we were getting a couple of grand more per passenger and still we couldn't cope with demand and as far as I know all of our imports got to a city and are living there now. That's another business lesson for you.

If I had been able to I would have sold franchises. When I did the MBA at Darwin Uni we had a whole unit on franchises and how that was a way to leverage a successful business, but how do you sell a people-smuggling system to people in the Caribbean or on the Med? Once, during the wet, when we closed down and anyway things were going well and I could leave Spanner to run the place, I flew to Tunis and asked around about how things were done. I discovered we were doing it better than any of them. We were unique and in part it was because I had set up a legitimate parallel business that allowed us to operate to and from the coast and to fly whenever we felt like between the camps and the station.

After Tunis I travelled as a backpacker through Morocco and the Western Sahara, then down through Senegal and Guinea and into Sierra Leone where the civil war had ended years ago. Sierra Leone was sparse but Guinea was beautiful in a way that the Northern Territory is not. Lush jungles, rugged forests and mountains, great backpacker lodges on fantastic beaches. Life was so simple there and I loved it. I couldn't understand why anyone would ever want to leave. Why do people ever want to leave that which they know, the place they are born?

One evening I was standing on the beach watching a one-armed fisherman working his nets. As I watched him I thought if ever there was a case to flee your own country there he was. I tried to recall if we had ever had any refugees come through the station with missing limbs. I couldn't remember any, but anyway, the bloody civil war, where ruthless gangs cut off the arms of their enemies, was before my time. Our clients came mostly from Iran and Afghanistan, and when that was over there would be some other place in the world where people would find a way to ruin paradise and we were assured a never-ending supply of customers.

The fisherman finished bundling up his net and came over to me, holding a basket of small fish with the stub of his arm. He smiled, and held up his hand with five fingers open.

'Five?'

He nodded. I gave him five one-thousand-leone notes. He put the basket on the ground and pulled a plastic bag from his pocket and indicated I should hold it. He tipped the fish in, nodded to me, and walked away happy. I took the fish back to my lodge and shared them and some beers with the other travellers, but all evening I was feeling sad.

By now I was starting to miss the harsh bright openness of the outback, where you can stand on an outcrop and see as far as there is to look, and where every little thing you see is significant. In Africa it was beautiful, lush, overgrown, vibrant, but eventually it got to be oppressive. When you trek to the top of a mountain there is a view and space but mostly to get there you are in jungle and the four green walls are all around you and it is like you are in the exercise yard of a prison cell and the other inmates are chattering monkeys. Perhaps it is that there is no place like home. What you are used to. Perhaps that was why these one-limbed cripples struggled on in their own land because I was sure if they really wanted to they could have found enough money to buy a ticket. But there is no place like home.

I travelled for six weeks until the wet was over and we could start up again. I had a day in Singapore on the way home and I went for a long walk along the waterfront. I liked looking at the activity, the ferries and the boats coming and going, the tourists. I came to the yacht club and at the bar ended up in conversation with another Australian businessman. He was on his way home from Vietnam where his company made fibreglass boats. They exported them all over the world but the thing he was most excited to tell me about was the racing yachts. Perhaps he thought I was a sailor.

'Carbon fibre, mate. Weigh less than two tonnes and cost me the same to build up there as a standard one in Oz. A glass hull is over four tonnes.' He pulled out pictures. 'Do you sail?'

'No,' I said. And then to justify me being at the bar in the yacht club, I added, 'I run tour boats.'

That was how we got the carbon fibre boats. I don't know if they really didn't show on radar but that's what we told people. Certainly we never got caught. But they cost me only what any other boat would cost, and running at high speed unladen back to Indonesia they used far less fuel, and the hull shape was excellent. They were so good that we could sell our trips as 'pay when you arrive'.

From Singapore I landed in Darwin and spent a few days sorting out my second-year MBA units. I placed a series of ads in newspapers and magazines for backpackers and grey nomads to visit what I called Palmenter Wildlife Conservancy. Slowly we started to mix our imports with legitimate travellers. Most of the time, you could camp out at one of the waterholes or up on a bluff with a brilliant view, watch the sunset over your camp with no one for miles and miles. People loved that, particularly after the wet when it was green for as far as the eye could see. We even got to have tourists during the wet, because we had set up the camps on high ground and Bitsy was able to get out to them when the roads became impassable. There was no other way to see the land in the wet season. People are interested to see stuff like that.

One time, two tourists came who had mountain bikes on the roof of their car. Serious-looking bikes. They had been at some desert cycle race in Alice and they camped out at Morgan's Well for a week, riding all over the place, carving out trails wherever they could find hard dirt or surface rocks. That was when Spanner and I came up with the idea of setting up a bike circuit for the tourists because we remembered how much fun it had been on those old bikes that Charles had brought up. We created single-lane bike paths where the sand and dirt was packed flat, and linked the outcamps with these bike trails. The distance along these trails between the camps was between ten and forty kilometres, so it was perfect for a rider who wanted to take in the whole place on a multi-day tour.

Eventually we had a fleet of hire bikes too because Charles brought in hundreds more of the wrecked bikes he picked up from streetside rubbish days in Melbourne. Councils rotate the collection times so there was always some locality where Charles could collect old bikes. He would load up the back of the truck, often having to put bikes inside the vans to make enough room to carry them all. Some trips there would be twenty or thirty old bikes that Spanner would fix up. Whatever bikes or bits he couldn't use he threw onto the gene pool.

When Spanner was full-time running the camps up at the coast he would often take a week off to come down to spend time with us. He would tinker in the shed rebuilding bikes from many bits. He taught Charles and some of the refugees enough about bike mechanics so they could fix most of them. Funny thing though was that it didn't help Charles choose better wrecks from the streetside. The pile of irredeemably lost bikes on top of the gene pool grew and grew.

We sent a bunch of bikes up to the coast to try out for when the fishing wasn't happening, but the coast was too rough, lots of steep limestone terrain or crocodile-infested mudflats.

It is important to notice what your customers are doing, what they want or are interested in, and then you build on that. Now we had backpackers doing cultural tours, bush tucker, grey nomads who wanted to sit with the view at Coffeehouse and hardcore cyclists who rode the back trails. And birdwatchers, walkers. All sorts. And imports. Even with all this going on it was only during the import weeks that it was crowded but no one minded. It is a big station. Lots of space.

We held one last genuine muster and thought we had sold all the cattle, but we kept finding a few at the waterholes and as I'd now started calling the place a Wildlife Conservancy we needed to get rid of them. I remembered that Palmenter had used to take hunters out after the imports and I wondered if we could add that to our activities, so I put a few feelers out to gun clubs in Darwin to gauge the interest. As you'd expect it wasn't quite as simple as that. Palmenter must have had some private arrangement with his cowboys who I had no desire to meet again, so for now it became Simms' job.

Simms would bring back fresh meat and whenever he did there was a free barbecue at the homestead. Cookie was in his element. He had rigged up a bell and would make fresh damper, ring the bell as the damper came hot from the camp oven. Tourists loved it. I bought some guitars and there was always someone who could play.

About the only thing I didn't get rid of was his name. Palmenter Wildlife Conservancy. I'd have liked to get rid of that too but supposedly Palmenter was alive calling the shots from somewhere and I was only his manager. You change what you can, forget the rest.

Newman did not come anymore. He had moved to Indonesia to live and he ran his end from there, and later he took on some other projects as well. We still used Rob and the same chopper to fly between the coast and the station but by then it was doing much more airtime in tours and joy flights that we sold to tourists. It was a ridiculous chopper for mustering anyway and wouldn't have fooled anyone. For mustering you want a nimble little two-seater and this was a six-seater. Massive great thing. We could fly a group of fishermen into the camps and the families would often come to the station. After the fishermen's week of man-time, the women and kids would be flown to join them and it worked so well. We set up some walks and stuff, wildlife and interpretive signs, printed guides and signposted the way. That was both on the coast and around the station. You have to give people things to do.

As I said, Cookie stayed on too, but I made him rip up his crop. You can't run a legit business and have a dope crop in the front yard, and I wanted the tourism thing to eventually take over. At first I didn't mind. I'd smoked a bit of it myself; in the bad days after Arif was shot it was the only way I could cope. Actually, we had all smoked quite a bit of it.

When I first took over – when I was worried that Simms or Charles or someone might not be fully on side, or that someone would ask too much detail about exactly where Palmenter had gone – then, I had Cookie lace the food with it.

Thing about marijuana is that it makes you happy, drowsy, it saps your energy but you feel so great. Mellow. It was brilliant for keeping everyone happy on the station and in line, but absolutely hopeless if I wanted to get anything done. Every evening meal Cookie'd dose the food and I had a compliant and willing workforce the next day. They did anything I asked them. Only it took them four times as long to do it.

You think I'm cruel doing that, particularly as only Cookie and I knew about it, but it's like money. People do anything for money. They'll do anything for another dose, drugs or money, it's the same thing. Wasn't that how Palmenter got me there in the first place? Wasn't that why we were all there? What is the difference between drip-feeding small amounts of cash and small amounts of dope? A wage, enough to get by on, but with the promise of a huge bonus. Money is a drug too. The junkie on the street and the high-flyer on the top floor are not that far apart.

I tried not to eat too much in the evenings but it was too difficult and eventually I was eating as much as everyone else and getting as stoned. I think Cookie had no idea how much to put in so he overdid it. I could tell you we had some memorable evenings but in truth, we usually fell asleep.

That was before the de-stock. That was before something happened and I decided we needed to change a few things. Up until then we had been always on the brink of leaving and we had been fearful of Palmenter's cowboys arriving unannounced.

We had so much money but the station was going broke. Palmenter had been feeding some of the cash in as cattle sales, faking income from the musters, but we had stopped doing that. I am sure we could have deposited all the money because no one was sitting out there in the scrub counting our cattle, how often we mustered or anything. But I wasn't giving any of my money to him, because once it was in the bank in his name how was I going to get it out? I had forged his signature on a few cheques but mostly I didn't bother to open the mail. You get into serious trouble for forging big cheques.

As so often happens in life the answer came to us. Literally. The bank came to us. Two suited gentlemen who at first I took to be thugs – the heavies we had all along been half expecting, the owners of the money, the cowboys who had come in on occasion with Palmenter. You know how in the movies thugs arrive at some place and they are well dressed and you think it is some legitimate business except that the music gives it away, they are there for something extremely nasty and end up slitting the nostrils of some innocent bystander to prove how tough they are? It's usually in a pizza joint and the other one will be eating pizza just to show how he doesn't care about the screaming and pain and blood over the floor. Well, that's what I thought these guys were when they drove in and if I hadn't been standing under the water tower talking with Sally I would have been out the back door and into my van and outta there.

'We apologise for dropping in unannounced. Is Alex Palmenter here?'

He apologised! Jeez, this must be serious and these must be

heavy dudes, I thought. We were so far out of the way no one ever simply dropped in.

'He's not here. I'm Dan Taylor, station manager. Perhaps I can help.' I put on my best voice but Sally was looking at me funny, what with me calling myself Dan.

The two men introduced themselves. Rural Bank of Northern Australia. Concern about the bank accounts and overdrawn amounts, significant arrears, security over the lease, on they went. Unless we can rectify, letters of demand left unanswered, serious breach of blah blah blah. Either the guy was an idiot, a city slicker who knew nothing about the real world, or thugs from some distant associate of Palmenter's here on a pretext, sussing out the situation, sizing us up. While he went on I considered the chance of outrunning them. They were in suits and stupid shoes, it was hot, I knew my way around and was young and fit. Easy. But Sally was still standing with us.

Although I looked older than I was, people probably thought I was too young to be in charge. Dan Taylor, who was that? Nick Smart was the one with the reputation. You have to be hard to survive in the underworld but in my case it was mostly by reputation. I used to yell a bit, get angry, strut around, stuff like that. I used to let people see me angry at Simms or Charles but I only ever hit anybody once, that's all it takes to make a reputation. One time Simms was being stupid as usual and I thought it wouldn't do any harm to make a bit of a point and I made sure Joseph and Chad saw me do it because they were a bit slack a lot of the time.

I thought, these guys must be here to check the lay of the land and then report back to whoever for when the real shit went down. Because of my reputation they were wise to check us out beforehand if there was going to be any rough stuff. But that goes both ways. I wondered who they were, who was the Mr Big I had not yet met? We could do a deal. I wondered how much I would have to pay. Perhaps it was Margaret. Would she want us to supply girls again? A few days ago there had been a husky-voiced phone call and someone had asked to talk to Palmenter. It might have been Margaret. I had never talked to her and for the life of me couldn't remember her voice.

'Well,' I said, 'come into the office. Mr Palmenter is away

overseas but I am sure I can sort this out.' I motioned them to the homestead. Two of us could play this game. 'Sally, can you bring us some tea? Or would you gentlemen prefer a beer?' They accepted tea, and I watched them as they watched Sally leave. I wondered how two thugs in the employ of Margaret would look at a sexy girl as she walked off to get tea. Not like that. Respectful. No, I didn't think they were from Margaret.

Where the hell had they come from? Banks don't do house calls particularly out here where the round trip from Darwin was a four-day minimum. Even if they were legit I had to get rid of them quickly. There was simply too much for them to see.

In the office I sat them to one side of the desk, facing both chairs inwards so that if I was going to abscond they wouldn't see me out of the window running across to where I kept my fuelled-up van hidden behind *Matilda*. One of them opened his briefcase and produced some ledgers and statements of account on bank letterheads. It looked to be legitimate. If this was some sort of scam they were certainly playing the charade out for all it was worth. Might as well play along, I thought, and anyway, if heavy shit was going to go down they would have already started. My mind was racing. I would offer them to stay the night and then sometime during the night, when they were asleep, I would slip out and leave, take the south track and fly standby from Alice.

Mr Serious Breach was rabbiting on about things, about not wanting to take this action and as employees we would be guaranteed our entitlements but that there would have to be someone here to be administrator.

'Hold on a minute,' I said. 'Are you saying you are going to take possession of the station?'

He shuffled uncomfortably. That was when I realised this was all legit. Thugs don't do uncomfortable.

'Of course if there is some other way, if there is a way to settle the outstanding amounts and bring accounts up to date, but if Mr ...'

'Well,' I said, 'although Mr Palmenter is away overseas, and I do have to admit I haven't had any communication with him for some time, but I am left under strict instructions to take care of all aspects of the business, including to make financial decisions. What I can tell you is that there is no shortage of funds. His international operations are going exceedingly well. Direct meat sales to Indonesia. Tourism is booming too. But as you will appreciate, living out here without internet and what with the pressure to run the place, we don't get into town too often. We are very busy and banking is not our biggest priority. And Margaret has been away in Melbourne because her mother is dying,' I added. There was no reaction from them at the mention of Margaret's name.

He shuffled even more uncomfortably while the second one remained mute.

'Unfortunately it might be too late. I have my instructions to either get the funds or serve you with notice. All our correspondence up until now has been ignored.'

Every month I went to Darwin for my MBA course and collected the mail from the post office. I threw most of it out. I only opened letters that might be from someone who was looking for or worried about Palmenter. Bank statements went straight in the bin.

'How much are we talking about?'

When he told me I nearly burst out laughing. Thirty-seven thousand plus penalties. Total fifty-two thousand. I could piss that on him. These were no thugs. Thugs would be asking for that in millions. Plus penalties. Don't make me laugh.

Banks are funny businesses. They are so keen to get your money they will do almost anything to get it and in the process overlook the obvious fact that our supposed overseas cattle buyers would be transferring money direct into our accounts, not paying cash. Who pays cash for anything nowadays? I gave him ninety-seven thousand two hundred and sixty dollars, an amount I made up to make it seem at least a little legitimate, but I deliberately miscounted it without him seeing so he had about ten grand extra. I also gave him some of the foreign currency and asked him to exchange it and deposit the proceeds. If he had smelled something fishy he didn't say anything and if later when he thought about it and was deciding what to do, when he counted the cash and discovered the extra he would pocket the difference and keep quiet. People are the same everywhere.

'I just haven't had the opportunity to get into town to deposit this,' I told him. 'We've had some issues with the bores along the south boundary and that has occupied our time. That and the general running of the place. What with the mining boom we are very short-staffed. You know how it is.'

I guarantee he had no idea how it was but he accepted the money and wrote out an interim receipt and said he would deposit it and post us the official receipt. I then went on to say if only we could make some sort of other arrangement, that I was investigating satellite systems for internet access, setting up our own internet service all the way out here and that perhaps that would solve our banking as well.

It pays to talk big, because in the end, Mr Serious Breach, Nathan was his name, agreed that the bank would fund half of the cost of a satellite dome that would give us our own internet access. What was so cool about that, apart from the movies we could download and all the other stuff we could now do, was that I could transfer money between linked accounts. Like, for example, between Palmenter Station and Palmenter Wildlife Conservancy and Wayne's Fishing World and a whole series of other accounts I set up at different banks to feed the cash in. I had to go to Darwin if I wanted to deposit any cash but I had been getting a bit sick of the monthly trips to hand in MBA assignments. Now I could do it all online.

They stayed the night and in the morning Charles and I took them for a tour out to Morgan's Well camp. I wanted to see how much a stranger might fall for the tourist venture charade. We had a barbecue down at the creek and Cookie outdid himself. We sat in the shade while Judy and her kid played in the waterhole, and after steaks bigger than the plates Cookie rolled some numbers so strong that soon we were giggling at nothing and then sleeping it off. They left midafternoon with a 'packed lunch', a half brick of some of Cookie's finest.

'Everyone likes to be given a prezzie,' said Cookie.

18

I realised that although a lot of money was coming in we were vulnerable because everyone was only as honest as the cash. If a problem arose we would throw cash at it, bribe people or offer more than the next man, but of course eventually that would catch up with us. We were giving stupid amounts of money for even the simplest things. Charles was buying the vans 'no questions asked' from a guy in Darwin who rounded them up from genuine backpackers who ended their Aussie adventure there. We were paying twice what they were worth and each month the price went up. There were lots of little deals happening like that, things that I had lost control of. Newman was paying some people up the coast to keep quiet and I'm not sure how Spanner was explaining burning so much fuel for three little fishing camps. If someone did talk it would be like rats deserting a sinking ship and no amount of money would keep everyone quiet. What would happen if business slumped? If the money ran out? Plus, now that most of the money was in the bank I needed to keep the business secure because there is a whole world of difference between having a few million in your backpack and having it in a bank account.

Of course, it wasn't only that. It was the whole thing getting so big and spiralling out of control. We were bringing in more than ever, demand for our products was limitless and so was our demand down the line. Everyone was making good money from it and, that was the thing, perhaps everyone was only in it for the money and no one was really on our side. No one believed in the product, in what we were doing. All they believed in was money. I had to change that. In business, your people have to believe in your product.

After the bank visit I sat everyone down. Spanner knew the truth and I had no choice but to trust in him, but I brought him back from the coast because I wanted him to be a part of it. I was pretty sure Newman was on side too but I didn't know about Rob. Cookie was happy, Judy and her little boy had moved in with him and most days he was wearing a bigger grin than when he'd be doped up and stupid leaning against the back door of the kitchen. Ingrid and Sally had by now well overstayed their visas and anyway I knew I could trust them. I liked Charles. He had plenty of opportunity to leave each time he was in the city but he always came back. Simms was a bit of an unknown, more because he might say or do something unwittingly. The ones I was most unsure of were the mustering mob. We didn't use them for mustering anymore but, after all, this was their land. Sort of. More than it was Palmenter's anyway. I thought that of all the people there, they were probably the least aware of what had been going on.

I needn't have worried. Everyone was on side. Turns out the mustering crew were very aware of what was happening and they were pretty smart about it too. After the main talk I took them aside and told them I needed a bit extra from them. People love to feel special and they love to feel involved, so you tell them you need a little bit more from them than from everyone else.

'You guys, we need some cultural stuff, tours and shit, places to take people. Forget cattle, we are now in the people business.' They loved that disparaging way of talking, pretending that it didn't matter too much. The funny thing was some of the cultural stuff they set up, the bush tucker and tour of sacred sites and traditional burial grounds, they became our most popular tours. Sometimes stuff you toss up as an afterthought becomes the best thing you ever did. Like the pizza oven. After the bank guys, I remembered about a movie where some thugs were eating pizza and I suggested we add a pizza oven to the barbecue area because woodfired pizza was all the rage in the city.

After the talk I took off by myself for a while, snuck out in the early morning while they were all hungover. I thought it was best if I wasn't around if any of them wanted out; they could quietly leave while I was gone and not feel any pressure from me watching them. If they stayed, it had to be because they wanted to. Also, if someone did leave and report all our activities I didn't want to be there if we were raided by the police or Immigration. I thought that would be unlikely but you never know. I took three hundred thousand dollars well wrapped in several layers of plastic and some food – tins and stuff that would keep – and I hid this along the way in a place I could hide out if I ever needed to. The other thing I hid with my secret stash was the little gold Buddha. I figured if the shit ever hit the fan I would only need to hide for a few weeks and then I could make my way south. I'd go to Perth where I had never been and no one knew me.

I headed out to the north-east. I hadn't been that way before as there were no bores out there. It was difficult terrain for the vans as the land rises slowly from the river flats and is very sandy. I was surprised to find quite a few tracks and even more surprised when I came to a ridge with a wonderful view to the north. Below me lay another river valley and if I looked long and hard enough into the horizon I could convince myself that was the ocean. It wasn't of course, but it felt like that. It felt as if this was the edge of the continent and the land below ran off into some new place.

This was where I camped. I parked the van where I had a great view as I sat in the back in the late afternoon. I pulled up some sticks and branches and spinifex and placed these over the van to hide it from the air, then threw handfuls of sand over it as well because I knew as the wind blew, a lot of the foliage would simply blow away. How like Palmenter or those five I was now, I thought, burying myself in my van out in the desert.

Only way anyone was going to find me was by walking up the limestone ridge from below, and that was what happened. I had been there five days when some of the muster crew simply walked right up to me as if they had known not only someone, but me, was camped there. Like you walk next door to visit your neighbour to have a chat.

The main man was Jimmy and he spoke in this growly slurred way that made the words difficult to understand but, you know, the funny thing was that unlike Charles, who at first I found difficult to understand, with Jimmy you didn't understand the words he used but you knew exactly what he meant.

'You come walk with us. We show you special place like walkabout tour. Like him you said.'

Jimmy led the way down the scree and over loose boulders. At the bottom of the slope there were caves of a sort, more half-caves, overhangs with smooth rock behind and shaded by large but spindly white-trunked trees. A group of women were sitting in the shade of one of these trees mixing some mud of different colours on some flat rocks.

'Touchup 'em drawings.'

Jimmy pointed to the smooth rocks behind and I saw that it was completely covered in pictures, stylised stick figures of lizards and kangaroos and people between handprints and random lines and dots. It was amazing. Pictures overlapped and the more I looked the more I saw I was seeing back in time, back over generations to a time long ago when the first of these might have been made.

'How old are these?' I asked Jimmy.

He laughed.

'Oh, 'em plenty old. Older than going back 'em old people and they old people and more old people after that. Plenty old. But we fixim for the tour. Make 'em plenty good.'

I remembered reading about the age of some of the Aboriginal art, up to thirty thousand years old, and how the people had been keeping the galleries continuously over generations of habitation. I was wondering what they thought of all these refugees, people who fled the place of their birth and abandoned their ancestors. Looking at the art and listening to Jimmy explain it to me I got the sense that they had been watching strangers come and go for all of those thirty thousand years, and that they accepted this in the same way they accepted the inevitability and passing of seasons.

'We bring people here, Jimmy?'

This was going to be brilliant for our tours, but I'd have to shift my secret stash to a safer place.

'Oh yes, I think plenty good for tour. You got good camp for 'em up there, we bring walk down here, walk around, sit down for story. This good place. Waterhole 'long there, plenty bird and tucker, bush tucker always plenty. Them tours always popular. Maybe sometime we catch bungarra, take uptop to cook him on fire.'

He took me for a walk along the creek, along a path to a beach and reed-lined pool. On the far side was a steep slope of rocks covered in a tangle of vegetation so the path was the only way in. It was a hidden oasis. Obviously they had known about it forever, but it was new to me. I wondered how many more secret places like this there were. We could open up a whole new part of the station and run a lot more tourists than we were currently. Both types of tourist.

But that was after. Before I talked to the muster crew, I talked to everyone together in the canteen. I had got them all in from the outcamps and the coast and wherever else they had been and in the afternoon we watched a movie in the canteen. I had brought a player and a projector up from Melbourne, and a whole bunch of DVDs, and the one I made them watch was *Blood Diamond*. That's where a group of South African mercenaries are looking for some smuggled diamonds, but it has a great scene in it where the Sierra Leone rebels are chopping off people's arms. 'Short sleeve or long sleeve?' they asked. Later, Simms killed a bullock and we had a big party. Then the next day I told them how things were.

'Look,' I said, 'you all know, to some extent, that Palmenter Station has been doing some stuff, bringing in people from overseas, asylum seekers and such. I am not sure exactly how much each of you knows or is aware of, but I want to be clear about where we all stand.'

Except for Spanner, all of them thought Palmenter was an absentee owner and I was doing his bidding. I wasn't going to change that belief, but I did want them to know I was calling the shots and that things were going to change. I went on.

'Palmenter is not here now. He's left me in charge and I want to make it a better place. Not just to work, but it includes that. I think we have to start with each and every one of us acknowledging what it is we do, and why we do it, and if you don't agree you should leave. You are free to go. I'll make sure you get all your pay and entitlements and Spanner will set you up a van and off you go. No problems. You won't hear from us again and we don't want to know about you and I know you will not say anything to anybody, ever, because, let's face it, we are all implicated in what we have been doing up to now.'

We were sitting in the canteen. It was morning, a time I figured they would have sobered up from the night before but not yet started for today. This bunch has probably never been in a meeting anything like this ever before and they sat looking at me, not talking, taking in everything I said. I wondered what they thought of me. Palmenter would speak to you alone, in twos or threes. I hoped I was coming across as powerful, competent. We had done some of this sort of motivational stuff in the business unit I was studying. Inside I was shaking. If this didn't work I would have to be the first to leave, faster and further than any of them. But it wasn't over yet. I hadn't finished with them.

'So that is the first thing. You are free to go, to find something else.'

I looked slowly around the room, at each and every one of them. I could see they were fidgety. I let them stew for a while. Next, I would offer them the freedom to come and go as they pleased and a share of the money if they stayed to help. They would be on easy street, they could never find anything half as good, but I wanted to make them think whether they wanted to be a part of this. For commitment, sometimes you have to push people a little harder than they are prepared to go, and I had deliberately chosen to pressure them while hungover from such a great party the night before.

When the tension in the room was almost unbearable I continued.

'But at least you have the freedom to do that, to be born into the lucky country and can live pretty well, do pretty much what you want. These people,' and I indicated with a raised arm the faraway coast and the boats coming in, 'these people have none of that and that is why we do this. To give them a chance at a better life. If you don't agree with that, if you think they are just fodder to fund our money-hungry materialistic lives and it is fair to rip them off and take everything we can from them and then set them free with even less than the nothing they had back home, if you think that, you ought to leave.' I was getting worked up. After the movie yesterday my words were producing the effect I wanted. It was even working on me. I was on a roll.

'If you think that, I don't want you here,' I said, 'and we are just going to trust you not to tell anyone, and off you go to live your quiet meaningful life in some place else.' I paused again, not as long, but long enough.

'If you don't leave, let's be really clear. You will be a part of it and I want you to stay because you think that what we are doing is good and worthwhile and a better thing to do with your life. It is the moral thing to do.'

I told them they were good at what they did and that my preference was they stayed, and I told them about some of the stories. From Lucy, from her family, and those that I had heard from those four in the van on the drive south. These stories were the reason we had to do this, I told them. I said it would not always be easy and that life on the station would not always be paradise, but if we were all in it together it would be as close to that as it could be. A life of outdoor freedom with trips to the coast as often as you wanted, even trips up to Sumba for surfing, mini-van collection trips to the cities every month if you wanted them, and a place at the homestead that they could always call home.

My guess was that if one left they all would. But they all stayed. Say any old shit often enough and you start to believe it. I was even getting teary myself. I was now the Mr Big of People Smuggling.

I say now, but of course that was back when, and now it is all gone. Closed down. Nothing there except them excavating the pit and uncovering bodies and I'm doing twenty years. But it's better than Spanner got. I don't regret any of what I've done, although I do sometimes think I should've acted sooner. Sometimes I think I'm a little too cautious and in the time it takes to decide things it becomes too late.

19

After the bank visit, we got our satellite dish and I set up email accounts for everyone so we were in touch with the outside world again. Palmenter had not allowed any personal mail through but I believe you must treat people with respect and trust them, so I allowed them to come into the office for their emails once a week.

That was how I found out that my father had kidney failure. I invited my parents to visit and they kept stalling. It was a big deal for us because of course we couldn't have them arrive right when the imports were coming through. By then we had camps away from the homestead and up on the coast, but even so it would require some coordination to show them around and not let them see anything.

I could tell something was wrong and eventually Mum admitted why they couldn't visit. Dad had to be within a day's travel of the dialysis unit and on call in case a donor kidney came up. It was a waiting game. For now he was okay but sooner or later he would need a transplant. Mum told me all of that on the phone one night, but it was Simon who emailed me and told me how sick Dad really was.

It was unlikely that he would ever get a kidney. The transplant waiting lists are years long as there are not enough people who die with good kidneys. Dad could not be moved up the list because of his age and other things – of course older people have more health issues! I wanted to fly down to Melbourne to argue with the doctors who made these choices but then I heard through someone that in Mumbai a transplant could be arranged almost immediately.

My second overseas trip was to India. On the way I arranged to meet Newman who was living in Indonesia and running that end of the operation. I thought he could put me in touch with some people up the line who might help. You get a bit of an idea about what is going on and then you ask a few more questions and piece the whole thing together. People who need the money were selling all kinds of things.

I emailed Newman and asked if we could meet in Bali. Of course I couldn't say why. Even in an email you have to be careful what you say.

Newman named a bar on the beach at Sanur. I arrived early and took an outside table where I had a view of the beach. From where I sat, near me at tables and in the clothing stalls opposite, far off in the surf or lying on the beach, everywhere I could see fat white westerners holidaying without a care in the world. Newman must have arrived and seen me because he came to the table with two beers.

'Been to Indo before?'

'No. Never.'

He didn't comment. He didn't seem in too much of a hurry to ask what this was about and I was happy to sit and watch. A group of women were negotiating the price of a massage with a man and a woman. Honeymooners by the look of them. As we watched I wondered if the ability to idly watch the world go on around was a skill learned from our time on Palmenter Station where every afternoon there was a beer with the same four blokes.

Eventually, though, I had to say something.

'My father is sick and needs a kidney transplant. I am on my way to Mumbai to see about getting it done there.'

'Is it safe there? Indian doctors, I mean?'

'I was hoping you could tell me. You ever been to Mumbai? A lot of our people come via Mumbai, don't they.'

'I'd say nearly all of them. Across the Arabian Sea or down via Pakistan. Mumbai's the main clearing house. But we don't get involved that early, they gotta get to Indo themselves. Jeez, if we opened up in Mumbai, the gates would really open.'

I smiled at that. Two western businessmen discussing their business. A man came by and offered us some watches from a wooden box he carried slung around his neck. Genuine, he said.

Newman said something to him in Indonesian and he left.

'Some of this gear is genuine. Probably comes from our people, they can wear it on the way here and then sell it to pay for the trip. Lot of good stuff ends up being sold on the beaches here. People don't know the difference, think it is all fake.'

Newman didn't seem to see where I was heading. Perhaps he thought I really wanted to meet to discuss our supply chain, see the ins and outs of how things went.

'I was wondering, y'know, about getting a kidney there for my dad. I've heard through the grapevine that it can be done. That's why I'm off to Mumbai.'

'You want to close down for a while? We've got them lined up all the way back,' he said. 'You can't stop now. Charles and Simms take care of your end?'

'No, that's okay. Whole thing runs itself now. You keep taking them in to Spanner, he'll coordinate the rest. I hear that you can buy body parts there. My dad needs a kidney,' I repeated.

'Mumbai?'

'Yeah, know anyone?'

'You want to bring in a kidney?' He looked at me inquisitively. I got the impression that it could be done.

'How would you do that? Could you buy a kidney?'

'You can buy anything, and I mean anything, in Mumbai. You gotta be just a little bit careful, pay the right people, you can't just barge in there and order a kidney. But wouldn't you have to keep it chilled? Have to fly it all the way, surely?'

I considered that. My idea was to fly my dad into a hospital in India and have the whole operation done there. For a start I didn't know how I would go about explaining the sudden acquisition of a kidney to the surgeon in Melbourne. Also, wasn't there some sort of compatibility thing with organs? But it was an attractive alternative. I didn't want to trust a surgeon in a third world country if I didn't have to.

'How much would a kidney be? Who sells them?'

He watched me for a moment without answering.

'Is that how they afford our trips?' I asked.

'Don't think so. Not usually.' I could tell it was only half the answer and waited for the other half. 'You do hear of some people selling one of their own kidneys. But most of it is they sell the whole lot. Two kidneys, liver, lungs and heart, eyes. Whatever they can that is still healthy.'

'But that would kill them!'

'You asked. Look, they take the old and sick to the hospital. They're gunna die anyway. Sometimes they let them live in a room at the hospital until they die, then they have the organs. Hospital feeds them, keeps them comfortable, gets them healthy. In return, their organs are used when they die. They don't need them anymore.'

'But they don't kill them? They wait for them to die?' Even that was a horrible thought.

He shrugged. 'Some children are sold as slaves into the Middle East. That's one way out. Die in the slums or a life working for some rich oil sheik. Others, if they are lucky enough, pretty ones are prostitutes, or the strong ones maybe work. While their bodies hold up.' He looked at me and followed my gaze around the holidaymakers. 'I don't think they kill anybody. That's the stuff of movies. The old people are happy to be given a home and to be well fed for a change, and the family get enough to come to a better life in a new country. It's a fucked-up world, but nothing you gunna do gunna change it. Take your dad there. I'll give you a few names, some contacts, some of my people who you can trust.'

In Mumbai I was met by a small Indian man who spoke with the same singsong accent that Charles did, and if it hadn't been for years of listening to and trying to understand Charles I doubt I would have understood anything he said. His name was Siddiqi and Newman must have told him what I was after.

'Everybody call me Sid,' he sang. 'First, I am taking you to the number one market. Here, I am thinking you will find what you want.'

He bundled me into a waiting taxi and talked quickly and at length with the driver who regarded me curiously in the rear-view mirror. The drive took over an hour, through crowded chaotic streets full of blaring horns and yelling, trucks and cattle and carts and people and bikes and scooters and of course thousands of taxis, but for all the noise and swearing not once did we actually stop. Always we edged ever forward, slowly, then accelerating through some gap in the traffic that would magically appear just as we got to it. How would you explain to this taxi driver that we drove on roads in Australia that for a whole day you might not see another car? If you told that to him would he be excited to go there, or terrified at the isolation and boredom? I wondered this as Sid chatted away like a canary, not seeming to need me to answer more than occasionally. I wondered what our imports were told to expect when they got to Australia. Or what was it that made them choose Australia in the first place. There had to be some attractive promise made by someone. I did not believe if you had grown up with the noise and bustle and chaos of Mumbai or Karachi or any of the cities or even the towns of these crowded places, that you would ever find satisfaction in the barren landscape of Australia. Not even in our cities where the homes were big and spread out and hidden from one another by high walls so that the suburbs were forever asleep. I could never have lived in Mumbai and I doubted that anybody at home in Mumbai could live happily in Australia.

Perhaps I was seeing things as I wanted to. I was in the people-moving business and I had to believe that those I was moving wanted to go where I was taking them, that anybody with the desire could have bought a ticket and that the reason they didn't was that we are all more comfortable with the familiar. Home is what you are born into. But as we drove past crowded slums of cardboard and plastic or the beggars in doorways I knew that these were the ones that could not afford to move, that their whole life was this, and I thought about what Newman had said. If you were ill, you knew you were going to die, wouldn't you too be grateful for a place to live out your days in comfort and with a full belly? Isn't that what we all do? We spend the intervening years between birth and death trying to make ourselves more comfortable. Buying a kidney off a dying man so my father could live comfortably for a few more years was a thing where everybody could end up happy. Win-win, as they say. But I was not prepared for where Sid took me.

The taxi stopped in an area where there were no other cars. The street had become a narrow lane between two foul-smelling gutters. Most of the traffic now was on foot and we joined them, Sid leading me down a side lane where high walls kept out the relentless sun. I would have preferred the sun. He pointed to the ground and instructed me to walk quickly but look where I was placing my feet, for one side of the lane was a sewer, and spilling from it, or flowing to it, filth waited to trap me. I hurried to keep up with Sid who walked placing his feet casually on rare dry ground, until I realised he was moving at whatever pace I was and if I slowed down so would he. He led me into an even darker and narrower lane and to a door where a giant stood guard, a man so fierce that he would have made Palmenter's cowboys look like puppies.

Inside was a paved courtyard. Around the perimeter were boys, teenagers or perhaps older, seated silently on stone blocks as if they were waiting for something and had been waiting for some time. They eyed me suspiciously, heads down except for furtive glances. I was reminded of the outback lizards that remain in the open but absolutely motionless in the hope you don't see them. None of the boys spoke. After the crowd and noise, the constant yelling and laughter outside in the street, this shrinking to be invisible was disturbing. I knew why, without being told.

While Sid talked to two men who sat by the other entrance, I looked at the boys. Many had missing arms or crippled legs. Several were blind. I could choose my own kidney in the way I might choose a live crayfish from a tank at a restaurant. It was abhorrent but even so I found myself assessing each for vigour or signs of disease.

Sid came to me with one of the men who offered me some tea.

'No, this is not what I want.'

'You prefer coffee?' Before I could answer he signalled another man who scurried off to collect coffee.

'No, I mean the boys.'

'They are good boys, healthy. This is the finest.'

'Finest?'

'Yes. Other market, I think not so good. Here, all healthy.' He motioned to one of the closest boys who limped across as if terrified. The man placed his hand across the boy's forehead and opened an eye wide with his thumb. 'See.'

'But …' I didn't know what to say. 'Who are they? They are just boys.'

'Oh yes, and very healthy too. Maybe they are too old, are not getting so much at the begging. So …' Sid shrugged. 'They only need one kidney.'

It was true. I should have realised that selling one of your kidneys was commonplace, but the reality was shocking nonetheless. These boys were maimed, had been beggars. I remembered a scene in *Slumdog Millionaire* where they blinded boys so they can beg.

'I guess when you have only one arm, or are blind, there is not much else you can do but beg.' I said it sort of to myself, sort of to say something, and sort of to test Sid, to test the horror theory forming in my head.

'Oh, yes, this is surely true, but when they are growing older the begging is not so good.'

'So they were unlucky enough to be born like this?'

'Oh, I think unlucky to be born, but their bosses do this for them. Unlucky for them, but lucky for your father. Come, drink coffee, then we make talk, discuss payment.'

The coffee was sweet but tasted bitter in my mouth. These teenagers were slaves who had been bought as children and maimed to increase their begging potential. When they got older, when they stopped bringing in money off the streets, this is what happened to them. A kidney. Not only a kidney. Everything. Of course they would tell me it was just one kidney but what was the value of a cripple who had no other body parts to sell? I knew how these people were thinking, because I was one of them. Sure, Palmenter had started everything but now it was me. I ran the business and I knew how these people thought. Boys and girls were sold by their desperate parents into slavery in the thin hope that they might live, and in many cases the money would be used to pay me to take the luckier members of the family to Australia.

I told Sid I wanted to think about it.

'Oh, no, we must make an offer. We cannot leave without making an offer and then, if it is too little, we leave and everyone is happy. But once you make an offer, you should make another offer a little bit more, because these are the best and much much better than those old ones and for your father it would be best to have the best one, no?'

'How much should I offer?' I could see I was not going to win any argument with him. I'd go through the charade and later, in the taxi, tell him I wasn't comfortable with it. It would have been so much easier to go to one of the hospitals and pay the money and fly my dad in and it would happen without my having to do anything other than pay the money. I had plenty of money. I would pay extra to do it like that, to have someone else do the dirty work.

Sid regarded me with something between amusement and concern. He had met me at the airport because Newman had told him to. Newman had told him what I was after, and I recalled a conversation we had one time on Palmenter Station. It might have been the last time Newman was there. We had the tourism and the import business both running full throttle. The de-stock was in full swing and we were putting on a free weekly barbecue for travellers. Sally was vegetarian and we would have great discussions about it, about the eating of meat and the ethics of killing creatures and in particular I remember Newman saying how it was ethical to eat meat if you were prepared to do the killing yourself. He was having a go at Sally because she said we shouldn't eat meat full stop. Pretty soon the whole conversation was about other things, about how we do so much in modern life where others have to do the dirty work. We pay the money and don't have to think about where things come from.

That was what I wanted now. And what was wrong with that? If you are lucky enough to be born on the right side of the fence. Those barbecues were great, the way all the backpackers and refugees and my staff would sit around the big open pit fire, and between songs on the guitar argue about all things under the sun. There was always someone who had something interesting, a retired judge or farmer or stockbroker on their grey nomad trip around the country, or gap-year students, graduated foreigners out to see the world.

'American dollars. This is best.'

'How many? A thousand?'

He spluttered. 'Oh, no, this is too much. Two hundred American dollars I think is plenty. Then you will get for your father a new kidney for two hundred and twenty dollars. This is plenty.'

A couple of hundred dollars for a life. To sell. And to buy. My father was paying a few hundred each week in tests and scans and dialysis.

My father died in India. Sid took me to a hospital and I talked to a doctor who understood enough English for me to feel comfortable with him, and then I had the difficult task of persuading Dad it was a good idea. I emailed Simon first, and then Mum, and told them what we could do. Of course they said no but I persisted, and first Simon and then Mum came around, but I don't think Dad would have agreed if he hadn't been getting steadily sicker. The waiting list in Australia was long and as an older patient he was classified as low priority. Low priority. That's what Palmenter used to call the imports. When it finally dawned on my father that he would die of kidney failure long before they offered him a transplant, he agreed to go to India. He and Mum flew into Mumbai on a Tuesday and I met them and introduced them to the doctor. My father was dead by the weekend.

20

I have some privileges here because of what they call 'good behaviour'. I admitted and then pleaded guilty to the murder of Palmenter, I cooperated with the police inquiry into everything else that had been going on at Palmenter Station, and now I do what I'm told by the people in charge. Good behaviour!

Once a week a tutor comes and we have creative writing classes. That is how I first came to write this down. I am allowed unlimited books so I read a lot. I'm hopeless at art but I enjoy the gardening.

I keep having flashbacks about things Palmenter said and one of them was about how you never learnt real things from books. In my first two years here I finished the MBA and I noticed that so many things Spanner and I had done were based on sound business principles. But the thing you don't learn, the thing Palmenter was not good at, was that none of it matters if you don't look after people. It doesn't matter how much money you make if you have no friends. People to visit you.

Mum comes up to visit as often as she can. We walk around the gardens where I can show her what I am growing. That is where I usually work. She brings books and magazines she thinks I will be interested in and we discuss them. She's joined a refugee advocacy group and she is the director of the charity. When Dad died I thought Mum might never speak to me again. She cried as we stood together in the office in Mumbai trying to sort out the paperwork. But now I know she never thought it was my fault. At the funeral when she hugged me she said, 'You gave him a chance.'

I keep hoping that someday Ingrid might come to see me. She and Sally have been deported for overstaying their visas but sometimes I dream that they could get some sort of special visa to return to Australia or, in some sort of bizarre twist, that they smuggle themselves in. I'm sure Newman could still arrange it. Between charity visits he's running surfing safaris off the coast of Roti. In carbon fibre boats. I think that's funny. Joseph and Chad got sent home as well and I guess they are doing all right.

I also hope that one day Charles or Simms will come to visit me. I know Cookie is dead. They shot him. And Judy and the kid. I heard the shots. But there is a chance that Charles and Simms got away and I hope that they will reappear out of the wilderness where they have been hiding, and visit me. Perhaps they did get away, perhaps they heard the gunshots and realised what was happening. But I know it is unlikely. Simms wasn't that sharp and Charles was too good a fellow to run away and hide if his mates were in trouble.

My brother has visited a few times. Working at the mine is now five weeks on and two weeks off but he still loves it. Has his freedom, he says, and then gets to spend two weeks with Michelle. They travel together to lots of places and have visited the hospital in India where Dad died and they were treated as celebrities. It is still tough there, but we continue to send money for medicines and supplies.

Michelle is terrific. We chat via email. I've only seen her once since the trial, that was when they did the trip to India – they flew via Darwin so they could see me. It was nice to see the two of them together but it left me very flat afterwards. They are so happy together. She's pregnant and the baby is due in November. I won't see the baby until it's older unless I can get exchange to Melbourne and they say there is not much chance of that. I should get parole before the twenty is up but, even so, he or she might be a teenager before we meet.

That first time Michelle met me she must have thought I was hopeless. I broke down on her doorstep and rambled and cried and then left all of a sudden, but when the truth came out and I admitted to the shooting of Palmenter she was completely supportive.

I have a computer and we have access to a whole range of courses, not online but packaged so we can work through the modules in our own time. I am allowed email, although it is all checked beforehand. Some of the guys have smuggled in phones so they get uncensored mobile internet but I haven't done that. They say to me, 'You're a smuggler, you could have whatever you want,' and it's true, prison is easier to get stuff in and out of than the country is, but I'm not interested. They don't get it, and neither did the lawyers. That was part of why I started to write my whole story down.

After my rescue and arrest, in the interviews, my lawyers wanted me to say things in a way that painted me in a better light. I was in the room with the lawyers and several police and I'd be explaining something, how some part of it worked or why something happened, and afterwards one of the lawyers would say to me, 'I just wish you had discussed that with me first.'

'Why, you want me to lie?'

'No. But there are ways of saying things, or perhaps just not saying everything. Leave out parts of it if it is not relevant. You should just wait for them to ask a question and then only answer what they have asked. You keep volunteering information.'

'Because I want them to know everything.'

'They will take what you say out of context.'

'Well, you will have to put it back in context.'

'It is not as simple as that. Once the impression is made, once the inference is there. They intend to make an example of you.'

'What? People smuggling is worse than shooting someone in the head?'

I wasn't the easiest of clients. They wanted me to plead not guilty, explain the extenuating circumstances and negotiate a lesser charge. Maybe they were right and I was about to get the book thrown at me, but I didn't care. I deserved it. I had shot Palmenter in cold blood. I had seen and been told of some pretty nasty things and Palmenter had been doing some of the nastiest, but if I was allowed to take justice into my own hands what then were the people who daily came through our business allowed to do? Surely those who had seen or been part of real violence to themselves or to their families, those who had witnessed far worse, they had far more right than I to exact revenge. But murder and violence, in cold blood or in anger, only ever escalates into a cruel tit-for-tat that leads to civil war. That was exactly what many of these people were trying to escape. There is no excuse. I said this to the lawyers but I did not argue with them, because you know when people argue with you that their case is weak. And, it didn't matter what Palmenter had done. Because, the truth is, I only found out about the full extent of it after I had shot him.

The lawyers were good. Simon said they were the best. During the case, they made me out like a saint. For example, when we described how we had de-stocked the station the prosecutor said that suddenly the Aboriginal stockmen were out of work and that we had only done it to keep the station isolated, and it was part of my single-minded and ruthless strategy, a strategy that began long before I shot Palmenter and continued afterwards. True, I had worked out that the cattle were costing us money and I had said so to Palmenter. But the fact was that in any case Palmenter never paid the stockmen, all they got was free drinks and a meal in the canteen and some promise of money, so when the prosecutor brought that up, my lawyers were able to turn it around on them and tell how the tourist business employed the locals and trained them and how Palmenter Wildlife Conservancy became one of the must-see places on the outback tourist circuit, and how it made a profit in its own right, and he made out it was all up to me, my big idea.

The prosecutor tried to show that I was a cold and calculating bastard who systematically removed anybody who was in my way. He even tried to cast doubt that Newman existed. Newman was some character I had invented to take the blame. If he did exist, the prosecutor said, he was probably another of my victims, his was one of the many bodies the police were still trying to identify. As to the rest of my story, that was completely fanciful and the extensive lies of a criminal mastermind who will say anything to avoid incrimination. That opened the doors for my guy. All that I had talked about in the hours and hours of interviews came out. About Spanner and his fishing camps and the bicycles and Newman and the health clinics and he even had statements from Ingrid and Sally about how the English classes were my idea. He took me from being the ringleader of a ruthless crime syndicate to a clueless patsy alongside Palmenter with the real Mr Bigs unknown and still at large. And then he turned me into the brains behind a tremendous humanitarian operation that was ever so slightly just outside of Australian law. It was remarkable. I even began to like myself. Despite how I was feeling about being a murderer.

It is hard to say exactly when I took charge. It certainly wasn't the day I shot Palmenter. I was in charge, I don't deny it. I was the Mr Big of People Smuggling. But it was built up over time and not to any plan, so in that regard the prosecutor was wrong. But he was right in that by the end I was clearly and systematically running the business. When the change happened I can't say for sure.

I could say it was the time I decided to de-stock the station and we began offering some genuine tourist experiences because I clearly remember the discussion Spanner and I had, but that was after I drove Lucy's family to Melbourne and I set them up in the house. I had made sure they were all right and was driving north with Ingrid and Sally and we visited Simon's camp and I determined to take charge of my life. I would enrol in university as I had always intended because Simon told me Dad was disappointed I had not come back to study as I had promised.

And there were a whole lot of other times, perhaps not pivotal moments but nonetheless times I can recall being aware of the slow change. Like, later, during the MBA, I was learning about project planning, writing out business plans and I remember at some point I realised that all my life I had been waiting for things to happen to me. I was learning about planning but had never planned my own life. So you might say that was when I took control, but that wasn't true either, because I recalled a time long before that lying awake all night in my swag, cold under a brilliant diamond sky.

It was things Zahra said, and the way she was, but more than that, not only these four I was travelling with: I was thinking about refugees and how they take their destinies into their own hands and set off across the planet in search of a better life, and here was I, living what to them must be a glorious life, and what did I want to do? Leave. That was my only plan. Leave, then what? A life on the run, always looking over my shoulder and worried for the time after someone discovered Palmenter's body and they came looking for me? Palmenter was gone but I would still be allowing someone else to decide what was going to happen in my life.

For what was the difference between me and them if we all just ran away? Were they really taking charge of destiny by fleeing to a foreign country unsure of what would happen next? Somewhere, someone had to take charge and help build the world that ought to be.

That sleepless night had come to me again when Ingrid and Sally and I saw the footage of that asylum boat smashing into the cliffs of Christmas Island.

'How can your country let that happen?' demanded Ingrid. I had no answer.

One time I had been standing on the verandah watching the arrival of another bewildered group. Charles and Simms were standing near the chopper directing them towards the canteen. Or rather, Charles was motioning them and Simms was standing there, watching. Palmenter yelled at Simms to do something, that he wasn't paying him to stand around gawking.

'There are only two types of people in this world, Son,' Palmenter said as he turned to me. 'The leaders, those who take charge and decide what is going to happen, where they want to be; and the rest. The followers. It's the leaders who will get on in this life.'

He was referring to Simms and Charles, and by implication me, but at that time I couldn't help thinking about the refugees. Surely of us all they were the ones who had done most to take possession of their own lives? That came back to me in my swag that night, and later when I was driving with Ingrid and Sally, feeling good about having found Lucy's family a place to stay and given them the chance to find some work.

'You haven't done a thing,' Ingrid said. 'You have left them in a strange city where they don't speak the language. They can only get low-paid menial work. They will be ripped off by everybody. You have condemned them to a life of poverty and fear.'

Of course I hadn't told the whole story, I had said the good bits, the bits that made me look good. I said I had found these refugees wandering aimlessly on our station and instead of handing them in I had taken them to the city. I made myself out to be the hero, but Ingrid ripped into me. They both did.

'You are the same as everyone. You half help. You help people just enough so you can feel good about yourself, but no more than that. Half help,' she repeated.

'Well, what would you do?'

'For a start, teach them English,' she said.

I was going to tell her that I tried, but she would have seen right through me same as she saw through me when I tried to impress her and Sally with my charity.

'Half tried,' she would say.

Half help. I could have pointed out that these people were illegal in our country and that I could hardly set up a school for them but I knew I couldn't win any argument and I risked saying too much if I tried. So it's funny that later I did just that, set up a school and Ingrid was the teacher but at no point can I say I directly decided to do it. It certainly wasn't part of some long-term plan.

In Mumbai after my father died I was definitely in charge and I had gone back to the clinic to confront the doctor who had botched the operation. I wanted answers.

When Dad died I was angry. At the doctor. At the clinic. At Newman for helping me, at the Australian doctors who didn't do a thing. At the officials who made it so complicated to bring a body back. There was I bringing live bodies into Australia and I couldn't even bring in my father. I wanted someone to blame, and when I realised there was no one to blame I got angry at myself and in my anger determined to shut the clinic down so that no one else would have to go through what I went through.

At the funeral my mother hugged me and told me it wasn't my fault, that at least I gave him a chance, but I flew back to Mumbai full of anger. During one of the weeks of the MBA workshops – I did the MBA by correspondence but twice a year for a fortnight we had to live in and attend group workshops – we played this game where you push against someone and they can't help but push back. Well, as I flew into Mumbai full of anger it was as if the world was pushing back at me. Outside the airport, on the crowded roads, sitting in the back of the taxi looking out at slums and poverty, beggars, the crowds outside the hospital. The whole world seemed to consist of struggle and poverty. By the time I got to the hospital I was somewhat less angry and as I sat waiting to see the doctor I saw how difficult things were for them. It was unbelievably busy. The power went off frequently. People arrived all the time, some so weak they could barely walk, others being carried or pushed on trolleys or makeshift wheelchairs. I watched the nurses treat injuries in the corridor opposite where I sat, washing out wounds and then selecting from a pile of clean rags torn into strips for bandages. There were no medicines, no antibiotics. By the time the doctor came to see me I wondered what right I'd had to jump this queue with my father. Even now to demand the doctor take some of his time to see me suddenly seemed unreasonable. Why did I expect that here they could do what the Australian system couldn't, and perform transplant surgery to heal a dying man?

The doctor was terrific. He remembered me and that in itself was remarkable. He sat with me in the corridor opposite the nurses who carried on treating patients. There was nowhere else to go, he didn't have an office and there was no staff room or private consulting room and I remembered the first time we met, when I stood at the entrance with him and we discussed in halting English what might be done for my father. He had said he could find a donor kidney, people were dying too often in his hospital. I had thought he was being meek in the discussion of money, now I realised it was that he was full of weariness and sorrow for the necessity of it. And he grieved for my father, for all his patients, for all the world.

'Why do you think the world is like this?' he asked me in faltering voice full of tiredness and curiosity, as if he and I were on the outside looking in and that all too soon we would be gone from it all. We were alien visitors and this was our chance to learn the truth.

It was a question that took me by surprise. He did not defend his surgery or the hospital or make excuses. What had happened had happened. Why was the world like this? I knew then that it was not his fault, he had tried his best and it was not enough and it was for him an all too common occurrence but yet still it hurt him.

'I don't know,' I said. I wanted to cry. What right did I have to cry?

We sat together amid the bustle, he leaning back with his eyes closed and me realising that in this place you paid what you could and that got you into the front of the queue, but once there everyone was equal. They all tried their very best.

Later, back home, Spanner had no hesitation agreeing to send medicines there. I had paid ten thousand for Dad's surgery and now I wanted to send a loaded boat back up the line, we could carry about a hundred thousand worth of drugs and bandages and equipment and perhaps it was sort of guilt money, but if you think too much about your motivation for doing things you never do anything at all.

It was Newman who said no.

'A hundred grand can go so much further if you let them spend it. Pay Aussie prices and you get nothing. Give them money. We can make sure it gets to the right people, smuggle it in so it doesn't get sucked up by all the layers of corrupt officials.'

He was right, but of course we couldn't send money all the way to Mumbai in a brown paper bag, so Newman agreed to take it himself. That was the first of many regular deliveries he did and so perhaps it is true to say that was the start of it all. I would get the notes together – exchanging the Aussie notes at the bank in Darwin on one of my visits – and seal them into a plastic bag and wrap them in brown paper lunch bags, so in emails we called them lunch. Later, for different amounts, we had dinner bags and breakfast, morning tea, afternoon tea and snacks. I'd email Newman something like 'I have morning tea packed for Barry.' Barry was our code for a clinic in Somalia. Each place had its own name. 'Dinner for Arnold is ready.' The prosecutor tried to make it sound bad that we had all these secret messages but of course we couldn't say in an email what we were doing. That backfired on him because of course my lawyers could then point out that all this money was going to people in need. I was not some ruthless illegal businessman but someone who was giving back.

I knew Spanner and Newman would agree to fund the clinic because they had been so enthusiastic the first time. That was when I got back from India after the first trip there.

When I was in Mumbai with Sid and trying to get Dad a new kidney, I bought all twenty-three of the maimed boys in the slave market. Five hundred dollars each. I now owned twenty-three slaves. We shifted them all the way from Mumbai to Indonesia by truck and then into Australia by boat. At the station we trained them in some things we thought might be useful. Funny, because the one with one leg, he became our best bike mechanic. Spanner loved him, said he was a genius. Spanner made him a special bike, balanced so he could ride with one leg. Cookie took on two of the blind ones and they became cooks. Cookie said they had the most amazing sense of smell. We taught them all first aid in our own clinic in the homestead. I had employed a nurse and we used the room that Margaret had set up for inspecting the girls. With so many people coming through there was always someone who needed treatment. If there was a refugee who showed a bit of interest or who had some first aid skill we'd get them to help in the clinic. Some of the refugees were smart but they had never had the opportunity to learn. After we taught them many agreed to return home.

The boys were the first ones who agreed to go home. We taught all of them English and then the girls taught them how to teach, and they agreed to go back to India where they could now make a living. I have twenty-three slaves living free in India.

You see, Spanner and I had talked about it with Newman and decided the best long-term way to help was to train the locals. Someone who belonged, not an outsider. Years ago Zahra had said she would be going back after she earned enough and I had briefly wondered at taking people both ways. Now we were doing it. Sure, the boats were full coming in and half full going out, but it was happening. We didn't charge for the return trip.

We were charging five thousand for each passenger, so each trip was bringing in over a hundred grand. People could do our lessons, learn English or mechanics or cooking, driving the tour bus or cleaning or housework and maintenance, all sorts of jobs that we could train them for. They could pay off the cost of the course by working for a while, then if they wanted they could head to the city, and when they had saved enough or for whatever reason they could come back and we would take them on the return trip for free.

In a way it was Palmenter who was doing all this because he

was the one who had paid for the station. All I had to do was make sure some of the money went into the bank each month to keep them happy. And the bank was happy, because for all they knew we had turned Palmenter Station into a thriving tourism destination.

I guess it was about a year after Spanner had moved to the coast that we decided to get rid of all the cattle. We no longer ran musters but every so often one of the former muster crew would visit, tell us the cattle were going wild or that such and such bore was dry. I wondered if it was a security risk to have them coming and going while we ran so many more imports. They hadn't been a problem in the past, but Palmenter had bribed them with free beer, girls, and the false promise of money. But to sell the cattle would be an admission to ourselves that we were not leaving, that we had taken control of the station and intended to continue running it. I had to discuss it with Spanner.

Ingrid and I caught a chopper ride to the coast and we sat with Spanner and a group of fishermen who had returned from a day on the water. Two large fish were barbecuing on an open fire and one of the tourists was rolling up dough balls to cook as damper.

'What's up?' Spanner said.

'I think we should sell all the cattle. They cost us money to muster each time and a wildlife conservancy shouldn't have cattle.'

I thought it was best with Spanner to get right to the point and discussing it in front of others was fine. The fishermen would overhear two businessmen planning their legitimate business.

'Sure,' Spanner said. 'You want a beer?'

I started laughing.

'What's wrong?'

'I thought it might be a big deal. You know, what with everything. That you'd want to discuss it.'

'Nah. Dead loss those cattle. And what the fuck with mustering all the time? As if everyone don't already know.' He handed me a beer. 'Tourism, that where it's at.'

He waved his hand to include the others in the conversation and they nodded agreement. Spanner was so relaxed, so comfortable, so happy.

'Awesome day out,' one of them said. The others agreed. Superb fishing. Brilliant guide. Great campsite.

'I thought you'd be against it.'

'Nah. Talk to Charles, he knows someone who can butcher on-site. Better than trucking them to Darwin and flooding the market. Get bugger all for them that way.'

'You've already discussed it?'

'Sure. Newman says we could take the meat, cryovac it and send it up to Indo.'

'Newman too?'

'Yeah. Of course.'

'Do they know about ...?'

What else had they discussed? And when? How long ago?

He looked at me. 'Of course not.'

Sometimes you think you are in charge only to discover that you are simply the fool at the top, that all the decisions are already made long before you get to them. But then, that is what good management is, to notice what people on the ground are saying, those doing the work, they are the ones who know what is going on and a good manager listens to them because long before you knew there was a problem they will be discussing it and having all the good ideas too. Your staff are always ahead of you. Someone wrote a book about it. Management by walking around.

I had flown up to the coast expecting to have a hard time of it and Spanner had reached the conclusion before me. He had talked with Charles and Newman and yet none of them had said anything to me. That was one moment I knew I was in charge. They were waiting for me to make a decision, to set the direction. Palmenter's words came back to me.

'There are two types of people in this world. Which one are you, Son?'

For the final muster we brought in the mobile abattoir. They do everything on-site right down to packing and freezing. We shipped the meat out, back up our import lines and it was brilliant, it gave us legitimacy and a reason for all those chopper flights and boats and we took the meat out to the islands and distributed it for free to remote and poor villages. On the books, it looked like we were selling it but that was the people-smuggling money coming in, suddenly I had a legitimate way to account for all that cash. If we had ever been investigated, though, we were selling each of the cattle several times over. I've never told anyone that before.

I would have liked to be able to send some of the meat further, into Africa, but of course the further your send it the more you lose control. Even in Indonesia unscrupulous people were selling it and making a lot of money out of our charity and you can be pretty sure none of it would have made it to the needy in Africa. That, and the problem of keeping it refrigerated.

What we did manage to send, though, was bicycles. Hundreds of them. All the way back to villages in Africa. We exported all the second-hand bikes Charles gathered on his trips to the city. We repaired them, and then sent them up on our boats. We found local charities we could trust in cities and towns and they distributed the bikes into smaller and more out of the way places. For many semi-rural people there is only one well for drinking water and this is kilometres from the houses. Usually it is even longer to school. A bike is a simple and reliable way to travel and it saves some of these people so much time and energy. I like to think we have helped someone live a better life because they can get around that little bit easier. I know we did, because people started complaining that their bikes broke down and asking us for another one. Newman discovered it was usually a flat tyre or a buckled rim. So from then on we sent each bike with its own pump and repair kit.

So bicycles was the second thing we did. Newman looked after the overseas part of that. He's still doing it, although it has been a lot harder recently with no money coming in. In emails we called him the lunchman, and when the prosecutor tried to use that as a criticism of me my lawyer got up and told them all about the hospital clinics in Mumbai and Africa.

You can make all the plans you like in this world but nothing will ever go as you think, and the more I think about that the more I think you have to be always ready to jump in the direction life is taking you. Spanner, Newman, Charles, even Simms. Cookie. We were all just doing what we thought was right. I don't consider the people smuggling to be wrong. It is illegal, but that's all. Killing people, no matter how rotten they are, that is wrong. I pleaded guilty to the murder of Palmenter and they also found me guilty of the people smuggling but the sentences are concurrent. I'm the one in jail so you might think that is justice, but I'm the lucky one.

The film studio want to make a movie, but of course I can't sell the story or make any money out of the movie because it's called proceeds of crime. The lawyers want to fight that in court but I did a deal.

Here am I, star in my own movie. Murderer, businessman, the Mr Big of People Smuggling, and all I ever wanted to do was get a few dollars so I could rent a place closer to university, graduate and then travel or go surfing on the weekends. The deal is five million dollars for the rights, plus ongoing royalties. Five million isn't much but the royalties will flow for as long as the movie runs and worldwide that might be for years. I don't get any of it, it goes to the charity and my mum and Newman will administer it. It will be enough to keep the charity running.

As well as the clinic in Mumbai there is also a yearly aid flight; the money will pay for the plane and the crew and the fuel. We will fill the plane with food and clothing collected from people, at schools, sporting clubs, through the Red Cross and other charities. Humans are humans and always somewhere they will be being nasty to each other and the weak will be fleeing the oppressors. Or they will be looking for something to eat. Might be natural disaster or because some war lord sets fire to the fields so people starve. Crops fail not because these people who have been living off the land for centuries suddenly forgot how to farm. If it doesn't rain, the crops won't grow, and there is no food. It has probably been happening forever, although maybe like they say it is getting worse with global warming. But whatever the reason, if we have excess we should share it with those in need.

So with this movie deal we can distribute aid. Perhaps we can make it that people like Noroz won't have to make those journeys and his father can look after his mother and not have to walk several hours each way every week, just to get food. When the money runs out I hope we can find a way to make sure all this work continues.

Because that is what I think about. How have we achieved anything at all, if what we achieve is not sustainable? And let's face it, what Spanner and I and the others were doing was good, but it wasn't sustainable. Eventually it was going to come crashing down.

21

In the wet you see great black clouds with streaks of rain rolling in from the horizon. Either side there is bright sunlight, shafts of light that are like beacons from the heavens. But it is all so oppressively humid until the rains hit that you see neither the light or the dark, nor the beauty of it. The rain is a relief but the reality is, it is not God smiling on you but about to dump on you. Sometimes the storms build from nothing, come out of nowhere, but the deeper you get into the wet the more you see them. If you get caught out in one of those storms you might be stuck for a while, the roads become boggy and impassable and the 4WD slews and slides all over, digs great ruts that later dry into bone-shattering holes that fill with bulldust and you don't see them until too late. When the wet arrives you have to submit to a force greater than yourself and live confined near to the station until it is over.

Then the dry arrives. It comes about the time the wet seems to go on forever and you think the seasons are all wrong and the wet will never end. The Aborigines have six seasons in a year but we white folk can manage only the wet or the dry. With the arrival of the dry the oppressive heat goes, the humidity goes, the early mornings and late evenings are cool and wonderful and life is worth living again.

With the arrival of our third dry came a big black 4WD, a massive Ford F250, a great threatening thing more like a ship than a car. It glided into the compound and five men got out. They were dressed as hunters, khaki greens and browns. It happened so quickly that I didn't have time to run. Or were we getting complacent?

One of them came directly to the office where I had been watching and the others carried large duffel bags into the canteen as if they owned the place.

'Where's Palmenter?'

'Up the coast. Can I help? I'm Nick, the station manager.'

I might have appeared calm but inside I was shitting myself. This guy looked as if he could have eaten Palmenter for breakfast. I knew something serious was about to happen. They were obviously not the police, Immigration or Customs. Ever since we took over I had lived in fear of this moment, when whoever Palmenter had been dealing with arrived and started asking questions. Someone owned the two million dollars we took and perhaps it wasn't Palmenter.

To begin with, when the phone in Palmenter's office rang it was easy to fob off callers. If it was to do with legitimate business I would explain that I was now the manager of the station, and as I had been dealing with the accounts these calls were simple to deal with. At first I had to forge Palmenter's signature on cheques but later I set up the satellite dish for the internet and made direct transfers. The less legitimate side was also simple to deal with. All I had to say was that there was some difficulty with Customs, or the police, that we had to lie low for a while. A few calls each week became calls once in a while, less frequent but curt.

'Palmenter.'

'He's not in. Can I be of assistance?'

'When is he in?'

'He doesn't come to the station himself much anymore.'

And the phone would go dead.

Or someone would call and say: 'Where is he?' Demanding. No introductory niceties, I would know who the caller meant.

'Melbourne I think.'

But these calls were few. I had expected that eventually someone would ring and ask me directly, someone from the brothels would ask about a delivery, perhaps mention by name one of the places so that I would know, without them saying the exact nature of the call, that they were after more girls. But that never happened and the calls became rare and we continued importing and sending mixed loads south to their new future. I was happy not to supply girls for the brothels and hoped that when they arrived in the city, men and women, they would all have a better chance.

I didn't think anyone would turn up unannounced but just in case I kept a share of the money packaged in envelopes ready to pay off someone. I had it neatly folded in different amounts, from a thousand to ten thousand each in its own envelope. If it cost more than ten thousand to buy someone I'd be doing a runner. More than ten grand, that amount of money wouldn't buy you out of trouble, you'd give them the money and then still be up shit creek.

This bloke wasn't interested in money.

'I know who you are. Who else is here?'

'No one. I'm in charge. How can I help?'

'What about Newman, where is he?'

How did this bloke know Newman?

'Indonesia. He lives up there.'

'Simms? Charles?'

This bloke was serious. He must have had some connection to what had gone before because he was naming all of the people from Palmenter's time. His buddies were probably outside talking to Cookie, so if I didn't tell him straight he would find out anyway and know I was spinning shit. I was a different person now to the one who had been intimidated by Palmenter, but this bloke made Palmenter and his intimidation seem like amateur hour.

'Simms is around somewhere. Charles is driving a tour, be back soon.' The girls were down at the waterhole with Joseph and Chad, but I wasn't going to volunteer that. I was going to ask why he wanted them, repeat that I was in charge, but this wasn't a bloke you asked questions to and I was beginning to think admitting to being in charge might not have been such a good idea.

'Okay. And Palmenter's up the coast?'

I nodded.

'Get the chopper in. We have to go see him.'

How did he know about the chopper?

I objected. Couldn't it wait until he got back, he didn't like to be disturbed, I wasn't exactly sure where he was, remote fishing, and so on, but they were having none of it.

'Get the chopper or you'll be out there at the pit with the others.' He paused and considered me. It was the only time he said anything that he thought about beforehand. 'The one that got away has been found. He left a notebook, wrote it all down. Now we've got to tidy up Palmenter's mess.'

He was testing me. If I didn't react quickly to the seriousness of this news, it was as good as admitting I didn't have a clue what he was talking about and I'd be sprung as no right-hand man of the absent Palmenter. Who was this bloke? He knew about the pit. These guys meant business. Bad business.

'Okay. The chopper will take about an hour to get here. You can wait in the canteen if you like, grab yourselves a beer.' I hurried off as if I knew how urgent this was. What did he mean, the one that got away?

While we waited, his four buddies set up cans on the fence posts and shot at them. It wasn't practice. They didn't need practice. They had high-powered rifles and each shot was a direct hit that completely obliterated the cans. They began using full beer cans, bottles of sauce from the barbecue and then watermelons from the garden. They shot at the targets even as one of them was setting up the next. Cookie and I sat in the canteen not talking. I was watching the cowboys through the window. I remembered I had seen at least one of them with Palmenter. We were a small town under siege in a wild west movie. Charles arrived from his tour with the empty bus but neither he nor Simms came to join us.

When the chopper arrived, the ringleader demanded that I come with them to the coast. I walked as casually as I could over to the chopper while he yelled to his gang.

'Finish up here,' he shouted.

The sound of the chopper drowned out the last of the gunfire and a few minutes later they marched over to us with their guns and duffel bags. They climbed in next to me and I thought there was a nod of recognition between them and Rob the pilot. Rob had flown for us ever since the Palmenter days, he was the one who had stood guard over the chopper while I talked to Newman after that last Palmenter muster, he was the one who had been least pleased that I had taken over. He hardly ever spoke to me and he had never, ever, asked after Palmenter or when or if he was coming back.

'All done. Not like the old days though,' one of the four said to the leader.

'A job to do boys. We do this job first, then maybe, just like the old days. One more time, who knows?'

I only half heard him. My mind was racing ahead, trying to plan what I might say or do when we got to the camp and they discovered Palmenter wasn't there. In the hour-long ride in sporadic conversation between them I gathered that a botanist had discovered the body of one of our refugees who had been hiding out in a cave. The botanist had been looking at plants on Palmenter Wildlife Conservancy and the way the head cowboy said 'Palmenter Wildlife Conservancy' left no doubt what he thought about the conserving of anything. The refugee had left a notebook.

'They can write?' asked one of the cowboys.

'Monkey language,' one of them said. The others laughed.

'Enough to put us in the shit,' said the boss.

The chopper wasn't due up at the coast for several days so Spanner came out to meet us, wondering what might have brought us out so early. Even before the chopper was on the ground the leader had jumped down and sprinted to Spanner but it was too noisy to speak. Spanner motioned us over to the tents.

'Where's Palmenter?'

Spanner looked at me and in that look he betrayed to everyone that Palmenter wasn't here, perhaps that he never was, that Spanner didn't get what was going on. He might have been shot there and then if I hadn't spoken up. The chopper motor was winding down and formed a high whine behind my words.

'It's okay, Wayne, these blokes know what's going on. Is he out on one of the boats?'

'Won't be back till sunset. You blokes want a beer?'

Fucking Spanner. The genius. That's the benefit of working close with someone for several years. You can read each other's minds, understand the messages hidden in your words. No one ever called him Wayne.

'Stick ya fuckin' beer up your arse. We wait. Get your kit, men, and deal with that.' He motioned towards the chopper that was now silent. Rob was climbing down to come and join us. I turned my back on them all and was walking to the kitchen tent. I didn't feel like a beer but I was going to get one because the less it looked like I was desperate to discuss anything with Spanner the better.

I was in the tent opening a beer when a shot rang out. A single shot. Trigger-happy bastards, I thought.

Spanner ran in.

'Fuck! They shot Rob. Come! Before they get here. Quick!' He led me out the back and along the path to the toilet tent, ducking quickly behind and then away, keeping the tents between us and where the men were dragging Rob's body to the water's edge.

'We're next if we don't get outta here.'

I had never seen Spanner so panicked. I had certainly never seen him run. Ever. Spanner was a great mechanic because he carefully and slowly did things. He considered things. He never rushed. His panic now put the fear in me and I ran too. I followed his short cuts as fast as I could but you can't run in thongs. I kicked them off. Eventually he stopped behind a tree at the top of a rise where we could look back to see if they were following.

'What's going on?' I said between gasps for air. I looked at my scratched and bloody feet.

'I've met those blokes before. They came in with Palmenter around the time of each muster. The short fat one brought money in. Then they'd arrive by chopper and take the vans out. Shit.'

'I thought Rob knew them. They shot him? Why?'

'Because he knew them. Knew too much. We're next.'

'But, why?'

Spanner looked at me, kindly, incredulous, like an older brother.

'You still don't know, do you?'

'What?'

'The hunting. The pit was only for the old ones. The old and the weak, those who wouldn't be any sport.' He said this out of breath, between breaths, both from our running and the effort to voice the unspeakable.

I still didn't get it. I did. But didn't want to.

'What do you mean?'

'That's what this is about and that is why now that they have found us, they won't stop until they get us. This is sport for them.

And we know too much.'

'Hunting?'

'More like target practice. The women went to Melbourne to be put to work, to pay off a debt they would never get rid of. The men who could run. Those who could put up a bit of a challenge.' He didn't finish the sentence.

He looked at me to see if I understood. He was leaning down as if short of breath, his hands on his knees to get deeper gasps, but it was as much in fear as with exhaustion.

'C'mon.'

He was running again, leading the way through the rough scrub and rocks. I was thankful he knew every path and track.

I followed close behind but it was too difficult to talk, to run and talk and to contemplate what he had just said. I felt so stupid. An idiot who uses this to avoid having to see the truth. The old and weak, the rest a bit of sport. Why had I not seen the obvious? That bloke had said the one that got away. Someone got away, left a notebook. Tying up loose ends. Gunshots back at the station before we got on the chopper. And now here, us. They would never stop chasing us, too much was at stake. And worse, now we were their sport.

I thought that Palmenter had changed over time. He had become ruder, angrier, short-tempered at everyone and more cagey about things. I remember saying something like that to Spanner once. We had been sitting under the tamarisk tree out behind his room. A hot wind was blowing and it echoed through the tree and all through the settlement. He had a beer but lately I had noticed he was drinking less, was more thoughtful of late and I said so. I said things seemed to be changing, Palmenter was more difficult and Spanner was drinking less. Perhaps nothing had changed and it had always been like this, that my first impression of the place was wrong. First impressions are like that, often wrong but difficult to move. I said it like that, as conversation.

'When I first met you I thought you drank too much, that you were a drunk, that that was why you never left here. He was an arrogant businessman and you were a drunk. Now it seems you are drinking less and he is getting more angry. He is angry all the time.'

Actually I had thought it might have been something to do with the shooting of Arif. Ever since then Palmenter had been unapproachable. You stayed out of his way and he only ever spoke to you if he wanted something directly.

'There's something,' Spanner had said. He had thought for a while before he responded to me and then waited before he added, 'They don't go to Sydney.'

'Where to then? Brisbane? Alice? Makes sense to make it a shorter journey.' Funny how we could discuss the business in a third party abstract way, as if it were not the illegal trafficking of people but the legitimate operation of a cattle station, as if the reality of it was nothing to do with us and all the things we knew about: the rip-offs; charging them every last dollar for an old car that we would take back; the bodies buried at the pit; Arif. Arif. Spanner didn't know about Arif. I had never told him, it was too shocking and the way to deal with that was to never think or talk or go there. Pretend it never happened and never think about it and eventually it would go away, sink deep into the thick mud that was the bottom of the mind, the thick ooze that hid all that was Palmenter Station.

'They were coming back too soon. The vans. I thought it was too quick, the vans coming back after one week. Can't get to Sydney and back in a week. So I thought Brisbane. But something else was wrong. I dunno, it just felt wrong. So I checked. I wrote down the odometers. They only go fifty, hundred klicks. Don't even leave the station.'

'Where are they going?'

'Beats me. Something's not right.'

The whole place was wrong and we both knew it and we both, to survive, knew not to talk about it. To do so was to stir the mud and this was the closest we had ever come to saying outright how bad things were.

It was some time after that, maybe a month or so, that Spanner told me something so shocking that at first I didn't believe him. He wouldn't joke about it, but he must be mistaken. Palmenter had told him to fill in the pit and dig a new one.

'I didn't understand why, I thought there was still plenty of room in the pit, could bury our rubbish there for years and so why bother to dig a new one? When I got out there it was mostly filled in already, roughly, dirt just pushed in from the sides. I started to tidy it up, scrape the dozer blade over the surface to flatten it so it could all grow over.' He looked at me, assessing me, seeing if he should say something.

'There's bodies. The dozer blade pushed up something and I got out to look. It was an arm. There was more. Several bodies.'

'Those five from out on the south track.' I knew it wasn't. We burned them inside their van. It wasn't Arif either. That was long ago.

'No, more. Recent. Several. Buried, like not properly, just sand pushed over the top.'

'People die on the boat trips. I guess they have to be buried somewhere.' I sounded more at ease than I was.

'Why fly them up here? If people die on the boat, just throw the bodies overboard. No, the fucker has been killing them and when he sent me out there to hide the evidence he knew I'd find them. He must have known I'd see them.'

I couldn't speak. I felt sick with the memory of Arif, how in the days after Palmenter shot him someone must have been out there to move the body. Who? Spanner? I was going to ask but the memory was too much. It came back in a flash and I saw Arif's eyes open and wondering, as if his soul looked out through those eyes and questioned. The fading of those eyes still haunted me and merged with the flyblown eyes of those five dead men, and now, added to that, Spanner was telling me there were more. How many? I didn't ask.

'We have to get outta here.'

Spanner had the vans, the keys to the fuel bowser. We could leave together, late one night when Palmenter was off somewhere. Hide a van off somewhere so the sound of the engine starting would not wake anyone. We could get several days headstart.

'He's a cunning bastard, letting us know little by little, waiting to see if we object and knowing if we ever left he would just deny it all. We could have left anytime is what he'd say. Cars, keys and fuel, no reason for us to stay. He meant for me to find them and he's challenging me to do something about it.'

Spanner was right, Palmenter was a cunning bastard. But at least now I knew there were two of us. He was doing the same thing to Spanner.

'We have to leave,' I said.

He took a swig of beer then tipped the rest of the can into the sand.

'Where to?' he asked. 'Where can we go from here? He'll track us down. You think you can go start a new life in the city, simple as that?'

It was one morning shortly after that that Palmenter came to me and said he needed someone he could trust. Maybe I was ready to take on more responsibility. He mentioned the job as station manager but I was only half listening because I was worried he had got wind of something, maybe he had seen Spanner getting a van ready for us. It was in the way Palmenter said he needed someone he could trust and sure enough, he then hinted at Arif and the buried bodies, said he knew I had never told anyone and in the same breath he offered me travel and more money.

'Congratulations, Son,' he said, 'You deserve it. I know you know how to keep quiet about what doesn't concern you. You are smart and we need that around here. A good honest worker will go far with me. It will mean more money. Some trips to the city. Might even see about adding Perth to our list. We'll talk about the details tomorrow.'

I managed to keep calm. More money? He never paid anyone. An honest worker who could keep quiet about the cold-blooded shooting of Arif? And, as I now knew, many more out at the pit. What he was really doing was threatening me. Why all of a sudden Perth? Spanner and I had agreed we would leave one night when no one was around, drive south-west to Perth where no one knew us and Palmenter might not have any influence.

I agreed to the promotion. That was in the morning. To get him off my back I had no choice but to agree. That night I would get Spanner and we'd leave. We couldn't delay any longer.

Palmenter had driven into the station in his flash 4WD and a muster was coming. Usually at muster he would fly in with the first lot on the chopper so I was expecting that he would leave by car during the night and reappear by chopper in a day or so. Spanner and I would bolt as soon as Palmenter drove out. With a day or two headstart even the chopper couldn't catch us.

I waited up all night for Palmenter to leave but he didn't. And in the morning he said he had a special job for me. A job only for someone he could trust.

22

We came to a rocky slope. At the bottom a muddy tidal creek flowed, the tide was nearly out and shiny mud banks lined each side of the creek. Away to the left we could make out the sea, sparkling blue. Spanner didn't hesitate and I was happy to follow. We turned and ran down the slope and then left along the hard rocks and sand above the mud at the edge of the water. When we got to the ocean we stopped. I was exhausted. I sat on a flat-topped rock and looked at the empty horizon in front of us.

We had a choice. Head back to the main camp along the coastline to our left or cross the mouth of the creek on the right. It was about two hundred metres wide at this point. In the middle was a conical scrub rock island. On the far side were broken red rock cliffs and a rocky slope rising behind.

'We should cross,' said Spanner between breaths. 'One of the camps is just beyond that ridge. About five kilometres. People there, clients. A bunch of lawyers and judges from Melbourne.'

He sat down next to me.

'What did you mean, this is sport?' I asked. 'Those who could run?' The sun was baking hot and my feet were bloody and sore, but it was nothing to my sense of dread.

'They won't ever give up. They'll come after us.'

'Why?'

'Because. The pit was only ever for those who couldn't run. The rest, they were sport. Hunting. Palmenter would give them a van, set them off. This lot, maybe more, Palmenter and a whole lot of others from all over, I dunno, they would hunt them. Give them a headstart then hunt them down. Soon as the van got bogged and they got out to walk, they didn't stand a chance. No one was ever going to miss them and if they got away, well, they would perish in the desert. No food or water. That's what this is about. Sport. And now they are coming after us.'

The sun went dark and the sky blackened and I needed not water for my thirst, but oxygen, air, life. I was suddenly at once both totally alive and aware and alert and at the same time not of this world. This world was dark and distant with the bright sky and the water and rocks and trees and birdcall retreating to reveal a parallel place that filled with the clues. Each of the obvious fell into place. Vans fuelled up as if for a long trip and given to hopeful refugees who had no idea. Newman asking, 'What about the hunters?' on that first day after and me saying, 'Tell them no hunting this season,' not knowing what he was talking about because I thought it was just one of the many extra things that went on, shooting for camel or bullock or buffalo or kangaroo. Humans. The look in the man's eye when he said, 'Just like the old days.' Gunshots at the homestead that I had thought was them shooting bottles. Cookie. Judy and her little boy. Simms. Charles.

'C'mon,' said Spanner. 'We need to get to this camp before they do.'

The tide was out. Thick leg-sucking mud pulled at us as we tried to wade to the water. I was there first and struck out, swam to the island and then splashed and dragged myself up the mud on my belly until I found the harder sand above the tideline. I stood waiting for him, scanning the ridgeline we had just stumbled down, looking for signs of the men following. I had seen them and their rifles. They could easily pick us off from up on the ridge. We had moved pretty quickly and Spanner knew where he was going, so I thought it unlikely they would be too close behind. That was when I saw it. Not the men. A crocodile. It slid noiselessly into the water not five metres from where we had been sitting on the flat-topped rock, slid into the water and disappeared except for two stone eyes that moved like floating rocks. Spanner was not a strong swimmer and was only about halfway across. I yelled. There was a flurry of white water, a small cut-off yell, a half gasp, a splash that in the time it took to turn and look, if you hadn't been looking right there, would have come and gone and then the world was bright and sunny again as if nothing had happened.

I found myself sitting on the beach, looking up as if Spanner would appear from the water any moment. I half expected him to emerge Tarzan-like dragging the conquered crocodile by the tail, to drag it up the beach then we would light a fire and roast its meat. But Spanner was gone.

I climbed up the small hill on the island and lay in the shade under a rocky overhang. Small shrubs hid me from view but I could see the beach and the water where I had last seen Spanner. There was no sign of the croc. I thought crocs didn't venture too far from the water and I thought I would be safe. I was suddenly so tired, so thirsty. A headache began and washed over me like a wave and left throbbing temples, all my sores spoke to me, my lips were parched, throat dry, feet and hands and legs scratched and raw and all of me covered in dried mud. I didn't know what to do.

Maybe I slept. The tide was halfway in when I next looked. I saw the glint of something across the water. Maybe a sound. I lay completely still. Nothing. Still I lay. Slowly I could make out the outline of a man, two men, sitting on the opposite side watching the water. Three men. The other two must be waiting back at camp for Palmenter if they still believed he was around, or maybe they were in some other lookout I hadn't spotted. Could they see me? It didn't seem so. I'd be dead if they could. I didn't move. Spanner was gone. Perhaps they were waiting for the tide to fall. I hoped for the crocodile to return. A whole family of crocs. What should I do if they decided to cross? Perhaps they could cross and go right by me and not see me, continue on to the camp. What then? Then where would I go?

I lay watching them for an eternity. Far off I heard the drone of a boat. Maybe the other two had gone back to get one of the fishing runabouts and were coming here.

The sound drifted off. It was probably one of the fishing boats from the next camp, full of lawyers from the city, judges unshaven and smelly with fish blood and salt and dirt and oh please come around here and see me, rescue me. The men didn't move. They had tracked us this far and knew we had crossed. How long would they wait?

By midafternoon the tide was right in. Clear water was now only a few metres from me, inviting me to dive in, to cool off and drink great long gulps of it. I saw a crocodile: the same one? Two stony eyes and a bit of a snout. That was the only time I saw the men move, one shifted his hand and pointed. They had seen it too. A little later they left, walked back the way they had come and then I was suddenly alone. The world was peaceful. Water flowed in and out and clouds came and went across the arching sky and birds and fish and insects flew and splashed and buzzed in the heat, and yet I was not of this world, I did not belong, or rather, this world did not care if I belonged or lived or died or breathed. I was irrelevant. A visitor. I was being ignored and it was funny how those men hunting me down were in some way comforting, to think that at least something, someone, wanted me.

I lay without moving for an even longer time. I was cocooned in a case of dried mud and I might not have been able to move before I did. That long time was essential, not for the care I was taking to be sure they had certainly left, but for every little thing inside me to rest, to regroup. To move up over that small hill to the other side and look out upon a crocodile-infested hundred metres of wilderness that stretched forever and ever and ever – that took everything. At every moment I expected the sharp ring of a gunshot. That noise I had never heard until the time when Palmenter shot Arif, and the noise I did not hear when I shot Palmenter. The noise you feel but don't hear, the noise that is over before you have time to know what it is. I heard it in a bird whistle, a fish splash, wind in trees, an insect silent call. The crack of dried mud falling off me was a bullet wound and the aches and pains and cuts and salt-stung scratches were punctures that got me before the sound of the shot that started them arrived. But there was nothing. I was utterly alone.

Once I was on the other side of the island and away from where the men might return, I sat in the shade of a small tree and considered what to do. I could swim, take a risk, try my luck with the crocodiles. Low tide, fifty metres, bit of mud. A minute. Two long minutes. Too long. And too weak, too tired. But only getting weaker. No water to drink. I waited. Trying to think.

I slept. I must have, because I woke with a start, like when Palmenter had shot Arif and afterwards I thought I couldn't sleep but I'd wake suddenly aware of something I could not name. This time I knew what it was. Jason. His cheerful smile came to me. 'I'm getting out of here,' he said.

Jason was the student who arrived the day after I did all those years ago. I had nearly forgotten about him. It was after the first muster that he came to Spanner and I one day when we were working at the gene pool. We were trying to get a starter motor from one of the wrecks so Spanner could install it in Bitsy and it was while we were doing this that Jason came up to us and announced he was leaving. I was standing by the bonnet and Spanner was underneath so all you could see of him were his lower legs and feet.

'I came to say goodbye. I'm leaving tomorrow. Palmenter's giving me a ride out to the highway in the morning.'

'You sure?' said Spanner from under the car.

'He said he'd drive me out in time to catch the bus.'

Spanner came out from under the car holding the starter motor. He put the starter down and began wiping his hands on a rag, but this merely smeared the dirt and oil over his hands.

'Bus? What bus?'

'In the morning.'

'Oh. Well, I can't shake your hand.' He held his palm flat to show how dirty it was. 'We'll have a beer for you tonight? You're buying.'

I wasn't paying attention because I was thinking about how I would like to be leaving too. I had only been there a couple of weeks and I thought it was derision in Spanner's voice. What would Spanner think of me if I also said I wanted to leave?

We didn't end up having a beer with him because we saw Palmenter and Jason drive out later that afternoon. It was quite late, and I remember wondering why he would want to wait all night in the darkness and cold before catching the bus in the morning. Of course I now know that Spanner was right, there was no bus along that road, the closest would be all the way up at Julia Creek and even then it ran only once a week, and now I woke sweating with the realisation that Palmenter drove back to the homestead a short while later and he had had only the time to drive to the pit. And that was before Arif. Long before.

Next morning I woke and the tide was out. I was parched, my mouth so dry, cardboard. Dried mud fell off me in sheets or dusted into my eyes. My head throbbed. Down near the water's edge I found some shellfish on the rocks and smashed these open, drank the salty brine and fishy mush. I remembered reading about how you could collect water to drink like this. But it wasn't good, it didn't help my thirst and then I remembered long ago, at school, reading about Burke and Wills and how they died because they got less energy from collecting food than they spent digging for it, they'd have been better off to rest in the shade and anyway, maybe it wasn't shellfish but fish blood. I couldn't remember. I could remember stuff, random stuff that was no use to me now, stuff that popped into my head but as soon as I tried to direct my thoughts, to think of something particular, my brain would disappear. My arms were so heavy I could hardly lift the rock to smash the shells. I could hardly walk. Perhaps if I waited in the shade I would get some strength back. The tide was out, for how long? It was only a short swim, but how long before the tide came in? The numbers were there in my head but I couldn't organise them. A day was how long? Two tides, twelve hours, did that make six hours or twelve hours between lows? I could not do the maths. Every time I'd get close something would distract me. I'd sit still and scratch with a stick to help but then find another shellfish. Forget them, I'm not wasting energy on them. Here is an old camp, where some people must have had a picnic or barbecue. Remains of a fire, some beer cans, fish bones. Think. The tide is twelve hours and the moon was full last night. Do crocodiles sleep at night? Dolphins don't sleep. At least I wouldn't see them coming. I could rest longer and get more strength, wait until evening. Swim across then, walk to the next camp. What time? What point? I didn't have a watch. I lay down to rest.

At some point, the obvious hit me. Maybe it was the sound of an outboard or maybe that was too far away and it was the ringing in my ears getting louder. I woke and could see far off the dot of a boat moving across the shimmering sea, heading around the point towards where Spanner had said the fishing camp was. I smashed open a beer can and used the shiny inner surface to flash in their direction. Was I dreaming? No, but it was like someone else doing all the stuff because I was watching the whole thing as if it were a movie. I saw the dot change direction towards me and grow until it was a fishing runabout. It pulled up to the mudflats and people came to me and talked and crowded around. I was too delirious to care. They took me in their boat to the camp and I ranted and rambled and they listened. They washed and fed and watered me, and put me to bed but I was so exhausted I could not sleep. The mud of the mangroves had dried and it fell away in sheets and then the rest washed away, but the quagmire at the bottom of my mind was also being drained and all and all and all came back, came out, flowed out in one big mix. Spanner, Arif, gunshots, the burial pit. I ranted and raved and they listened, and because they were lawyers and not doctors they gave me beers and not tranquilisers and didn't insist that I rest. We drank beer and they listened while I talked and there was only one thing I wanted to talk about.

Palmenter came to me early on that afternoon and invited me to sit with him at the table on the verandah. He had hinted at something the day before and again that morning but you never sat at a table with him. Spanner had told me about the bodies out in the pit and I had waited up all night for Palmenter to drive out but he hadn't.

'Son, you're doing a good job with the bookwork.' He waited a while to see my response.

'Things seems to be going pretty smoothly,' I replied carefully. A compliment from Palmenter was always the prelude to something.

He grunted assent.

In fact, during musters I didn't have a lot to do as the imports didn't come into the station anymore. The usual thing now was that Palmenter and his cowboys would arrive on the first chopper and take the vans out to somewhere off-site. Newman and Rob would refuel several times during the day and after it was all over Palmenter would reappear to drive off with Margaret and the girls who had been flown in a few days earlier.

'I know I can trust you not to speak out of place. Soon we might see about you taking on an even bigger role. Oversee some of the trips. International stuff.' He was working up to something big. 'Make you manager of the station, put you in charge.'

'Cookie and Spanner have been here a lot longer,' I ventured.

'Son, some people will never amount to anything.'

He sat looking at me and I became very uncomfortable but I met his eye. This was not a simple conversation about taking on a greater role. It never was. Nothing about Palmenter was straightforward.

'We got a problem, Son. That double-crossing son-of-a-bitch Newman wants out.'

At some level I didn't see a problem with that. Like me, Newman seemed to have little to do. He arrived with each import in the chopper but exactly what his role was I didn't know. But I knew the reality. No one left this place.

'Do we need him? What does he do?' I asked. As I said it a wave of nausea came over me. What had I just suggested? That we drive out to the pit with him like we did with Arif? What had I become? I sat most days in my little office off the back verandah and had little to do with the people. By hiding in my office, shuffling numbers and invoices around in neat columns, I could avoid thinking about all that was. The deaths. The murder. The refugees. Guilt and compassion pushed aside by keeping busy.

'Unless we do something he'll take us down. Threatening to spill the beans. He wants to set up a rival operation.'

Behind him across the compound I could see the faded sign on the canteen. *Hotel California*. I remembered the day I first arrived, when I saw that sign and heard the music from inside.

Palmenter had said something and pushed a gun across the table to me. The dark metal had a presence, a here and now insistence that drew me back to Palmenter who was looking at me for a response.

'Son?'

'Spill the beans?'

'You should know what that means.' It was a threat.

'Can we do anything about it? Can we talk him out of it?'

I said 'we'. I had to. I had the feeling he was setting me up to act alone.

'Already talked to him. He's a cunt. He's going to set up his own operation. Dob us in and set up his own operation, and unlike us he's got no reason other than to make money. The money-grabbing double-crossing arsehole. You used one of these before?'

He pushed the gun closer.

'Sure,' I lied. To avoid looking at him I picked the gun up. It was cold and heavy.

'When he comes in, he'll demand money. Cash. He won't trust me but he'll trust you. Get him out to the pit. Wait until after he's refuelled and then drive him out, tell him you are taking him out to where we hide the cash.'

He was telling me to shoot Newman. To do to Newman what he did to Arif. I continued to turn the gun in my hands.

'Don't do it till you are out there. Not before. You understand, Son?'

I felt sick. I might have nodded.

'You sure you used one of these before?'

'Sure.'

I lifted the gun and aimed across the compound at the *Hotel California* sign. I squeezed the trigger.

BANG!

'Jesus, Son.'

'I didn't think it would be loaded.'

'Jesus, Son, what you doing?'

'Bullseye.' I signalled the sign across the way. He turned to look. I had no idea if I'd hit the building, let alone the sign, but he turned to look. His bull neck was sweaty. I saw wispy grey hairs and folds of fat and ugliness. He grunted, like a pig. That was the last thing he ever did.

I talked. I became even more incoherent with beer and exhaustion but also strangely aware, as if I was a person outside of myself watching a group of fishermen trying to make sense of my garbled words. I saw the camp guide become increasingly worried that he could not raise Spanner on the radio. Had they not believed me about the crocodile? When a helicopter – not ours but a small black one – flew in low from the east and disappeared towards the main camp his mood changed and he pulled out the satellite phone, but I did not care because I was in the middle of telling them about Cookie and Judy and their kid playing and laughing and 'Finish up here' and muffled gunshots under the sound of the chopper and they were now dead and I was sobbing. They never had a chance.

Maybe Charles and Simms got away. At least down at the waterhole Ingrid and Sally would be okay. But then I thought of all the others, those five unnamed, and Arif, and then how many more? People who had escaped from one crisis to build themselves a second chance, only to have Palmenter take it away.

And as I watched myself see all of this, I remembered Spanner. We were talking that time when he told me about the extra bodies in the pit. How hard had it been for him to discover that, and then to tell me about what he had seen? That was the moment we decided we had to escape to Perth. At the end of that conversation he had carefully poured his beer out in that considered way he did so many things. But the way he did it, watching the flow of beer dissolve into the earth, it was like it was the end of one thing and the beginning of another. As I remembered that, I came back into my exhausted self and then I poured my beer slowly and deliberately into the sand.

Great reads from Fremantle Press

Conway inhabits an apocalyptic future in a continent caught up in a violent struggle for control of water. On the run from the Water Board flunkies who hate him, but who need his water divining skills to survive, Conway dreams his way back to the arrival of Europeans in Western Australia when Captain Charles Fremantle chooses to throw off the mantle of Empire and join the Nyoongar people.

'Docker conjures up a tantalising vision of what might have been.'
— *Sydney Morning Herald*

9781921696947 pbk • 9781921696954 e

It is 1968. All around the world people are marching, protesting, fighting for freedom and free love.

Jack Muir arrives in the islands fresh out of Grammar School: a failure, a virgin, and a reluctant employee of The Colonial Bank of Australia. Life in the islands is raw, sensuous, real. Here, the white man takes what he wants. But the veneer of whiteness is flimsy, and brutality never far from the surface.

'... a relentless rawness ... that make its moments of tenderness hit their mark even more keenly.'
— *Bookseller+Publisher*

9781921888779 pbk • 9781921888922 e

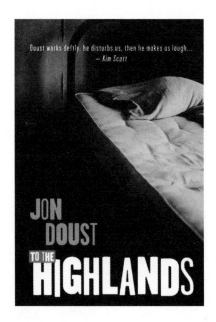

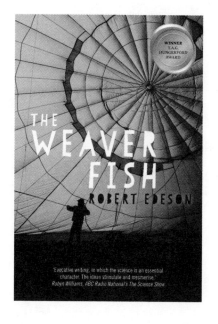

Cambridge linguist Edvard Tøssentern, presumed dead, reappears after a balloon crash. When he staggers in from a remote swamp, gravely ill and swollen beyond recognition, his colleagues at the research station are overjoyed. But Edvard's discovery about a rare giant bird throws them all into the path of an international crime ring.

'Evocative writing, in which the science is an essential character. The ideas stimulate and mesmerise.'
— *Robyn Williams, ABC Radio National, The Science Show*

9781922089526 pbk • 9781922089533 e

For six special people, reality is about to become a bit more real.

Without their knowledge, Kathy, Mario, Garry, Hannah, Robert and Julia are about to participate in the ultimate game of manipulation. A stranger brings them together, but can this ruthless puppeteer really be held responsible for the choices they make?

In the end, who is to blame for their actions: for their deceit, infidelity and crime?

At the heart of this thought-provoking novel lie questions of fate and self-determination.

9781922089373 pbk • 9781922089380 e

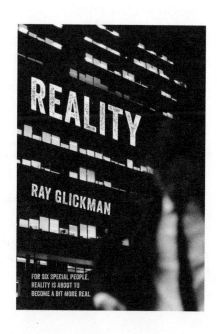

First published 2014 by
FREMANTLE PRESS
25 Quarry Street, Fremantle 6160
(PO Box 158, North Fremantle 6159)
Western Australia
www.fremantlepress.com.au

Also available as an ebook.

Consultant editor Georgia Richter
Cover design Ally Crimp
Printed by Everbest Printing Company, China

National Library of Australia
Cataloguing-in-Publication entry

Chambers, Martin, author.
How I became the Mr Big of People Smuggling / Martin Chambers, author.

9781922089540 (paperback)

Jackeroos—Australia—Fiction.
Ranches—Australia—Fiction.
Human smuggling—Fiction.

A823.4

 Government of **Western Australia**
Department of **Culture and the Arts**

Fremantle Press is supported by the State Government through the Department of
Culture and the Arts.

Publication of this title was assisted by the Commonwealth Government through
the Australia Council, its arts funding and advisory body.